"Maybe [   ] **than we** [   ] **bought my services. A cattle drive in wild country…it's got certain risks to it. Accidents can happen, maybe even fatal ones."**

Samantha faced him squarely. "Not to me, because I'll be safe here in San Antonio. And I don't appreciate your suggesting I might be in danger just so you can—"

"Collect a fee? I don't operate that way, Ms. Howard." Roark's eyes narrowed in a flash of cold anger, and then, just as swiftly, they softened. "But it's too bad you and I won't be on that drive together."

There it was again, she noticed. Something smoldering on his strong face and in the brazen gaze that made her breath quicken. She made an effort to steady her breathing, to respond carelessly. "Is it?"

"Oh, yeah," he said, his voice low and disturbingly husky, almost seductive. "All those long nights under the stars. People share things in situations like that. Things that can get downright interesting."

Dear Harlequin Intrigue Reader,

We wind up a great summer with a *bang* this month! Linda O. Johnston continues the hugely popular COLORADO CONFIDENTIAL series with *Special Agent Nanny*. Don't forget to look for the Harlequin special-release anthology next month featuring *USA TODAY* bestselling author Jasmine Cresswell, our very own Amanda Stevens and Harlequin Historicals author Debra Lee Brown. And not to worry, the series continues with two more Harlequin Intrigue titles in November and December.

Joyce Sullivan concludes her companion series THE COLLINGWOOD HEIRS with *Operation Bassinet*. Find out how this family solves a fiendish plot and finds happiness in one fell swoop. Rounding out the month are two exciting stories. Rising star Delores Fossen takes a unique perspective on the classic secret-baby plot in *Confiscated Conception*, and a very sexy *Cowboy PI* is determined to get to the bottom of one woman's mystery in an all-Western story by Jean Barrett.

Finally, in case you haven't heard, next month Harlequin Intrigue is increasing its publishing schedule to include two more fantastic romantic suspense books. That's *six* titles per month! More variety, more of your favorite authors and of course, more excitement.

It's a thrilling time for us, and we want to thank all of our loyal readers for remaining true to Harlequin Intrigue. And if you are just learning about our brand of breathtaking romantic suspense, fasten your seat belts for an edge-of-your-seat reading experience. Welcome aboard!

Sincerely,

Denise O'Sullivan
Senior Editor, Harlequin Intrigue

COWBOY PI
JEAN BARRETT

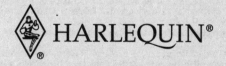

HARLEQUIN®

TORONTO • NEW YORK • LONDON
AMSTERDAM • PARIS • SYDNEY • HAMBURG
STOCKHOLM • ATHENS • TOKYO • MILAN • MADRID
PRAGUE • WARSAW • BUDAPEST • AUCKLAND

ISBN 0-373-22728-0

COWBOY PI

Copyright © 2003 by Jean Barrett

This edition published by arrangement with Harlequin Books S.A.

® and TM are trademarks of the publisher. Trademarks indicated with
® are registered in the United States Patent and Trademark Office, the
Canadian Trade Marks Office and in other countries.

Visit us at www.eHarlequin.com

Printed in U.S.A.

ABOUT THE AUTHOR

If setting has anything to do with it, Jean Barrett claims she has no reason not to be inspired. She and her husband live on Wisconsin's scenic Door Peninsula in an antique-filled country cottage overlooking Lake Michigan. A teacher for many years, she left the classroom to write full-time. She is the author of a number of romance novels.

Write to Jean at P.O. Box 623, Sister Bay, WI 54234. SASE appreciated.

Books by Jean Barrett

HARLEQUIN INTRIGUE

308—THE SHELTER OF HER ARMS
351—WHITE WEDDING
384—MAN OF THE MIDNIGHT SUN
475—FUGITIVE FATHER
528—MY LOVER'S SECRET
605—THE HUNT FOR HAWKE'S DAUGHTER*
652—PRIVATE INVESTIGATIONS*
692—OFFICIAL ESCORT*
728—COWBOY PI*

*The Hawke Detective Agency

CLASSIFIEDS

CAST OF CHARACTERS

Samantha Howard—Spending days in the wilderness with a man who represents everything she hates—especially when he's a virile cowboy—challenges her on every level.

Roark Hawke—The PI and part-time rancher is experienced in dealing with danger, but he never counted on falling for the alluring woman he has sworn to protect.

Joe Walker—He wants his granddaughter to inherit his ranch, but she has to be protected while she earns her spurs.

Wendell Oakes—Roark's trainee is eager to make a success of his assignment.

Shep Thomas—Is it more than just his responsibility for the cattle drive that worries the trail boss?

Cappy Davis—The tough old man has been a fixture on the Walking W for more years than anyone remembers.

Ramona Chacon—Is the housekeeper hiding a secret?

Alex McKenzie—The young drover has a crush on Samantha.

Dick Brewster—The good-natured horse wrangler is in charge of the drive's remuda.

Ernie Chacon—He has a bad reputation and a volatile temper.

To my brother-in-law, Ray,
my sister-in-law, Judy, and their family.
May the fish always bite for all of you.

Acknowledgment

My sincere appreciation
goes to Nancy and Lonnie Stellpflug for demonstrating
how a front-end loader works and for so patiently
answering all my questions about horses.

Prologue

Joe Walker was dying.

Roark had been warned the old man wouldn't make it, but he hadn't believed it. The rancher was a local legend, so tough and cantankerous that, in spite of his advanced age, it seemed he would go on forever. Now, standing over the hospital bed, Roark couldn't deny the reality. Joe was dying.

As little as three, maybe four, years ago, he would have survived the broken hip he'd suffered. There would not have been any tubes connected to him supplying him with oxygen and liquid nourishment. No complications resulting from his accident. But not now. Now he was simply too old to withstand the pneumonia raging through his system.

When had that strong body become frail? Roark wondered, gazing with compassion at the shrunken figure on the bed, its face as seamed and desiccated as a Texas landscape.

The elderly rancher's eyes were closed. Roark thought he was sleeping. But Joe must have been awake, and sensed his presence. The withered lids lifted, revealing a gaze that was steady and lucid.

"Took your time getting here," he croaked. "And I got

precious little of that to waste." The effort caused him to
wheeze painfully.

"I shouldn't be here at all. Look, why don't I come
back when you're feeling better?"

Joe Walker wasn't a man of humor, never had been. But
Roark's suggestion must have amused him. He recovered
enough wind to cackle softly. "There is no better, cowboy.
This is as good as it gets. Sit," he commanded.

No, Roark thought, time was something Joe didn't have,
and the rancher knew that better than his doctor. Roark
drew up a chair beside the elevated bed and folded his
rangy length in it.

There was one thing that was still vital about the dour
old man: a pair of pewter-gray eyes that regarded Roark
shrewdly. "That spread of yours over on the other side of
the McKenzie place," he rasped. "Not worth a cowpat.
Not enough range for your beeves."

Roark's own small ranch suited him just fine, but he
offered no objection. He simply waited, well aware that
Joe's opinion of his operation wasn't why he had sum-
moned him to his bedside.

"But you're sticking to it, and you know your stuff,"
Joe said. "Not bad for a weekend cowboy. Hear you also
know what you're doing with that PI agency of yours
down in San Antonio. That combination makes you the
man I need."

The rancher paused, his inflamed lungs struggling for
the oxygen that would permit him to continue.

"My lawyer explain the setup to you?" he whispered.

"Yes." Roark had had his share of strange cases, but
nothing as eccentric as this one. He probably wouldn't
have considered the proposal at all if he hadn't grown up
on John Wayne movies, and the chance to actually experience... Well, the offer was damn tempting.

"Then you know what I want. I won't send her up there
without protection. Made that a requirement in the will."

The "her" was his granddaughter, Roark thought. Samantha Howard. He had never met the woman, but he was angry with her. Why wasn't she here at Joe's bedside?

The old man, still wheezing through the pain that must be stabbing his lungs with every breath, understood Roark's tight-jawed, unspoken judgment. "No use for each other, Samantha and me," he said. "Never had." He paused, plucking at the sheet tucked around him. "But she's the only family I got. And I don't aim for the Walking W to leave the family, not if it can be helped. Want her to inherit everything. But if she stands any chance at all of running the ranch, she's got to toughen up. Way I see it, and I thought about this carefully, I got no choice but to send her on this trek. It's the best way to harden her."

He stopped to regain enough strength to go on. There was a long silence interrupted by his fitful breathing. "Every man has his secrets," he muttered.

Was he wandering? Roark wondered. Had that sharp old brain been dulled by illness and fatigue?

"Figure," Joe said, "there's maybe someone out there with a secret I don't like. Maybe up to mischief. Maybe not. Even so, there's always risks on a haul of this kind. Enough, cowboy, that you got to watch my granddaughter's back while she's earning her spurs."

Understanding him now, Roark leaned earnestly toward the bed. "Joe, she doesn't need a bodyguard. She's not in danger. The fall you took from your horse was an accident. The sheriff's investigation—"

"Didn't mean squat!"

The old man's sudden, obstinate anger resulted in a hacking cough that alarmed Roark. He started to get to his feet to call a nurse, but Joe clutched at him, pulling him back.

"Stay," he gasped, managing to quiet himself after a moment.

"You sure?"

"Not sure of anything," he said between shallow

breaths, "except this damn ache in my chest that never goes away. But before I stop fighting it, you got to tell me you'll look out for her. Could be there's nothing to worry about. Probably isn't, but I won't send her to Colorado without easing my mind on the subject. Promise me, cowboy...."

WHAT THE HELL had just happened? Roark asked himself as he came away from the hospital ten minutes later. But he knew exactly what had happened. He had gone and pledged his services to Joe Walker. Or, more precisely, to Joe's granddaughter. He just didn't know why he had been fool enough to guarantee his protection of the woman.

But that wasn't true either, Roark thought as he paused in the parking lot, hand resting on the door of his pickup truck. Though he hated to admit it, he realized all too clearly why he had accepted the assignment. It was simple. He had been unable to refuse the urgent appeal of a dying man.

He would do it, Roark told himself as he climbed behind the wheel of the truck, but he didn't like it. He'd decided by now that this condition Joe had insisted his granddaughter fulfill in order to inherit his estate was extreme, if not downright bizarre. That was one thing. And for another, he was dealing with an issue of his own. A personal conflict that had been tearing him up inside for weeks now. How was he supposed to come to grips with that while playing bodyguard in the wilderness for a woman he already resented?

No, he thought, speeding away from the hospital, he wasn't looking forward to Samantha Howard.

Chapter One

What was the expression? Oh, yes, now she remembered. *In the toilet.*

Blunt but accurate, Samantha thought. Because that's exactly where the real estate agency she had spent the past year and a half struggling to save had been headed. Battered by a slow market and tough competition from the national chains, the agency had been slowly sinking in spite of her every effort.

But not now. Now things were looking up. This afternoon she would be meeting with the buyer to sign the papers on a mansion in the King William District, an estate they'd carried for over six months without being able to move. The sale would earn her a sizable commission, money the agency badly needed.

Even better was the property she was examining this morning. Clipboard in hand to jot down particulars, she toured the facility to determine its value. A Tex-Mex restaurant had recently vacated the premises. Rather than leasing it to another occupant, the Houston-based landlord had decided to sell the building.

Samantha resisted the urge to celebrate. She didn't have the property on her books yet, but the owner had practically guaranteed her the listing. He had a team of painters currently redoing the main dining room, giving it a fresh look that would appeal to the eye of a prospective buyer.

That was good, but not nearly as important as the location, which was clearly evident when she stepped through one of the open doors onto the balcony. The structure overlooked the city's famed River Walk. This was prime real estate.

Samantha was enjoying the reason for that valuable advantage, gazing at a gondola gliding along the olive waters of the winding San Antonio River, when the serenity of the scene was destroyed by a deep male voice demanding loudly "Where is she?"

Twisting around from the railing at which she stood, she searched in the direction of the disturbance. The speaker, his back turned, had been addressing one of the painters on a scaffold in the dining room. His brusque inquiry was answered by a startled look and then a paintbrush pointed with hesitant slowness in the direction of the outdoor balcony.

With a muttered thanks, the tall visitor swung around and headed across the expanse of the dining room. She watched him moving purposefully toward her with a long-legged, confident gait. One glimpse of his lean, narrow-hipped figure was enough to stiffen Samantha's spine.

Cowboys were far from rare in San Antonio, and occasionally they were the genuine article, sometimes even as sexy as legend promised. This one definitely qualified in that department, at least in appearance.

He had a mane of tousled black hair that had been crammed under a hastily removed Stetson, a dark stubble on his square jaw, stains on his faded jeans and denim shirt, and a coating of dust on a pair of well-worn boots. They were the collective result of a man who had been out wrestling steers, or at least herding them. And Samantha neither liked nor trusted any aspect of that image, and wouldn't have liked it even if this cowboy had been one of the harmless urban variety.

She stood her ground as he strode out onto the balcony, a pair of disarming blue eyes colliding with hers. "Samantha Howard?"

The timbre of his voice was sensual, in keeping with all the rest of the cowboy package. But she didn't care for his abrupt manner, though she tried to be pleasant. She couldn't afford to offend someone who might turn out to be a client. "Yes, that's right. What can I—"

She got no further. He stopped her by leaning over and slapping a small rectangle of cream-colored pasteboard onto the little wrought-iron table at her side. Samantha glanced down at his form of introduction: a business card with an emblem of a swooping golden hawk and the words *Hawke Detective Agency.* He was not a client.

When she looked up, the glacial blue eyes were still fastened on her. She was aware all over again that he was unshaven, sweaty and incredibly virile. Samantha had once been susceptible to that kind of masculine allure, but no more. These days she made it a habit to stay away from cowboys. *Far* away from them. And this one was standing much too close to her, so close that she could swear she felt the heat of his hard body.

Only, he wasn't a cowboy, she reminded herself. Not entirely, anyway, though she'd been told he had a ranch near the Walking W. Roark Hawke. She should have guessed his identity the minute he'd asked for her.

How he'd gotten into the restaurant was no mystery. With all the doors left wide-open to vent the paint fumes, anyone could walk into the place. But his knowledge of her presence here was another matter. "How did you find me?"

A pair of broad shoulders lifted in a little shrug. "I'm a private investigator, which means it's my business to find people. In this case, I didn't have to search very hard. Your office manager told me you'd be here."

Samantha reminded herself to speak to Gail about her habit of being entirely too receptive to persuasive callers.

Particularly those who knew how to use a husky Texas drawl to their advantage.

"Why should you want to find me, Mr. Hawke? Didn't my grandfather's lawyer tell you that—"

"Oh, he told me all right. Caught me out at my ranch working on a stubborn windmill."

Which meant his appearance was neither the result of wrestling steers nor herding them. "So, without stopping to clean up, you jump into your pickup—I'm assuming you do drive a pickup—"

"Don't know of a rancher in Texas who doesn't."

"You jump into your pickup and tear down here to San Antonio to…what? What could be so urgent? Unless, of course, the lawyer didn't make my decision clear to you."

"Ebbersole is too thorough for that."

There was another heavy table just behind him. He leaned his weight against it, long legs crossed at the ankle, and proceeded to measure her with those bold blue eyes. His scrutiny was both direct and speculative. Samantha found herself clutching the clipboard defensively against her breasts.

"Then why are you here?"

He was in no hurry to answer her. She watched him slowly, absently rub the brim of the Stetson against his muscular thigh. "See, I figured you and I would eventually run into each other at the hospital."

While she was visiting her grandfather. That's what he meant. Only, Samantha had never visited her grandfather.

"When that didn't happen," Roark said, "I thought for sure I'd meet you at the funeral."

His tone was casual, nonjudgmental, but she could feel his anger. Roark Hawke was angry with her because she had failed to visit her dying grandfather, hadn't even bothered to attend his funeral. He had probably liked and admired Joe Walker, thought him a wonderful old character and his granddaughter heartless for her neglect of him. He didn't know the truth, and she had no intention of explaining it to him. Her anguish was none of his business.

"Now," Roark said, "it looks like I won't be getting to know you in Colorado, either."

Samantha went rigid, resenting him for his anger with her. He had no right to it. "Is that why you chased down here from Purgatory? Just for the opportunity to meet me?"

"Guess so. On the other hand—" he paused to toss the Stetson into a chair "—maybe I just wanted to try to understand why a smart businesswoman would go and throw away a valuable inheritance. Kind of puzzles me."

"And you hoped I would enlighten you. Or maybe you hoped to change my mind."

"Can I?"

"Not a chance. I don't want any part of my grandfather's money. I know what that sounds like, but I have my reasons." And Roark Hawke didn't need to hear them, even though those thick black eyebrows of his had knit in a little frown of puzzlement.

"Looks like you and Joe shared something."

"I don't think so. We had nothing in common."

There was a little smile now on his wide mouth. It was a smile that didn't reach his eyes. "How about obstinacy?"

"I like to think of it as being independent. I've worked very hard to be just that, and I intend to keep it that way."

"Which you wouldn't be if you were saddled with the responsibility of the Walking W, is that it?"

"Independence requires trust, Mr. Hawke. At least by my definition, it does. Would you say that's what my grandfather was doing, trusting me, when his will specifies that in order to inherit, I have to go up to Colorado and play cowboy in the wilderness?"

"You're asking the wrong guy. I like to play cowboy."

"And this whole thing doesn't strike you as...oh, I don't know, a little peculiar? Slightly preposterous, maybe?

A cattle drive? We're talking about a *cattle drive!* Hasn't anyone in Purgatory heard that the Chisholm Trail is now an interstate?''

''Think that rumor did reach us,'' he said dryly. ''But this is one of those cases where a drive is necessary. Joe bought the herd before his accident. Now the steers have to be moved out of there.''

''What happened to cattle trucks?''

''Too costly for a herd that size, even if a fleet of trucks could get in there, which they can't. They tell me the only road into this ranch is under construction. It's rugged country. Of course, once the drive reaches the rail line, stock cars will ship the steers to Purgatory.''

''Oh, of course. Just a matter of— How far did the lawyer say the rail line was? I'm afraid at that point in my conversation with him I wasn't listening too carefully.''

''A hundred miles. More or less.''

''That little?''

''Uh-huh.''

''Through rough country?''

''Yeah.''

She stared at him. He stared back, a clear challenge in those potent blue eyes. What was she doing, standing here crossing swords with him? The man was brash, almost to the point of being rude. Not only had he made it his business—which it wasn't—to track her here, he actually expected her to explain herself.

Samantha didn't like this, defending her decision to a stranger to whom she owed absolutely nothing. She didn't care for the gaze that remained locked with hers and was so intense it positively sizzled. She was unprepared for the impact of that gaze on her senses, and in the end her courage deserted her. She looked down at the tiles on the floor of the balcony, pretending to be very thoughtful.

''Why?'' she asked.

''Come again?''

''Why add more cattle to the Walking W when there

must be plenty of cows already on the ranch?'' She didn't care to know why. She'd simply needed to end the silence that had stretched between them so tautly. ''You seem to have made it your business to learn all the particulars, so why would my grandfather have acquired another herd?''

''They're special. Longhorns.''

She found it safe enough now to look up again, though she avoided meeting those compelling blue eyes. ''Even I know that longhorns aren't special. They're back on the scene, including right here in Texas where they started.''

''They tell me this herd *is* special. Took years for the Colorado ranch to develop the strain. They've got more meat on them than the traditional longhorns, plus they're able to withstand the extremes of both heat and cold, and they can graze on what other cattle won't touch. Interested?''

''Fascinated. But not enough to chase longhorns through the Rocky Mountains so I can be tested to see if I'm fit enough to inherit Joe Walker's kingdom. Because *that,* Mr. Hawke, is really what this cattle drive is all about.''

''And you want nothing to do with it.''

''I want nothing to do with it. And even if I did, I wouldn't need the services of a bodyguard.''

''Guess Ebbersole didn't explain that part of it.''

''Oh, he made it very clear. How my grandfather's broken hip was the result of a fall from his horse, which he shouldn't have been riding at all at his age, and certainly not on his own through a ravine that, if I remember correctly, is in an isolated corner of the ranch. And how he insisted it was no accident and that gunfire spooked his horse. *Deliberate* is the word I think he used to the sheriff.''

''And you don't buy that.''

''I have no reason to, not when his faculties were probably no longer reliable. Not when the sheriff looked into it, found not a single spent bullet in the area, and was satisfied that if someone had been shooting out there, it was probably a hunter after rabbits.''

''And not after Joe, you mean?''

Samantha gestured impatiently with the clipboard. ''My grandfather must have had his share of enemies. He was ornery enough. But I can't imagine any of them would have tried to kill him. Or have any reason to be a threat to his granddaughter.''

''You're probably right,'' Roark said casually, sliding his hands into the pockets of his jeans. ''More than likely, the whole thing was just the paranoia of an old man. On the other hand…''

She set the clipboard on the table and faced him squarely again. ''What? You're determined to say it, so go ahead.''

''Maybe that old man was smarter than we gave him credit for when he bought my services. A thing like a cattle drive in wild country…well, it's got to have certain risks to it, doesn't it? Accidents can happen, maybe even fatal ones.''

''Not to me, because I'll be right here, safe in San Antonio. And I don't appreciate your suggesting I might be in any danger just so you can—''

''Collect a fee? I don't operate that way, Ms. Howard.'' His eyes narrowed in a flash of cold anger, and then just as swiftly they softened. ''But all else aside, it's too bad you and I won't be on that drive together.''

There it was again, she noticed. Something smoldering on his strong face and in the brazen gaze that made her breath quicken. To avoid it, she lowered her own eyes again. But just slightly this time, to prevent him from thinking she was in any way intimidated by him. Only, this was worse. She found her eyes fastened on his deeply tanned throat where his Adam's apple bobbed slowly as he swallowed. The action was like a pulse, both mesmerizing and arousing.

She made an effort to steady her breathing, to respond carelessly. "Is it?"

"Oh, yeah," he said, his voice slow and disturbingly husky, almost seductive. "I think it would have been some experience all right. All those long nights under the stars. People share things in situations like that. Things that can get downright interesting."

Intimate things. That's what he was saying. This had gone far enough. "Sounds like fun," she said with a lightness she was far from feeling. "It's a shame I'll have to miss it."

He was silent for a few seconds, taking her measure again. This time she managed to hold his gaze. "Then your decision is definite?"

"Very," she said with emphasis.

"Guess I'm wasting my time here."

To her relief, he leaned down and collected his Stetson from the chair. When he turned to go, she reminded him quickly, "You're forgetting your business card."

"Keep it," he said, tugging the hat over his dark hair. "You never know."

Watching his tall form stride away through the dining room, Samantha felt as though she had just escaped from something potentially dangerous to her. Roark Hawke had had that kind of effect on her, and she wasn't happy about it.

Since the scene below the balcony was much safer than the sight of his departing figure, she turned to it. Looking down through the feathery foliage of an ancient cypress, she watched the tourists strolling along the cobbled, sun-dappled walkways on both sides of the stream. She saw them wander in and out of the souvenir shops, or focus their cameras on flower beds vibrant with color.

Only, it wasn't a safer scene, because the image of Roark Hawke intruded on it. His lean face with its sensual mouth called up memories of another cowboy. Unwanted memories carrying a pain that was connected with her grandfather. She hadn't thought about Hank Barrie in ages, and she didn't want to think about him now. She had put all that suffering behind her long ago, and she meant to keep it in the past.

No, she wasn't going there. And she was going to forget all about Roark Hawke and how he had made her pulse accelerate. But when Samantha turned resolutely away from the railing, her eye fell on the business card he'd left on the table.

You never know.

But she did know. She had absolutely no intention of ever calling the number on that card.

WHAT THE HELL had he been thinking? Roark asked himself as he moved swiftly along the River Walk, needing to vent his anger with some form of action, even if it was no more than stretching his legs among the tourists.

Racing down here from Purgatory like that! Storming into the restaurant and cornering Samantha Howard in order to—what?

Throw her over his shoulder and haul her shapely little backside all the way to Colorado and that cattle drive?

Okay, so he'd been tempted to do just that and instead had tried to convince her to change her mind. Which was bad enough. Why hadn't he anticipated that maybe Joe Walker's granddaughter wouldn't want his protection? And why hadn't he just dropped the whole thing when the lawyer had informed him of her refusal?

Because she was right. She didn't need his services. Samantha was in no more danger from some unknown enemy than Joe had been. Who would want to harm her, particularly when she intended to surrender all claim to her grandfather's estate?

Roark didn't know the answers to any of those questions. Not why he had so explosively charged into the restaurant or, even worse than that, why he had actually come on to the woman.

Well, yeah, he guessed he did know the answer to the last question. She'd been dynamite waiting for a match in that sexy little power suit. The abbreviated skirt had afforded him a clear view of long legs in heels and a tantalizing glimpse of silken thighs.

There were also the attractions of a luscious mouth, a pair of beguiling brown eyes, and a mass of gleaming chestnut hair—not to mention the sparks they'd rubbed off each other throughout their whole brief encounter, all of which would have meant trouble for him on a cattle drive.

Passing under one of the bridges, Roark unconsciously slowed his steps. He paid no attention to the street player strumming his guitar for the benefit of the tourists. He was far too occupied with the heat that gripped him over the image of Samantha Howard's lush body.

Damn, what was he doing? She had turned him down. He was off the hook. He should be congratulating himself that she was no longer his problem, that he could concentrate now on his own troubling issue.

Right. Let it go.

Determined to do exactly that, Roark swung around and headed toward the city garage where he had parked his truck.

Except he couldn't let it go. There was still his promise to a dying old man who had trusted him. It nagged at him all the way back to his pickup.

Chapter Two

"Tell me they absolutely loved it," Gail pleaded. "Tell me they've already made an offer on it."

Samantha, cell phone pressed to her ear, hesitated before answering. What could she report to her anxious officer manager about the high-rise condo she had just finished showing? What could she say to Gail that wouldn't sound too dismal?

"They said they would think about it."

What the elderly couple had actually told her was that they wanted to shop around a bit more before deciding, which meant they weren't interested. Samantha didn't blame them. The price on the condo was too high, and it was in need of updating.

"Well, that's encouraging," Gail said brightly. "Isn't that encouraging?"

"I'm hopeful," Samantha lied, wondering how in a span of less than twenty-four hours everything that had been so promising could end up being so bleak.

Yet it had, starting with yesterday afternoon when her buyer for the mansion in the King William District had backed out of the sale. Something about a deal going sour on him and his software company being in trouble. Okay, so she had lost that one, but she still had the hot property on the River Walk. Only, she didn't. The owner had called this morning to tell her he was listing with her chief rival, the Van Nugent Agency.

She hated this! All right, so she hadn't gone into the business to become rich. She'd opened her agency primarily for the joy of putting people into their dream houses. But she had expected to make a living out of it and to provide decent incomes for her employees. Like Gail, a widow in her fifties supporting an ailing mother. And the young woman who worked for her part-time and needed her salary to pay for the college degree she was earning. And her other agent, a handicapped father raising two kids. The job market wasn't good for any of them. They were depending on Samantha. As was the bank, who expected regular payments on that business loan she had secured from them last month.

Bad, but she wasn't sunk yet. Another potential buyer for the mansion had surfaced this morning, which was why she was calling her office manager at the agency.

"Where are you?" Gail asked.

"In my car and ready to head over to King William. I'm just checking in to make sure this guy hasn't canceled the appointment. Please tell me he hasn't canceled." The way things were going, it wouldn't have surprised her.

"He hasn't canceled."

"Then there still is a real estate fairy. Tell me the name again. Is it Mulroony or Mulroney? I don't want to risk any errors on this."

"Mulroney."

"Anything else you can tell me about him that would help?"

"Just what you already know, that his wife will be accompanying him and they prefer to meet you at the property. Like I said earlier, I didn't meet him. He made the appointment by phone after seeing our ad."

Samantha didn't like going blind into a showing, but it couldn't be helped. "Keep your fingers crossed."

"If it helps, I'll cross my toes as well."

Samantha rang off and eased out into the flow of traffic, passing the Tower of the Americas in Hemisfair Plaza as she headed away from the downtown area. The soaring structure, along with the more famous Alamo, was the pride of San Antonio.

Samantha seldom failed to take pleasure in her city. Only, not today. Today her attention was focused on saving her agency.

There is a solution, you know. It's right there in front of you, waiting to solve all your problems. All you have to do is—

No! Tempting though that inheritance from her grandfather was, *really* tempting now, she was going to make it on her own. She wasn't going to play Joe Walker's game. If she could nail this sale, the commission would be enough to keep her going until—what? Something else came along? Yes, why not.

There was something else holding her back from calling the lawyer and telling him she had changed her mind. Something that, in spite of her best efforts, had been stealing into her consciousness since yesterday morning on the River Walk. The memory of a tall, black-haired figure who, according to her grandfather's instructions, must accompany her on the cattle drive. Roark Hawke, with fire in his cobalt-blue eyes and a bold mouth that didn't bear thinking about.

So don't think about him, because you need to concentrate on making the best impression possible on the Mulroneys. These people could be your salvation.

Leaving the main stream of traffic, she turned into the King William District, a twenty-five-block area of fabulous Victorian mansions built by prominent German merchants over a century ago. The house listed by her agency, the last one on a dead-end street, was a brick Queen Anne sheltered by live oaks.

There was no car waiting out front when Samantha arrived. But then she was a few minutes early for the appointment. Sliding out of her car, she went and stood by the iron gate that led to the front door. There was no one else around, the street quiet except for the thunder overhead of a jet from one of the nearby air force bases.

The house was unoccupied, its owner moved away. A vacant property never made the most desirable showing. However, it would seem less empty if she opened up the place and waited inside to welcome them. Removing the keys from her purse, she followed the brick walk to the deep porch and unlocked the front door, leaving it ajar by way of invitation to the Mulroneys.

The interior she entered was spacious and handsome, many of the period furnishings still in place. All the same, it had a hollow, somewhat gloomy aspect and, with the air-conditioning turned off, it felt stuffy. She could do something about that.

Quitting the wide entrance hall, she crossed the shadowy double parlor into a tall bay that overlooked the side of the property. The bay, too, was dim because of the lowered blinds at its windows. Leaning over the window seat, she raised the blinds to permit cheerful sunlight to stream into the room, released the catches on the sashes and lifted the windows. Better, much better. Fresh air drifted through the openings.

Wrought-iron grilles had been fitted over the long windows on the outside of the bay. Samantha was admiring their delicate tracery when the deep silence behind her was ruptured by a sudden, ominous buzzing. Something electrical? A problem? That was what occurred to her, until she turned around to investigate.

She saw it at once. How could she not see it when it was coiled there on the floor less than three feet away? Threatened by her intrusion, it must have slithered out from its hiding place behind the folds of the velvet portieres that framed the bay.

A diamondback rattler! A very large and very deadly diamondback!

Samantha was instantly seized by the same heart-stopping terror she had experienced as a child whenever she'd encountered snakes at the Walking W. A paralyzing terror that had earned her her grandfather's contempt. But snakes were expected on a ranch, not here in the city. Along with that shock was the mystery of how it could have gotten inside a closed house.

All this raced through her mind, together with the re-alization that she was in a serious position. Cornered, in fact, because the grilles over the windows behind her pre-vented any escape that way. And if she attempted to edge around the thing, or even tried to climb up on the window seat…uh-uh, no way. Any action at all, even the slightest movement, and it would strike.

Sick though she was with a cold fear, Samantha obeyed the lesson of her childhood and managed to remain per-fectly still. Her only option, it seemed. And all the while the diamondback measured her, its thick, ugly head weav-ing slowly back and forth, its upraised rattles vibrating a steady warning.

Damn, how long was she supposed to stand here like this? She should be doing something. What?

Before she could decide, she heard the sound of the front door she'd left ajar opening and closing, followed by the tread of feet on the floor of the hall. The Mulroneys.

A risk, but she had to caution them. "Careful!" she called out. "There's a snake loose in here! A poisonous one!"

Well, that should effectively spoil the chance of any sale.

Her warning was met by a brief silence. Then a figure appeared in the archway between hall and parlor, treating her to another shock. This was not one of the Mulroneys. Roark Hawke stood there asking no questions, his hard gaze swiftly assessing the situation.

Slowly, and with care, he advanced into the room. "Just keep still," he instructed her. "Not a muscle, okay?"

Did trembling count? Samantha wondered. Because she was certain that by now she was quivering all over as she watched him withdraw a revolver from a shoulder holster inside his suit coat. What was he doing carrying a gun? Never mind, just be grateful he had one.

When he was several yards away from the bay, he stopped and took aim. "Don't worry," he assured her with what she could swear was nonchalance. "I'm a good shot."

She took his word for it and prayed. The diamondback had detected his presence. Head lifted from its tight coil, it issued a sibilant alarm as it whipped around. In the next second it had no head at all. It was blown away by the bark of the revolver in Roark's steady hand.

Samantha permitted herself to shudder in earnest before going limp with relief. "If that was a demonstration of your skills as a bodyguard, I'm impressed."

"I don't like to destroy nature," he said, nodding solemnly toward the snake whose heavy body was still twisting in spasms, "but in this case…"

"Exactly." She watched him tuck the revolver back inside the holster. "Do you always come prepared like that?"

"I'm a PI, remember?"

Samantha doubted that private investigators carried guns with them everywhere they went. On the other hand, he was no ordinary PI. Yesterday he had been clad in denim. Today he wore a trim business suit whose coat emphasized the breadth of his shoulders, making him no less potent than yesterday's cowboy in jeans. The contrast was rather startling, reminding her that this was a man who inhabited two worlds.

Roark glanced around, discovering the marble fireplace with its tools still in place at the side of the hearth. He went and got the poker and shovel, returning with them to scrape up the remains of the snake.

"Big sucker," he said. "Maybe not lethal if it had managed to sink its fangs in you, but you'd have suffered some serious consequences.''

Her silence must have made him realize his observation was not a welcome one. He looked up from his task, searching her face. "I'll get rid of this thing. You okay?"

"Dandy."

She wasn't. She could see that for herself the moment he left, disappearing into the hallway. There was a pier glass directly opposite the bay, and even across the width of the parlor she could tell that the tall, slender woman in jacketed dress and low heels, long chestnut hair coiled at the back of her head, was badly shaken, shoulders sagging, legs looking like they were in danger of no longer supporting her.

Samantha lowered herself into the window seat. Roark found her huddled there when he returned to the parlor.

"Dumped it in the shrubbery outside," he reported, replacing the poker and shovel.

She didn't invite him to join her on the seat, but that was where he ended up, his big, solid body squeezed so close beside her that she could feel his heat, smell the clean, masculine scent of his soap. Quite a change from the unshaven, grimy Roark Hawke of yesterday but every bit as unsettling, though she couldn't argue that his nearness was also comforting.

"Feeling better?" he asked, turning to her.

There it was again, that Adam's apple bobbing in his throat, hypnotizing her with its slow action that shouldn't have been in any way alluring but somehow was.

"Much," she lied. "Thank you for playing knight to the rescue and slaying the—well, I guess it would be serpent in this case and not dragon." She tilted her head to one side, favoring him with a grateful smile. "And now would you please tell me just what the hell you think you're doing?"

"Care to clarify that?"

"Turning up here like this. It's not by chance that you happened to walk through that front door."

"Ah, that. It's because of the watering hole I visited last night. Some interesting people hang out there, and sometimes they provide me with useful bits of information. Seems to be a favorite haunt of one of your competitors. It only took him a couple of drinks before he was bragging to anyone who would listen that you'd just lost a major sale, that he'd taken another important listing away from you and that your agency was on the ropes."

Van Nugent! Bad news traveled fast in the business, particularly when vipers like Nugent got hold of it. Apparently, he'd learned before she did that she wouldn't get the River Walk property.

"So you decided I'd be desperate enough by now to change my mind about my grandfather's inheritance."

"It did occur to me to look you up again."

"And I suppose it was Gail again who told you where to find me."

"Nice lady, your office manager. Very helpful. Remind me to send her flowers."

"Did Gail also tell you to be sure to pack a gun when you came looking for me?"

"Now, see, that was my idea. I kind of had this uncomfortable feeling by then that, if you did go and change your mind, maybe you weren't as safe in San Antonio as you figured. Looks like I was right, huh?"

"Are you suggesting the snake was—"

"Deliberate? Why not? You think that thing just happened to crawl in here? I bet if you looked through the house you'd find a window or door somewhere that's been forced open." He turned his head, sweeping his gaze around the parlor. "So where are they?"

"Who?"

"The couple Gail told me you were scheduled to meet here."

His shifts in topics were so abrupt that Samantha had

trouble following them, particularly when she was feeling limp again. And vulnerable. *Decidedly* vulnerable. She glanced at her watch. "I guess they're late."

"You ever meet them?"

"No, they arranged the appointment by phone through Gail."

"Wanna bet they never turn up? That they don't even exist?"

She stared at him. "But that would mean—"

"Oh, yeah, a setup, because your office manager must have mentioned the house was unoccupied, and you go and walk into it with a diamondback rattler waiting for you in the parlor."

"If that's true," she said, feeling weaker by the moment, "then it's also possible…" She couldn't name it, didn't want to believe that anything so fantastic could be a reality.

Roark, however, had no hesitation about putting it into words. "That Joe Walker wasn't imagining someone was after him. The same someone who wants to prevent you from qualifying for your grandfather's estate."

"But I told the lawyer that I intend to sign away any claim to the estate."

"Either this guy hasn't learned that yet, or he's trying to make sure you don't change your mind. Because, even though he must have realized it was unlikely the rattler would have killed you if it had managed to sting you, there was a good chance it would land you in the hospital or, if not that, scare you into not joining the cattle drive."

"Well, his threat was an effective one." She was silent for a moment, absorbing his conjecture and not liking it one bit. "Oh, this is crazy. Who could possibly have a motive for wanting either my grandfather or me out of the way?"

"Someone who benefits, of course. Did Ebbersole explain the contents of your grandfather's will?"

"In more detail than I wanted to know."

"So, who inherits if you default?"

Samantha frowned, trying to remember all that the lawyer had shared with her. "There are some cash legacies to my grandfather's employees at the ranch. None of the legacies are all that large. In any case, they're guaranteed no matter who inherits."

"No motive there, then. What about the big stuff?"

"It's to be divided. The investments would go to St. James Monastery and the ranch itself and all its contents to the Western Museum in Purgatory. But you can't think—"

"That either a community of Catholic brothers or a nonprofit public museum would go to any lengths to inherit Joe Walker's estate?" He shook his head. "Not likely."

"Then, if they're above suspicion—and they must be—none of it makes sense."

Roark didn't respond. She eyed him as he sat there, slowly flexing the fingers of his right hand as he pondered the problem. Was the action an unconscious habit that permitted him to deliberate, or some form of exercise?

The hand captivated her. It was large and tanned from the sun, the fingers that repeatedly curled into a fist and opened again were long and with an obvious strength. Fingers that were capable of being both tough or stroking a woman's sensitive flesh.

The sudden image of such a seduction was so arousing that it alarmed Samantha. Catching her breath, she inched away from him on the window seat. She didn't think he was aware of her hasty retreat until his hand went still. He turned his head and looked at her, a smile of amusement hovering on his wide mouth.

It was a smile that, like everything else about him, unnerved her. She made an effort to remedy her unwanted state as she said quickly, "Shouldn't I be calling the police?"

"Why?"

"If there was a break-in here, I ought to report it."

"Then that much is probably a good idea."

But not the rest. That's what he was saying, that the police would be able to offer her no more answers than he could at the moment. Or, without either a suspect or evidence, their help, either. She knew he was right.

"So, are you?" he wanted to know.

Out of nowhere he had changed the subject again, because she realized he wasn't talking about phoning the police. "What?"

"Desperate enough by now to go after that inheritance?"

Samantha looked away from him, her gaze traveling around the parlor. The Mulroneys didn't exist. She wouldn't be selling the house to them today. That hope had evaporated along with all her other prospects. All she had now was a debt to the bank, employees who were depending on her, and an agency she couldn't bear to lose. She had no choice but to swallow her pride and accept the terms of her grandfather's will.

"I suppose I am," she said.

"Scared?"

"Yes," she admitted.

"Then maybe it isn't worth it."

"That wasn't your argument yesterday."

"Yesterday I wasn't convinced there was any danger out there."

"I'll have to risk it, because I need the money. Besides—" she was angry suddenly, an anger that fueled her decision, turning it into a fierce resolve "—I don't like it that someone thinks he can frighten me into giving him what he wants."

Roark nodded, seeming to understand her determination without needing any further explanation, even admiring her for it, if the gleam in his eyes was any indication. "Then it looks like you and I are going on a cattle drive, Samantha Howard."

She stared at him, chagrined. She had momentarily for-

gotten that the terms of her grandfather's will required her
to accept the protection of Roark Hawke. There was no
choice about it, and she didn't like it. Why? Certainly not
because he was a private investigator.

*Then what? Because he's a cowboy. But how can you
mind that when there will be others like him on the drive?*

Oh, but they would be essential, with impersonal identities. She could distance herself from them, at least emotionally. But this man was something else altogether. She
wasn't even sure she liked him. No, she probably didn't,
despite his provocative effect on her. And she wouldn't be
able to distance herself from him. He would be close and
constant, forever at her side through the long days and
nights they spent out there in the wilderness.

He had to know what she was thinking. She could see
that in the way those compelling blue eyes of his devoured
her in the intense silence that stretched between them as
they sat there regarding each other.

Roark finally ended the silence in a low, husky tone.
"You'll have to go all the way with me, you know."

She swallowed, her mouth dry. "I will *what?*"

He chuckled. "The cattle drive, Samantha. You have to
stick with it all the way to the rail line or lose the inheritance. That's the stipulation, remember?"

Damn him. He'd gone and put a deliberate spin on his
words and was now enjoying the result.

"You and I together," he said softly.

A cowboy. Maybe only by avocation, but in soul and
spirit Roark Hawke was a cowboy with all the raw, sensual
appeal of his breed, along with a wicked smile and a sinful
body that did things to her insides. And she had promised
herself long ago that, no matter how susceptible she was
to this combination, she would never permit it to hurt her
again.

"I'm looking forward to it," Samantha said in a steady
voice.

That's what she said, facing him with a cool, calm de-

tachment, but all the while she feared more than the perils
of a cattle drive. Roark Hawke was another kind of jeop-
ardy. How was she ever going to survive him?

HER CRY OF DISBELIEF was so piercing that Roark held the
phone away from his ear.

"You can't be serious!" She rushed on with barely a
pause to recover from her shock. "Being a PI is who you
are, who we *all* are, and to give that up…"

He sat there in his swivel chair, one hand curled around
the phone he'd restored to his ear, the other flipping
through the day's mail on his office desk as he listened to
her. No use in attempting to explain himself until she had
exhausted all of her arguments.

Roark had already shared his announcement with the
other members of his family. He'd saved the most difficult
call for the last, knowing that his youngest sister, Christy,
was likely to treat it as a bombshell. He wasn't wrong.

She finally came up for air after one last, mournful
"Rory, why are you doing this?"

Christy wouldn't understand his dilemma. She had always loved being a private investigator, had never wanted
to be anything else, and couldn't imagine any member of
the family thinking about another career. But he tried.

"Honey, I'm a frustrated rancher who needs to devote
time and energy to his spread. I can't do that if I've got
clients to serve here in the city."

"Are you sure that's all it is?"

It wasn't. There was another issue in the picture, and
the guilt related to it that had been eating at him for weeks
now. Making him wonder how he could bear to go being
a PI after his fatal mistake, whether he even deserved to
be. But he couldn't bring himself to talk about that.

"Very," he lied. "Look, it's not final yet."

"It sounds like it is. What do Ma and Pop say? Have
you told Devlin and Mitch yet? Talked to Eden about it?"

Christy was referring to their parents, who managed the

home office of Hawke Detective Agency in Chicago, and their brothers and sister who, like them, operated branches of the agency in various parts of the country.

"They'll support me in whatever I decide."

Christy issued a sigh of reluctant resignation. "All right. I don't like it, but you have my support, too." He had known she would come around in the end. They were that kind of loyal, loving family. "What about the San Antonio office? Will you just shut it down?"

"I'm training a replacement."

"But not family. It won't be the same."

No, Roark silently agreed after ending the call a moment later, it wouldn't be the same. He regretted that. *If* it happened. He still had that tough decision to make, and he figured that a cattle drive, out there away from everything, would be a good place to deal with it. He promised himself that by the end of the drive he would have the answers, both for himself and his client. Providing, that is, he wasn't too distracted on a personal level.

Samantha Howard. Oh, yeah, she definitely qualified as a distraction, a risky one for a man who needed to concentrate on what might be his last case.

Getting to his feet, Roark went to the window behind his desk. The agency's fourth-floor location offered an appealing view of the city, but it wasn't San Antonio that interested him as he stood there unconsciously exercising the fingers of his right hand. His mind was entirely occupied with the image of the woman he had escorted back to her office less than an hour ago. He couldn't get her out of his head.

Not beautiful, he decided. Not in the conventional sense, anyway, but eye-catching all the same with her mane of burnished chestnut hair. The kind of hair a man longed to release from that tight coil so that it tumbled into his hands, his fingers sifting through its mass while those velvet-brown eyes stroked him with her gaze. Eyes that were vulnerable but at the same time wore a strength of character.

He tried to remember her face, and all he could picture was pride and a composure that he wanted to believe concealed hot emotions. The wild fires that challenged a man.

Careful, Hawke. You're letting an imagination you can't afford control your senses. You're being hired to protect her, not seduce her.

Damn, he was getting himself all aroused. There were problems enough in this case without involving himself in that direction. He reminded himself that he needed to be concerned not with those long, silky legs and a pair of tantalizing breasts but with the welfare of the woman behind them. He had guessed almost from the start she was hiding some painful secret and that maybe it was connected with her resentment of him.

Issues from the past were bound to complicate things on this fool cattle drive. Yeah, he could count on it. And why, in the first place, had he ever urged her to accept the terms of her grandfather's will, particularly now when they knew the threat to her was real? So real that he had a man watching out for her while he made preparations for his absence from the agency.

Roark thought about the snake. Someone was playing a deadly game, and he'd have his work cut out for him safeguarding her. But it was too late to retreat. Not when he'd promised the old man, not when his granddaughter was determined now to win that inheritance.

He was still absently clenching and unclenching his hand, still thinking about Samantha when the door opened behind him. He swung away from the window, one eyebrow climbing in amusement as Wendell entered the office huffing like a wounded bull, his flushed face nearly the color of the hair that flamed on his head.

''That stinking elevator!'' he gasped.

''Not working again?''

"The next time we lease office space, can it please be at ground level?"

Roark's young trainee dumped his load of parcels on the surface of the desk. Roark came around the desk to inspect them. "Are we in business?"

"Managed to get everything you wanted. The map was the hardest. You have any idea how tough it is to locate a simple thing like a detailed map of Colorado? Bet I went into three stores before I found it."

"Necessary, Wendell. I should be able to keep in contact with you by cell phone, but we'll need to locate and agree on any places along the route where I stand a chance of picking up your e-mails."

"I'll be sending them," his eager young trainee promised.

"This is your chance, Wendell. While I'm investigating on my end, you're going to be investigating for me on this end, which makes you my eyes and ears back here while I'm on that trail."

"And your legs."

"And my legs," Roark conceded, knowing the trainee was thinking of the three destinations he had assigned him to look into. "Just be careful how and where they carry you. Remember, Wendell, until we know otherwise, we assume we're dealing here with someone who's desperate enough to kill. And maybe he's not alone."

Because if there is more than one of them, Roark thought, Wendell could be as much at risk back here in Texas as he and his client were in Colorado.

Samantha Howard. The thought of sharing anything with her on the long trail, even danger, already had his blood racing. With that kind of temptation to be resisted, it was going to be one hell of a cattle drive.

HE CAME HERE whenever he was in town. It wasn't just because he admired the structure, though the Tower of the Americas was a marvelous feat of engineering. Like a gigantic, long-stemmmed mushroom, it soared above the humble and the mundane.

What he relished was standing here like this, all alone on the observation deck hundreds of feet above the sprawling city, gazing out at the far horizon. It represented the pinnacle of success he was striving for, and he wasn't going to be cheated of it. Not this time.

He'd failed before, and the reminder of that failure, the crushing sense of disappointment, made him feel sick all over again. Made him grip the rail of the lofty deck with rage and frustration.

But he was going to correct all that. He had already begun. He'd hoped to scare her off with the snake, but it wasn't enough. He'd have to get serious now. Only, he had to be careful, not risk anything that would direct suspicion at him.

She had to be stopped, though, before someone learned of the secret he was protecting. The timing was critical, and she stood in his way. He promised himself that before it was all over, she would no longer be an obstacle.

"You can count on it, Samantha," he whispered into the wind.

And then he smiled. Yeah, he liked being here on top of the world. The height exhilarated him, made him feel tall and powerful. Made him feel he could do whatever he had to do.

Chapter Three

It's a long way to fall.

She would go and tell herself that, Samantha thought wryly. It was something she wouldn't have done if the bridge under here had been solid, because heights didn't ordinarily bother her.

There were no guardrails, and the planks over which they bumped felt about as secure as toothpicks. She supposed that's why the gorge they were crossing seemed much wider than it probably was and the river at its bottom an unnerving distance below them.

"Don't worry, folks," their young driver assured them from the front seat. "There's a brand-new steel structure supporting us. The boards are just temporary until the crews get around to pouring the floor and installing the rails. Now, the old bridge this one replaced...that was something to worry about."

He had been cheerfully informing them of the progress of the road's reconstruction ever since he had collected them from the airport in his sturdy SUV. That had been miles ago. Long miles through a spectacular mountain wilderness of dizzy ascents and breathless turns.

The Morning Star Ranch, where the other drovers were waiting for them, was their destination. It had been purchased by a company that was developing the property into Colorado's next ski resort. The company was responsible for the new road and this hellish bridge that was making her giddy, Samantha thought. Would they never finish crawling across its length?

"You okay?" Roark asked beside her. He had to have noticed how rigid she was.

"Couldn't be better."

Oh, you're just great. If you can't handle this, what are you going to be like piloting a couple of hundred long-horns?

But she didn't want to think about that. Not until she had to. Anyway, it wasn't just the condition of the route that had her on edge. Her companion squeezed in beside her was partly to blame for that.

With every jolt in the road, every sharp bend, his solid bulk had come bumping up against her side. Making her far too aware of the heat of his hard body, of the distinctive scent that she already associated with him—a masculine blend of faint musk and the stronger odor of a woodsy soap. Heady stuff, and on him far too arousing.

"Sorry," he kept apologizing, though she wondered if those contacts were sometimes deliberate.

She might have challenged them, except the SUV was carrying so many supplies from town, along with their own gear piled beside the driver, that she and Roark had a minimum of space on the back seat. And with so little room for them to occupy, she could scarcely blame him for his closeness, even if it did leave her light-headed.

Samantha was able to breathe easier when the vehicle reached the other side of the gorge. The bridge behind them, they traveled another half mile along the rough gravel and then were halted where the crew was working with heavy equipment that blocked the road.

"Looks like we'll be sitting here for a few minutes," their driver indicated.

"Care to stretch your legs?" Roark asked Samantha.

She welcomed his suggestion. It would be a relief to escape the disturbing intimacy of their position on the crowded back seat. They left the driver with the car and strolled back along the road, away from the dust and roar of the machinery.

There was a gap in the evergreens, and they stopped at an overlook that commanded a view of the mountains. Along the lower slopes were groves of aspen, their thick ranks so golden with autumn tints that the sight was almost blinding.

For a moment they were silent, their attention focused on the dazzling display, and then Roark turned to her and said quietly, "Want to talk about it?"

Stretching their legs had been just an excuse then, Samantha realized. He had sensed she was worried, that the closer they got to the ranch the more troubled she became.

"What's bothering you?" he persisted. "Besides this god-awful road, I mean? It's the risk of the cattle drive, isn't it? The fear that someone wants you out of the way and that this drive could give him an opportunity to strike? Look, I know that's a very real possibility, that the threat is there, but I want you to know I'm going to stick close to you. I'm going to see to it that, whoever he is, he doesn't touch you."

It would be easy to lie, to let him think this was exactly what had her so unhappy. But why bother when tomorrow he would see the truth anyway? All right, so her pride was going to suffer, but it was better to get it out in the open now.

"That should be what's worrying me, but it isn't." Samantha drew a slow breath, released it and confessed her fear. "It's the horse."

He was clearly perplexed. "Are we talking about a particular horse?"

"Yes, the one I'm going to be expected to mount tomorrow morning when we move those cattle out."

He stared at her. "Are you telling me you don't ride? That you're about to join a cattle drive, and you have no experience in the saddle?"

"Let's just say I'm not comfortable in the saddle. That I hate being in the saddle and that the horse, any horse, knows it."

"How can that be when you grew up on the Walking W? Or was I misinformed about that?"

"Yes, I was raised on the ranch, and I was taught to ride. I wasn't given any choice about that. But there was never a moment when I wasn't plain scared up there in those stirrups. You can imagine how my grandfather liked that."

"Yeah, Joe Walker wouldn't have appreciated a grand-daughter who wasn't at home in the saddle. I guess that explains why the two of you ended up being alienated, why you didn't visit him in the hospital or attend his funeral. Or does it?"

It didn't begin to explain Samantha's estrangement from her grandfather, barely touched on the reasons for her intense dislike of everything connected with ranching. But those wounds were too deep, too personal to discuss with Roark Hawke. She avoided the subject by giving him another truth. One she shared in an angry voice.

"I did try to visit him when I learned he was ill. But he made it clear through his lawyer that he didn't want me there. I shouldn't have been surprised. To the end he was too stubborn to want anything from me, especially my sympathy. That's how it was with us."

"I didn't know that."

No, and you didn't know that I was at his funeral. Or as close anyway, Samantha remembered, as she could bring herself to go. Unnoticed by the mourners, she had watched her grandfather's burial from a hill overlooking the cemetery before fleeing from a scene she could no longer handle. The memories had simply been too painful. But Roark didn't have to hear this either.

"A real joke, isn't it?" she said grimly. "I've got to climb up on a horse—a horse, mind you, that isn't going to like me being on his back any more than I want to be there—and pretend I know what I'm doing while I escort two hundred unwilling cows through a howling wilderness. Now that qualifies as funny, don't you think?''

"You'll manage."

"You sound very sure about that."

"Why not?" His gaze traveled from her face down the entire length of her figure, his appraisal so slow and thorough that Samantha could feel herself flushing. "You have a body built for the saddle."

And other things. That's what his hot eyes seemed to be telling her. Before she could stop him, he reached out and captured her hands, imprisoning them in his own big hands as he bent his head to inspect them.

"And you have a pair of hands meant for holding reins. Strong hands, I'd say."

His touch was warm and steady and far too provocative.

"What you learned as a girl will come back to you. You won't have forgotten those lessons, whether you liked them or not. And if this time around you have a little patience with yourself…yeah, you'll manage just fine."

His easy confidence in her was hard to resist, his husky voice and deep, blue-eyed gaze even harder.

"Besides…"

"What?"

"You won't be alone out there in that howling wilderness. I'll be riding beside you."

Not as close as he was now, Samantha hoped, which was too close. She could smell his scent again, and she swore that this time she detected more than just musk and soap. That he bore the odors of leather and horses. Aromas that had poignant associations for her. They set off a warning inside her head.

He's not just a PI and a bodyguard. He's also a cowboy who was your grandfather's friend. Stay away from him.

Their driver sounded the horn of the SUV, signaling them that the road was clear again. It wasn't necessary to snatch her hands away. To her relief, Roark released them.

The cattle drive was waiting for her, Samantha remembered as they walked back to the car. She was still nervous about it, but determined. She could do it. She *had* to do it. If for no other reason, she needed to overcome the ghosts of her past.

NONE OF THEM QUESTIONED his presence. And Roark wondered about that. Asked himself if any of them around the table suspected his real reason for being here. That he'd been hired to protect Samantha on the drive because of a threat to her. That there was someone who might want her eliminated.

Just how had the lawyer explained him to the others who had arrived here from Texas ahead of Samantha and him? Had he told them Roark Hawke was joining the outfit simply to help out? Well, that wasn't so improbable. He was a rancher himself, a neighbor of Joe Walker's. After all, another neighbor, who was caring for the Walking W in their absence, had sent his son for that same purpose. The young Alex McKenzie was seated on the other side of Samantha.

Whatever the members of the company supposed, Roark had no intention of enlightening them. They would understand soon enough. For now, it was enough they accepted him as one of them. This they'd readily done when he'd been introduced to them. It had occurred as they'd gathered at the picnic table under the cottonwoods for the last kitchen-prepared supper they would enjoy before they reached Alamo Junction a hundred miles south of here.

The faces around the table were familiar to Samantha. She had known these people from the Walking W and could share their easy camaraderie. But for Roark, who had been too busy every weekend on his own spread to meet more than a handful of his neighbors, they had yet to emerge as distinct individuals. Observant, which he had to be as a PI, he worked now on their identities as he listened to their exchanges.

"How much trail you reckon we can cover per day?"

The question was issued around a chunk of steak, which had replaced the wad of chewing tobacco that had earlier been parked in a corner of the speaker's mouth. It came from Cappy Davis, whose face was as seamed as bark. He'd been a fixture on the Walking W since his boyhood, which, if his tough old frame was any indication, must have been before the Flood.

Shep Thomas, the Walking W's earnest ranch foreman who was serving as the drive's trail boss, considered the question that had been directed at him. "Anywhere from ten to twenty miles a day. Depends on what we encounter. Most of it is public land, and we have permission to cross that, as well as the private stuff. But I won't kid you. This country is some of the meanest in the Rockies."

Cappy grunted and went back to his steak.

"Problem is," Shep continued, cradling his mug of coffee, "we got us a time line. A *crucial* one. We either deliver the cows to Alamo Junction by the contract date, or those stock cars don't wait for us. It will call for some hard driving."

The man across from Shep, as jocular as the trail boss was sober, treated the outfit to a long, slow whistle. Roark knew he was the Walking W's horse wrangler in charge of the drive's remuda, but for a moment he couldn't recall his name. Brewster? That was it. Dick Brewster.

"I know what that means. Our butts will be in slings from all that riding."

Samantha was silent, but Roark could see that Brewster's comment had her worried all over again. Not that she needed any reminders of tomorrow's ordeal.

Morning Star's ranch house, whose golden sandstone walls were just behind them, was situated on the brow of a hill that overlooked a valley. The longhorns were down there. Restless from being rounded up from the open range, they milled about in the lingering twilight, lowing their objections. Roark was aware that Samantha had been nervously eyeing the herd since the meal had been served.

He was not the only one who sensed her discomfort. Alex McKenzie, that friendly young puppy on the other side of her, tried to come to her rescue. "If it's going to be all that rugged, Samantha shouldn't have to put up with it. Not on horseback. She can ride in the chuck wagon with Ramona."

Dick Brewster hooted with laughter. "That old heap? She'd be jounced to a jelly before noontime of our first day out. That is, if the thing makes it that far."

All eyes at the table slid in the direction of a sturdy but battered pickup truck parked under a ponderosa pine several yards away. The vehicle's back end had been fitted up as a rolling pantry. The only gaze that didn't turn toward the truck belonged to Ramona Chacon, the Walking W's round-faced cook. Her eyes were busy glaring at the horse wrangler.

"My baby can go anywhere your horses and cows can go, Dick Brewster. And you'd better start having a little respect for her if you expect to keep your belly full on this drive."

Roark could see that the woman wasn't genuinely offended. He had already decided that Ramona was too sweet tempered to mind Brewster's teasing.

Alex returned to the subject of Samantha's uneasiness. "Rules don't say Sam has to be in the saddle, just that she has to finish the drive."

Roark wasn't sure he appreciated McKenzie's concern for Samantha, even though she had explained to him at the start of the meal that Alex's interest in her welfare was the innocent result of a boyhood crush he'd had on her when he was a teenager. Fine. Except McKenzie was no longer a teenager, and Samantha looked as if she was enjoying his attention too much. And, damn it, why should he care?

Ramona added her invitation to Alex's plan. "I'd be pleased to have your company in the chuck wagon, Sam." Wise or not, Roark could no longer keep silent. "Good suggestion. The only thing is, Samantha has already decided she intends to make this drive on horseback along with the rest of us. Isn't that what you told me on the trip up here, Samantha?"

She turned to him, meeting his challenge. For a moment she said nothing. He'd noticed she had an unconscious habit—whenever she was particularly tense about something—of catching the lobe of her right ear between her forefinger and her middle finger and tugging on it slowly. She was doing that now.

Roark was experiencing his own tension, wondering if she was about to tell him she'd didn't appreciate his veto on her behalf, that she would express her own decisions. He knew she would be right if she did blast him, but he hoped instead she would agree with him. That she would have the courage to conquer her fear.

Her fingers dropped from the lobe of her ear. "Roark is right," she said quietly. "I promised myself I would do this on horseback. I'll stick with that."

"Then it's settled," Roark said, wondering if she had any idea how much he admired her for her resolve. A resolve that he knew couldn't have been easy for her.

One of the staff at the ranch appeared from the kitchen with a loaded tray. The outfit turned their attentions to the desserts she served them. Roark used the opportunity to study the faces around the table.

The expressions were cheerfully eager as they anticipated tomorrow's drive. But Roark wondered, Did one of them have another agenda? Could one of this pleasant company be dangerous?

AFTER MAKING SURE that Samantha had safely locked herself in the bedroom that had been assigned to her for the night, Roark went back to his own room next door.

The old ranch house had no electricity. Hard to believe in this day and age, but its last owner, a contemporary of Joe Walker's, had preferred it this way. Roark had to use a flashlight to find his way across the room to the oil lamp that had been provided for him on his bedside table.

There were matches beside the lamp. He struck one of them and lit the lamp. Its soft, flickering glow permitted him to perform one last, essential task before he turned in for the night. Reaching for his cell phone, he perched on the edge of the bed and punched in the digits for the number he wanted at a condo back in San Antonio.

As instructed, Wendell was waiting for his call. The young trainee answered on the first ring. "How's it going?" he asked after Roark identified himself.

He knew Wendell was hoping to hear about some exciting development. Too bad he had to disappoint him. "Fine. We're all one big, happy family here." *So far,* Roark thought. "How about your end? Did you get out to the Walking W?"

"Visited that gulch just like you wanted," Wendell reported, referring to the deep ravine where Joe Walker had been thrown from his horse. "I was careful not to be seen. Not much chance I would be. It's in the middle of nowhere. Heck of a long hike out there."

"Find anything?"

"I think maybe I did. There was a lot of wall to cover down in there, some of it pretty high. But I found this spot where the rocks looked like they'd been freshly chipped off by bullets. And if they were, that means the old man's horse *was* spooked by gunfire and someone *could* have been shooting at him."

Wendell was so enthusiastic about his discovery Roark hadn't the heart to tell him that chipped rocks weren't necessarily evidence of gunfire. "Could you tell whether the rock was scored? You know, as if bullets had left channels in it?"

"The marks weren't clear. Maybe you'll be able to tell

something. I took a bunch of photographs. As soon as they're developed, I'll e-mail them for you to study. They should be waiting for you at your first stop.''

''That's fine.'' Roark would examine those photographs, but he doubted they would give him anything useful. But Wendell, being Wendell, was so eager to succeed that, again, Roark didn't want to discourage the overly zealous trainee.

''Tomorrow I'll tackle the monastery and the Western Museum,'' Wendell continued, referring to the institutions that would receive Joe Walker's estate if Samantha failed to meet the terms of her grandfather's will. ''I'll let you know what I learn.''

Cautioning him to be careful about how he handled those interviews, Roark promised to keep in touch and ended the call. He hoped he would be able to maintain regular contact with Wendell. He'd had no problem tonight, but a cell phone might not be dependable in a remote mountain area like this. There was also the matter of power, though Ramona Chacon had told him he could keep the instrument recharged using the lighter in her truck.

Roark went on sitting there for a moment on the edge of the bed, listening. Although it wasn't all that late, a silence had settled over the house. The members of the outfit, knowing that the drive would be underway at first light, had retired early. Which, Roark told himself, was what he needed to do.

Shedding his clothes, he blew out the lamp and crawled under the covers. His phone call to Wendell hadn't produced anything worthwhile. Not that he had expected it to, but a PI overlooked nothing. It was a beginning, and on the drive he would seize every opportunity to advance his investigation.

His last thoughts before he drifted off were for Samantha next door. He hoped she was sleeping peacefully, not worrying about tomorrow. He also wished he could think of her as nothing but a client who needed his protection instead of a woman he wanted beside him in this bed. Damn.

SAMANTHA DIDN'T BOTHER switching on the flashlight on her bedside table to check her watch, but she knew it was late. Probably close to midnight, if not after.

She had managed to drowse for a couple of hours, though fitfully, but now she was wide-awake. The moon had risen, its light streaming through the uncurtained windows. She might have blamed its brightness for her sleeplessness, except that wouldn't be true.

Nor could she blame the cattle in the valley below, at least not entirely. Although if their occasional bawling was any indication, they continued to be as restless as she was, reminding her of what tomorrow would demand of her. And tonight?

She had to face it. The fundamental reason for her waking was a physical one—she needed a bathroom. In any other circumstances, this wouldn't have been a problem. In this place it was. The ranch house had neither bathrooms nor electricity and only rudimentary plumbing in the kitchen. Relieving herself meant a trip to an old-fashioned privy out back. Not something she wanted to risk in the middle of the night.

You can wait until morning.

That's what she told herself, and she believed it. For a while. But the more she tried not to think about it, the more she wanted that privy. When her need became urgent, she gave in.

This is ridiculous. You have to go, so go.

Swinging her legs over the side of the bed, she shoved her feet into her slippers, scooped up the flashlight and, after putting a coat on over her pajamas, headed for the door.

The lock was as outdated as the rest of the house, the

kind that came equipped with a key. It had to be persuaded before it would turn and let Samantha out into the passage.

There were doors along both sides of the corridor, all of them closed, the rooms behind them silent. She looked at the door next to hers, knowing she had to rouse Roark and ask him to accompany her. He would have her head if she didn't. She had raised her hand to knock when the door directly across the hall opened. Ramona emerged, surprised to find her there.

"I need a trip out to the privy," Samantha whispered.

"Me, too," Ramona whispered back, securing the sash on her bathrobe. "I'd welcome the company. I wasn't looking forward to going out there alone."

Samantha decided that as long as Ramona was with her she needn't disturb Roark. She didn't know Ramona well, but she knew enough to trust her.

The gleam of the flashlight led them into Morning Star's living room where Samantha could make out the shapes of a stone fireplace, Navajo rugs on the floor, heavy pottery and dark oil paintings on the walls, the kind of Western scenes her grandfather had favored. In fact, the whole place reminded her of the Walking W's ranch house, and she found that depressing. Still, it would be a shame when all this was pulled down and replaced with a ski lodge and condos, which was scheduled to happen when the new road was finished.

Crossing the room, they let themselves out of the house through a French door, which they left ajar for their return. A gibbous moon swam in the night sky, casting a glow strong enough to permit Samantha to make out the forms of the longhorns in the valley below. They were hushed now, as if waiting for something.

For a quick moment she experienced a sense of uneasiness. It was her imagination. She was letting her imagination get the best of her, seeing an enemy lurking in the thick shadows under the trees where there was none. Besides, Ramona was close at her side.

Samantha remembered the way from an earlier daylight visit. With the flashlight to guide them, they went around the house and along the path. Samantha was thankful for the coat over her pajamas. The day had been almost balmy, but a sharp chill had set in after twilight. It was the autumn weather that made her shiver. Or nerves. Whatever the explanation, she was relieved when they reached the facility at the end of the path.

"You go first," Samantha instructed her companion, handing her the flashlight.

Ramona disappeared inside the privy. Samantha waited outside, wishing she would hurry. When the woman finally reappeared, she returned the flashlight with a warning.

"The batteries must be weakening. I'm afraid it's getting kind of dim."

So dim, Samantha discovered, that managing the privy was a challenge once she was inside and with the door closed. After making use of the facility, she was able to wash her hands using the basin and a can of water one of the staff had provided on a shelf.

By this time the flashlight was worthless. She switched it off and tucked it into a pocket of her coat. They didn't really need it, anyway. The glow from the moon would be more than adequate enough to light their way back to the house.

That's what she thought until she stepped out of the privy and found Ramona nowhere in sight. What had become of her? Had she returned to the house without her?

"Ramona," she called softly, "are you there?"

There was no answer. And Samantha suddenly missed the reassuring beam of the flashlight. She also decided that the night seemed much too quiet, so quiet that she could hear nothing but the sound of her own breathing. She didn't like it. Didn't like how heavy the shadows were in that grove of trees off to her right, shadows that could conceal a menace lurking in their depths.

She was being silly again. But she couldn't shake her

sense of uneasiness, the eerie feeling that she was being watched, that she was no longer alone out here. The feeling became a certainty when one of those dark shadows moved, detaching itself from the others.

Samantha didn't pause to learn the identity of that furtive shadow or why Ramona hadn't waited for her. Swinging around, she fled up the path as if every nightmare from her childhood were at her heels. She was so fearful of the thing behind her that she didn't concern herself with what might be in front of her. Until she flew around the corner of the house and smacked into a wall that hadn't been there before. A towering wall of living, breathing flesh.

She knew it was flesh, because when she raised her hands to defend herself against her attacker, they encountered a chest. A hard, totally bare male chest. She was dragged up against its heat when a pair of strong hands gripped her upper arms to steady her. Gasping, she struggled against his hold.

"Easy," he said.

Samantha went still. She recognized his voice.

"What were you running from?"

"Something back there under the trees."

"What?" Roark demanded sharply.

"I don't know. I couldn't tell. Maybe it was human, maybe not."

Her relief that Roark was here had been both enormous and sweet, but, aware now that she was still pressed against his naked chest, Samantha experienced another kind of danger. One from which she needed to disengage herself. "I'm all right now," she insisted. "It was probably just an animal. You can let me go."

He released her. "What in hell are you doing out here, anyway?"

"I needed to visit the privy."

"Then you should have had me go with you. That's what I'm here for, remember?"

"I didn't go out alone. Ramona was with me."

"Where is she?"

"I don't know. She seems to have dis—"

"Here I am," Ramona said, trotting around the corner of the house.

"Where on earth have you been? Didn't you hear me call you?"

"I'm sorry. There was a nightjar singing in one of the trees, and I stepped around the other side of the house to see if I could catch a glimpse of—" She broke off, as if she realized that Samantha was upset and that Roark had arrived on the scene and was looking far too rigid standing there. "Is something wrong?"

"Samantha spotted something she didn't like under the trees. Did you see anyone back there? Or maybe an animal?"

"No, nothing."

Roark nodded, and then before Samantha could prevent it, he grabbed her hand and hauled her in the direction of the open French door. "What are you—"

"I'm taking you back inside. Putting you behind a locked door where you belong."

He must have the eyes of an owl, she thought. He needed no flashlight to aid him as he swiftly conducted her through the door and across the living room into the corridor, pausing only long enough to make certain that Ramona was close behind them. Samantha waited until the bemused cook was safely back inside her room before she confronted her rescuer.

"Why are you so angry with me? I told you I'm all right now."

"You're not all right. You're shaking all over. And Ramona or no Ramona, you had no business being out there without me. Or are you forgetting what happened back in Texas? That threat could have followed you here to Colorado."

"How did you know Ramona and I were—"

"I caught a glimpse of your flashlight passing under my

window so I left my room to investigate and saw the
French door open.''

The light must have awakened him, which demonstrated
an alertness on her behalf she had no choice but to be
grateful for. She expressed her appreciation with a meek
thank-you.

By then he had steered her back into her bedroom. Or
what she assumed was her bedroom until he lighted the
oil lamp, and she learned that it was his room.

She also discovered, turning to him, that he was a riv-
eting sight in nothing but a pair of snug jeans. In his haste
he hadn't bothered to don anything else, unless she
counted the gun tucked into his waistband. Samantha
wasn't sure whether her slight wooziness was the result of
the terror she had just experienced or the slabs of hard
muscle above the waistband of his jeans.

"Uh, I assume you have a reason for bringing me here
instead of next door. A *good* one."

"I want you on that bed."

"I said I was grateful for your rescue, but I'm not *that*
grateful."

"Sitting there, Samantha, not lying there. If someone
happens to be prowling around looking for you, maybe
even knows which room is yours, then you're safer waiting
here while I check outside. I want to find out what you
saw in that grove of trees. Try to relax, huh? I'll only be
a few minutes."

He was gone then, taking the key with him. She heard
him locking the door from the hallway outside. Eyeing the
bed, Samantha decided that his command was probably a
sensible one. She was feeling just weak enough to need a
support, and there was no chair in the small room.

That was better, she thought when she'd lowered herself
onto the edge of the mattress. What didn't feel so comfortable was the memory of Roark Hawke's high-handed
treatment of her. All right, so she had made a mistake, but
he didn't have to be so brusque about it. It was bad enough

having a bodyguard without his expecting her to ask permission every time she went to the bathroom.

She didn't like any of it, but she had her resentment under control when he returned a short while later. "Nothing," he reported. "Whatever was out there is gone. It was probably nothing more sinister than an animal."

"A big one, by the size of that shadow."

"Well, it *is* bear country."

"Is that supposed to be reassuring? Though, come to think of it, I guess a bear would be more friendly than a two-legged stalker. It doesn't make sense, you know."

"What doesn't?"

"That someone should want me out of the way. I talked to the lawyer again before we left Texas. He told me that my grandfather's investments were still sound but nowhere near what they'd been worth a few years ago when the market was high. The value of the ranch itself is solid, but there are debts against it that will have to be paid off by whoever inherits. What it all comes down to is that the estate is important to me because of my situation, but to someone else—"

"It doesn't represent the kind of fortune they'd go to extreme lengths to get their hands on."

"Exactly. So what's the explanation?"

Roark shook his head, as much at a loss for a motive as she was.

Samantha stared at him. Though she hadn't been aware of it happening, he was seated beside her on the bed…too close. She was conscious again of all that expanse of naked chest. "How can you go around like that? Aren't you freezing?"

"I'm warm enough."

"I'm bundled in a coat, and I'm still like ice. My hands are, anyway."

By the time she realized her admission was a mistake, it was too late. He had already captured her hands between his own.

"So let me share some of my heat."

His strong fingers began to massage her hands, briskly at first and then more slowly and deeply. She should have stopped him, but his treatment felt too good, as soothing as a warm bath.

"Better?"

"Mmm."

Another error probably, because he must have read her languid acknowledgment as an invitation. His performance became decidedly sensual, his hands stroking hers with a series of caresses that could only be defined as seductive. Her gaze met his, searching his eyes that had become so dark a blue they were like midnight, intense with his unmistakable arousal.

"What are you thinking?" she challenged him nervously.

"That I'd like to share more than just the heat of my hands." He leaned toward her, his mouth mere inches from hers, his voice low and raspy. "What are *you* thinking, Samantha?"

He was so close now she could feel the male heat radiating from the sleek flesh of his naked chest, searing her with his desire. In another moment his mouth would cover hers, their breaths mingling as he devoured her with his lips and tongue. She had never been so tempted, nor so terrified of the consequences.

"I'm thinking," she answered him firmly, removing her hands from his and pulling away from his potent nearness, "that I'm not going to risk getting burned."

He stared at her for a long minute, frowning. She could see he was trying to understand. "What just happened? Because I've got to tell you, I thought you were as interested as I was in getting—"

"Intimate?"

"Well, yeah."

"You're a cowboy, Roark. You may be a PI, but at heart and in soul you're a cowboy."

"What's wrong with cowboys?"

"I don't get involved with them. Ever."

"Why? Why do you have this resistance to everything connected with ranching? And don't tell me it's because of the sour relationship you had with your grandfather. I don't buy it. There's a better explanation than that."

"I'm sorry, but it's the only explanation I have." She got to her feet, needing to get away, needing to escape from her treacherous susceptibility to him. "I'm going back to my room. I think we should both try to get some sleep with what's left of the night."

And that wouldn't be easy, Samantha realized. Not with her emotions threatening to betray her every time she came within touching distance of Roark Hawke.

CONCEALED IN THE SHADOWS, he stood on the slope above the ranch house and watched the light go out in her window.

He had missed an easy opportunity tonight. If the PI hadn't rushed to her rescue…

Hawke was a frustration all right. Always there, guarding her. A definite problem. Never mind, there would be other opportunities. He would wait for them, and he would get to her in the end. But he had to be careful. No one must guess. An accident would be best. If he could arrange an accident…

Whatever it took. Because she had to be eliminated before the end of the drive. Everything depended on that.

Chapter Four

There was a mist in the valley where they gathered in the chill dawn.

"It'll burn off when the sun clears the horizon," Roark said, studying the sky. "We should have clear weather for our first day."

Samantha, standing beside him, nodded. She knew he was no more interested in the weather at this moment than she was. He was merely trying to keep her distracted. She silently blessed him for that, and for making no mention of what had happened between them last night...or, what had *almost* happened.

Roark's effort, however, was a wasted one. Nothing could divert her attention from the longhorns milling restlessly behind the barbed wire barricade that kept them in the valley. Close up like this, they weren't a sight that encouraged her with their long legs, mottled hides in a variety of colors and patterns, and wicked-looking horns. They seemed to be watching her as unhappily as she eyed them.

"They sense they're about to be moved out," Roark explained. "Cattle are resistant to leaving their home range."

She didn't blame them. Given a choice, she would have remained here herself.

"They'll settle down after an hour or two on the trail."

Samantha seriously doubted that she would accept the situation in a similar fashion. She was certain of it when their horse wrangler rode toward them where they waited. The bony-faced Dick Brewster was leading the two mounts he had cut out of his remuda for their use. One of them was a big, handsome roan, the other a dainty mare. Both were already saddled.

Dick wore his usual carefree grin when he reached them and dismounted. "This here is Dolly," he introduced Samantha to the mare. "Don't worry, Sam, she's as gentle as she looks. She won't give you any trouble."

"You ready?" Roark asked her quietly.

The morning air had a sharp bite to it, but Samantha's hands were perspiring. Nerves, of course. She wore a lady's low-crowned Stetson tied under her chin. She'd left it hanging down over the single thick braid that swung from the back of her head. But now, catching the brim in her hand, she pulled the hat forward and settled it firmly in place at a jaunty angle. A gesture of determination. She hoped.

"Ready," she said.

"Want a boost up?"

Shaking her head, Samantha placed her foot in the stirrup, gripped the saddle horn, and swung her leg up and over the mare's back. To her relief, Dolly accepted her presence without an objection. She prayed that all those detestable lessons of her childhood wouldn't desert her as she gathered the reins loosely in her hand and tried to act as if she knew what she was doing.

"Looking good," Roark congratulated her.

She watched him mount his own horse with an ease she could never duplicate. Whatever the accident of his urban birth, his rangy body had been designed by nature for the saddle. And no matter how she felt about cowboys, it was a sight she couldn't help admiring.

The others had joined them by then, their quarter horses

moving in close so that the riders could receive their orders from the trail boss.

"Here's the plan," Shep Thomas instructed them in his somber manner. "Ramona is going on ahead with the chuck wagon. Come midmorning, she'll be set up and waiting for us with coffee and goodies. But don't count on coffee stops after this. We won't have the time for them. It's just that, this being the first day and all, I figure we'll be more than ready for a morning break."

"Ramona know the route?" Cappy Davis asked, his jaws working on a chaw of tobacco.

"I've given her a map. She'll find the way. Dick," the trail boss continued, turning to the horse wrangler, "you'll be out front, of course, with the remuda. I'll ride point. Cappy, you take left flank, and, Alex, you handle right flank. Roark and Samantha will ride drag."

The young Alex McKenzie, mindful of Samantha's comfort, expressed his concern. "But that leaves Sam swallowing the dust."

"I know, but there's less pressure there for an inexperienced rider trying to keep up." Shep regarded her solemnly. "You don't mind riding drag, do you, Sam?"

"Be happy to."

"Fine. Let's roll then."

Shep and Cappy headed for the gates on the other side of the pasture. Dick, with a good-natured wink in Samantha's direction, trotted after them. Jamming his hat over his unruly curls, Alex saluted her with his own boyish smile of encouragement, wheeled his horse, and rode off to take up his post.

When they were gone, Roark leaned toward her from his saddle. "You don't have a clue what just happened here, do you?"

"My education at the Walking W didn't include Cattle Drive 101," she admitted. "So, if you'd care to translate…"

While the others moved into position, Roark enlightened

her. "Horses not working are too impatient to follow slow cattle, so the remuda is always out in front. Riding point means leading the herd. Flank riders are at the sides to keep the herd from bulging. Drag brings up the rear to discourage strays and keep the herd moving. And swallowing dust—"

"That I've already figured out. It's what you and I are going to be doing back here behind all these cows."

"Well, two hundred longhorns are going to raise some clouds." He stood in his stirrups to see over the herd. "Gates are down. You all set?"

"Absolutely," she lied, clutching the reins.

From the far side of the pasture came Shep Thomas's shout. "Move 'em on out!"

Someone—Dick Brewster probably, Samantha guessed—raised a yell worthy of the best cattle drive movies. The others took it up, urging the longhorns forward. They poured through the open gates, streaming south along the trail.

The drive was underway.

WITHIN THE FIRST ARDUOUS HOUR of the trek, Samantha decided that someone had made a serious mistake. Unlike its aggressive ancestors, this new strain of longhorn had been bred to be docile. Trouble was, the cows didn't seem to know that. Looking out over a sea of backsides, she was convinced that no beasts could be more stubborn, more stupid or just plain downright ornery.

By now, Samantha had added another word to her growing cattle drive vocabulary. *Cowbrutes.* And that's exactly what the longhorns were. They were forever challenging their drovers by either making repeated attempts to turn back, straggling from the herd to graze on vegetation no respectable steer would touch, or, for no apparent reason, simply coming to a complete standstill.

She supposed she had no good reason to complain. It was, after all, Roark who so capably dealt with these problems whenever they occurred at the rear of the herd. Samantha wasn't able to help him, even had she known what to do. She was far too busy amid all the noise, smells and dirt just staying on her horse.

So far she was managing to keep her seat, which Roark was largely responsible for. When he wasn't dashing off after strays, he stuck close to her side, offering her patient advice.

"Not so tight on the reins. Trust Dolly. She knows what to do."

And again. "Try to relax. You're holding yourself so rigid, you'll be worn out before our first break."

And finally. "That's it. You're getting it. You'll be a drover yet."

Samantha doubted that, but he did have an easy faith in her that heartened her, and a lopsided smile that tugged dangerously at her insides.

The sun was well above the horizon when the others dropped back for a brief conference on the progress of the drive.

"Most of 'em is starting to settle down nicely," Cappy observed, "but we got us a headache with that one there." The old man spit tobacco juice in the direction of a reddish heifer. "She's forever up to mischief."

Shep nodded. "She's a late calf. Recently weaned by the looks of her and probably too young for the drive. But I couldn't leave her behind with Morning Star shutting down its operation."

"Yeah, but chasing after one heifer is taking up too much time and effort we need for the other beeves. What're we gonna do about her?"

There was a moment of silence while they considered the problem. It ended when Samantha said carelessly, "I'll be responsible for her."

The men stared at her in disbelief. Samantha was as surprised as they were. What had possessed her to make such a startling offer? But she knew the answer to that

question. Guilt. Guilt and a feeling of uselessness. They
had expected nothing of her. She was simply there because
she had to be there, and they had accepted that.

She had accepted it herself. But she was tired of being
helpless, of watching them do all the work while she
trailed after them on Dolly's back, of no value to either
them or herself.

Shep cleared his throat. "I don't think—"

"Damn it," she cut him off, squaring her shoulders with
determination. "I can look after one heifer, can't I?"

"I think we should let her," Roark said, and there was
a note of pride in his voice that warmed Samantha like a
comforting glow.

The trail boss shrugged. "All right," he agreed. "She's
all yours, Sam."

In the half hour that followed, Samantha had cause to
regret the mission for which she had so readily volunteered. How much trouble could one young cow be? she
had asked herself. Plenty, she learned as she played hide-
and-seek with the heifer around a pile of boulders, chased
her out of a deep hollow and freed her from a juniper
thicket in which she had trapped herself.

It wasn't that the animal was mean tempered. She simply had difficulty understanding why she should keep on
the move when there were so many fascinating things to
investigate. Samantha could sympathize with her reluctance, which was probably why, with a combination of
coaxing and scolding, she began to achieve a measure of
success with her charge.

"I think Irma is going to be all right," she reported
happily to Roark. "Only one detour since that incident at
the creek."

Roark stared at her. "*Irma?* You've gone and called a
cow *Irma?*"

"I got tired of using cuss words."

"Samantha, drovers don't make pets of their cattle."

"What pet? She isn't a pet. It's just that she needed a

name and 'Irma' seemed to fit. Really, Roark, she does respond better with a name. Well, that and a little patience.''

"Heaven help us, she's gone and bonded with a beef!''

Let him tease her, Samantha thought. What could it hurt to be fond of a little heifer, particularly when it made her feel less anxious about this drive? And able, for the first time, to appreciate its setting.

Until now she'd been so concerned with staying on her horse and managing the heifer that she hadn't spared a moment for her surroundings. And they deserved her attention.

The land over which they were traveling was a narrow, lush park located between two long mountain ranges. Maple and oak trees, flaming with autumn colors, rimmed the grassy valley. On the slopes behind them were the forests of quaking aspen, their foliage masses of radiant gold. Higher still were the dark ranks of spruce and fir. And above it all the majestic Colorado peaks under a luminous blue sky.

From time to time, Samantha caught glimpses of wildlife—a red-tailed hawk, elk, even what might have been a bighorn sheep, though it was so far away she couldn't be sure. But she was certain of the horse she spotted.

There was a high ridge that paralleled their route, sometimes open and in other places wooded with the aspens. The horse was on that ridge, and it wasn't alone. A rider was on its back.

At first Samantha thought nothing about the distant figure. There was no reason someone shouldn't be up there. She forgot about him when he vanished into the aspens. But then he emerged on the other side of the grove. After that, though she lost sight of him again and again, he never failed to reappear, always moving abreast of them along the ridge. By then she had the uneasy feeling that the presence of the rider was no coincidence.

After checking on Irma to be sure the heifer was staying

with the herd, Samantha guided her mare over to the side of Roark's roan. "There's someone up on that ridge."

"I know," he said. "I've been aware of him."

"Am I imagining it, or is he deliberately shadowing us?"

"No, we're being tracked."

"But why? Roark, you don't suppose he's our visitor at the ranch last night?"

"We don't know there was any visitor. This could be just someone curious about our drive, maybe a rancher worried about where we're going."

"Then why doesn't he just come down here and ask?"

"Maybe he's shy."

She thought Roark was being maddeningly complacent about the whole thing. "Aren't you at all concerned about him?"

"Yeah, I'm concerned, but it's public land. He has a right to be up there, and as long as he doesn't bother us and keeps his distance…"

She supposed Roark was right. Their rider was too far away to be a threat. Unless, that is, he was armed with a high-powered rifle. Damn, she would go and think that. On the other hand, if he wanted to pick one of them off— and remembering all that had happened, she guessed that would be her—he could have done it long ago without his presence ever being detected. Just the same, Samantha wasn't happy with the idea of being a potential target.

"Do you think we should tell the others?"

"I imagine they already know."

"So we do nothing about him?"

"We stay vigilant, Samantha. That's what we do. And I don't want you out of my sight. That includes no more chasing alone after Irma. If the heifer wanders off somewhere, you call me to help. Otherwise," he said, looking out over the herd as if the longhorns were his only real interest, "it's business as usual."

But Roark proved to be less cavalier about their mystery

rider than Samantha had assumed. She was with him when he spoke to the trail boss during the coffee break a short time later.

"Shep, I suppose you've noticed we have company on the ridge."

"Oh, him. Is he still up there?"

"Last time I looked."

"He's not a problem, is he?"

"Not yet."

"Well, then…"

Samantha could see that the trail boss had his mind strictly on the cattle drive and not on some harmless rider who was keeping his distance. Nor were the others in the outfit interested in anything but swapping stories about their morning's experiences with the longhorns as they stood around gulping coffee from their mugs.

Samantha went over to the cook wagon where Ramona Chacon was dispensing coffee and doughnuts. Was she the exception in the company? The Walking W's plump, olive-skinned housekeeper did not seem to be her perpetually cheerful self. She looked sober, preoccupied.

"You're so quiet, Ramona. You're not bothered by that man on the ridge, are you?"

"What are you talking about?"

"Haven't you noticed him? He's been following the drive."

"I didn't see anyone. How could I? I've been ahead of you with the truck, remember? You ready for a refill?"

Ramona didn't seem to want to talk about it. Or, for that matter, anything, which was odd. She was ordinarily so garrulous that Samantha had to snatch at excuses to get away from her.

Nor was the cook any more forthcoming at midday when they caught up with her again where she had lunch waiting for them in the form of burritos and black beans. By now the rider on the ridge had become the cattle drive's faithful follower, though he never came within shouting distance of them and most of the time remained either out of sight among the trees or no more than an unrecognizable silhouette.

Who is he? Samantha wondered. Why is he watching us?

He continued to haunt them that afternoon as the drive pushed on through the valley. And then, to Samantha's relief, he disappeared. She kept eyeing the ridge, thinking he would reappear as he had before. But when an hour passed and there was no further sign of him, she was ready to believe he had finally given up and rode away.

After that she forgot about him. The trail had become so rugged it claimed the full attention of everyone in the outfit. Samantha spent the rest of the afternoon struggling to keep in the saddle while praying that Irma behaved herself.

The sun was low in the sky when they neared the stream where they would make camp for the night. And that's when Samantha saw him, a distant but unmistakable figure high on the ridge. They hadn't lost him, after all. She felt vulnerable all over again.

Samantha found a moment to talk to Roark while the cattle were being watered at the stream. "Our friend is back."

"I saw."

"There's something else. Ramona claimed she didn't know what I was talking about when I mentioned him to her, but I think she's lying. I think she has noticed him up there. I don't know if this is what has her so strained, but she's upset about something."

Roark was thoughtful for a few seconds. "Looks like we need to discuss the subject with Ramona."

"I tried that at the break this morning and then again at lunch. She has nothing to say."

"Let's see if this time we can persuade her."

They waited until the herd had been settled on the broad meadow beside the stream where the longhorns were content to graze, and then Roark drew the trail boss aside and explained the matter to him. Shep was reluctant at first and then agreed to accompany them. They approached the truck where it was parked on the far side of the meadow. Roark came right to the point.

"Ramona, what do you know about this guy who's been shadowing us all day?"

The cook looked up from the stew she was preparing for their supper, a defensive expression on her round face. "Nothing. Why should I know anything?"

"Then you wouldn't have, say, any connection with him?"

"That's crazy. Where did you get such an idea?"

"It's just that it's funny, him being out there all this time," Shep said.

"Well, what has that got to do with me?"

"Just wondering," the trail boss mumbled.

"You can stop wondering. Anyway, I don't know why you can't leave him alone. He isn't hurting anyone being out there, is he? He hasn't even tried to come anywhere near us, so why all the fuss?"

Ramona's sudden anger was uncharacteristic, not at all like her, Samantha realized. Shep tried again.

"If you would just—"

She stopped him brusquely. "Excuse me. I've got work to do." Seizing a triangle, she banged on it with a large spoon in the time-honored practice of a chuck wagon summoning the drovers to their meal.

For Ramona the subject was ended. But not for Roark. He waited until the others arrived on the scene, and when the cook was occupied serving them their supper, he took Samantha and the trail boss off to one side.

"Shep, you know Ramona. Would you say she *is* hiding something?"

"Maybe," Shep said, unwilling to commit himself beyond that.

"I think she's worried, anyway," Samantha said.

Roark nodded. ''Which means it's possible that, even if he was in the distance, she got enough of a glimpse of this guy to not like what she saw.''

''Are you saying he's someone she recognized?'' Samantha asked. ''Because if that's true, why wouldn't she just admit it?''

''Who knows?''

The lanky trail boss ran a hand through his graying hair and frowned. ''You think we really do have a problem here?''

Roark didn't immediately reply. He gazed for a moment in the direction of the grazing herd. ''Now that we're not tied down with the cattle, what do you say, Shep, after supper you and I pay a visit to our friend up on the ridge? I think it's time we had some answers from him.''

Shep had no objection. ''I guess we have enough daylight left for that.''

After eating, and just before the two men rode off together, Samantha found herself promising Roark that, yes, she would keep alert in his absence and, no, she would not leave camp for any reason or fail to make certain she remained in the company of the entire outfit.

Dirty, exhausted, stiff and sore from her long day in the saddle, Samantha would have liked nothing better than to crawl inside her sleeping bag and stay there until morning. But even though she was ready to collapse, she was much too anxious to rest. She kept thinking about Roark and Shep, hoping they were safe, although they had armed themselves before riding away.

She busied herself helping Ramona put the chuck wagon to bed for the night. Ramona asked no questions, though she had to be aware that the two men had slipped off after supper. Alex brought Samantha a bucket of water from the stream, and she used it to give herself a quick sponge bath behind a blanket strung on a line.

And all the while she worried about Roark and Shep,

wondered about the man on the ridge. Who was he? What did he want?

Her concern deepened with the twilight. She was fast approaching a state of alarm when, just before full darkness, the two men rode back to camp.

"Nothing," Roark reported to her as he dismounted from his horse. "We couldn't find a sign of him. He's either well hidden up there, or he's left the area."

"I think he's gone," Shep said. "I'm ready to believe we've seen the last of him. Is there any coffee left in the pot?"

Night settled over the camp. Tired though she was, Samantha lay awake in her sleeping bag. Dick Brewster had the first shift watching over the cattle. As he slowly circled the herd on horseback, she could hear him in the tradition of an old-time drover softly serenading his cows to keep them peaceful. The horse wrangler had a good voice.

"The Red River Valley," a soothing song. Very effective with the longhorns, but it didn't work with Samantha. Probably just because it was a cowboy song, and that made her aware of the man who lay next to her in his own sleeping bag. Made her remember how protective of her he was, never wanting her out of his sight, shielding her from any potential threat, forever concerned about her well-being.

All right, so he was being paid to keep her safe, but he had no need to care about her in any other regard. And yet all day he had been quietly attentive, assisting her whenever she needed help, backing off when she didn't, and always ready with a word of praise or encouragement. Believing in her.

Protective and attentive. A potent combination, one almost any woman would be susceptible to, especially when it came packaged in a man with Roark Hawke's tantalizing assets.

It was also a treacherous combination when Samantha was unable to forget that Roark was a cowboy. He belonged to this scene in a way that she, although raised to it, never could. Dear Lord, he even walked with the sexy swagger of a cowboy. And there had been moments today when she had detected on him the faint aroma of male sweat mingled with saddle soap. Memories. He brought back memories she didn't want, couldn't deal with.

But how was she to avoid them when the man responsible for them lay so close beside her that she could touch him without effort? *Longed* to touch him because, even asleep as he was, he tugged at her senses.

There was one advantage anyway in Roark's disturbing, late-night nearness. She was so busy resisting it that she forgot about the man on the ridge, prepared by now to believe that Shep was right and that they'd seen the last of him.

YESTERDAY WAS A PICNIC, *only, I didn't have the sense to realize it.*

Samantha had every reason to frequently remind herself of those words the following day, most of which she spent being miserable with water dripping from the brim of her hat and smelling the unpleasant odor of wet horses and cattle.

They had awakened to the sight of clouds piling over the mountains, and by the time they'd finished breakfast, the blue bowl of the sky overhead had disappeared under a heavy overcast. The first rain fell as they struck camp and headed along the trail. It continued to fall throughout the morning and into the afternoon. By then, the fine weather of their first day on the drive was only a memory.

There was nothing now but this dreary drizzle as cattle and horses pushed on through the endless valley. The ridge was buried in low cloud so much of the time that it wasn't possible to know whether their mysterious rider was still out there. Nor, on those infrequent occasions when the curtain did lift, was there any sign of him.

If he is still there, Samantha thought, he's either keeping a low profile, or else he was a phantom, after all.

It was easier to tell herself he'd only been an illusion, since none of them could afford to worry about him. Not when they had to deal with all the difficulties of herding cattle over land that hundreds of hooves churned into a mire. Samantha played what part she could in keeping the longhorns on the move, sodden and uncomfortable though she was.

The spirits of the entire outfit lifted when, late in the afternoon, the clouds parted. The backs of the longhorns steamed under the warmth of the sun that finally appeared. Samantha welcomed its glow, and by the time they made camp and she was able to change into dry clothes, she was smiling again.

"Hate to spoil all that cheer," Roark said when she emerged from behind the blanket, "but you and I have drawn the dogwatch tonight."

"I won't ask what that means."

He told her anyway. "We get the late shift guarding the herd."

She managed not to groan. "I don't have to sing to them, do I? Please tell me I don't have to sing to them."

Roark chuckled. "Not unless your Irma has a special request. Hey, it won't be so bad. If we turn in early, we'll have four or five hours of sleep before our— What's the matter?"

He'd noticed that she was no longer listening, that something else had captured her attention.

"Up there on the ridge," she said.

He turned around, gazing in the direction she indicated. A thin column of smoke rose from behind the distant trees.

"It's *him* again, isn't it? He's still with us."

"Samantha, it could be anyone's campfire. Or maybe someone has a cabin up there."

"I suppose." She wasn't convinced, but she tried to

forget about the smoke. It was no longer evident, anyway, when Ramona called them to supper.

Roark roused her just after midnight. By the time she got into her clothes, he had their horses saddled and waiting. The watch turned out to be not as unpleasant an obligation as she'd feared. Once they were mounted and in place at the edge of the herd, and with the sleep cleared from her brain, Samantha was actually able to appreciate the beauty of the scene.

The moon had risen. It was a full moon, with the light it shed so bright she could easily distinguish the shapes and patterns of the longhorns browsing contentedly on the rain-freshened grass. She recognized Irma among them. Roark teased her about Irma, and it was true she was protective of her. Maybe just because she'd noticed that the older, larger longhorns sometimes bullied the heifer, which was probably why Irma had a tendency to wander from the herd.

The heifer was peaceful now, as quiet as the rest of the herd in the stillness of the night. There was no sound either from the direction of the sleeping camp. Roark's deep voice broke the silence.

"Cold? I have a thermos of hot coffee in my saddlebag if you need it."

"Maybe later."

Although there was an autumn sharpness in the late-night air, she didn't seem to be feeling it. Maybe his nearness had something to do with that. Even though they were both on horseback, he was so close she swore she could actually feel his body heat. That might have been just her imagination. But what she saw, when she turned her head and looked at him in a light almost as bright as day, was not.

She had noticed it before, the way his Adam's apple bobbed slowly in his tanned throat, like a pulse rising and falling. The sight was as fascinating to her now as it had been then. And as arousing.

Samantha quickly lowered her gaze, only to discover another action she had observed before. The big hand that had been resting lightly on the pommel of his saddle was now busy making fists as he slowly, repeatedly closed and unclosed his fingers. Was he even aware he was doing it? Roark noticed the direction of her attention. "Does this bother you?"

It did, but not in the way he meant.

"It's not a nervous habit," he went on to explain, "though by now I guess it is an unconscious one. I broke the bones of this hand a few years back, and sometimes the fingers go a little stiff on me. It helps to exercise them like this."

"An accident?"

"Thrown from a bronc in a competition I entered up in Montana. I thought I was rodeo material. I found out the hard way I wasn't."

Samantha's response was immediate and explosive, surprising both of them in its fierceness. "A rodeo!" she cried before she could stop herself. "You could have been killed! People are killed in rodeos!"

"Hey, relax. You've startled the horses. It was a rodeo, Samantha, not a war."

He thought she was overreacting. He didn't know. Nor could she bring herself to tell him. "Yes, that was a little excessive," she murmured. "Sorry."

He stared at her, and she could feel him wondering. "Tell me about it, Samantha," he urged her. "Tell me what happened between you and your grandfather that's left you with this legacy of loathing for everything connected with his world. I'd like to understand."

Things that had to do with ranching, he meant. Things like rodeos. That particular subject she wouldn't discuss, because it meant opening herself to a pain that was too private, too unbearable. But the rest?

Yes, she decided, maybe it was time he knew. Maybe she wanted him to stop thinking of her as less than she was. Or maybe it was just the spell of the moonlit night they shared that invited confidences, made it easy to talk to him.

"My grandfather was a hard man," she said. "I don't think he ever stopped resenting my mother for being a daughter and not the son he wanted. And then when she married my father, who was a teacher instead of the rancher he expected her to choose…"

"More to resent, huh?"

"Oh, he took her back on the Walking W when my father died and she had nowhere else to go, no money, no job skills and with a daughter of her own to raise. But he made her pay for that. She earned her way as his house-keeper—that was long before Ramona—and I hated watching her forever trying to please him and always failing. My mother was a gentle woman. My grandfather didn't see that. He saw her as weak willed, and in the end he broke her spirit."

"But not yours."

"My mother was a lesson to me. A cruel one. I promised myself I wasn't going to be like her. That I would never be dependent on Joe Walker." Samantha sighed. "And yet here I am on this cattle drive doing just that."

"While not forgiving either him or anything he represented."

"Meaning he's dead and gone, and I should just let it go, is that it?"

"I didn't say that, Samantha. I can understand the issues you have with your grandfather, but to hate ranching and everything associated with it just because of how much he valued it—"

"He more than valued it," she cut him off sharply. "It was like a religion to him. It is with ranchers. It's that way with you, too, isn't it? In your blood. Which is why—"

"What?"

"Nothing."

She turned her head away and was stubbornly silent.

Painfully silent. Gazing at her, Roark sensed that she
hadn't told him everything. There was more. He didn't
press her, though. He understood about secrets and the
need sometimes to hold them inside. He had his own deep
ache he was guarding.

"It must be hard," she said after a moment.

"What is?"

"Being a private investigator at the same time you're
living and breathing cattle."

He wasn't alone in being perceptive. "It gets tricky,"
he admitted, but he didn't tell her just how torn he was or
about the decision he had yet to make.

"My grandfather didn't have to worry about being divided like that," she said wryly. "Nothing mattered to him
but his precious spread, even when he was dying. I know
why he put me on this drive. It wasn't to harden me. That's
just a small part of a much bigger motive."

"Which is?"

"He was hoping that before the drive was over I'd fall
in love with cattle and ranching. Or at least that I would
learn to appreciate them enough I'd want to keep the
Walking W in the family. Treat it just like he did and
refuse to part with a single cherished acre. That's how Joe
Walker's mind worked."

"And will you preserve it?"

She shook her head. "I'll sacrifice it. Not because it's
a way to get back at him either, but because I won't have
a choice. With his investments having lost a lot of their
value, there won't be enough to save my agency if I don't
sell the whole operation."

"Too bad."

"You think I'm being callous, don't you?"

Roark told her, no, and that he understood her need to
rescue the business she had worked so hard to establish.
Told her it was regrettable Joe had never given her any
reason to share his sentiments, that it wasn't fair to expect
her now to preserve something his treatment of both her

and her mother had taught her to hate. Told her that, in any case, what she chose to do about the ranch was none of his business.

And all the time he was telling her this, what Roark actually wanted was to hear her say she was ready to forget the sins of the past. That she was prepared to fight for the Walking W, that whatever effort it took she would hang on to it. Because, given her opportunity, that's exactly what he would do himself.

But then he and Samantha had opposite views about ranching. So totally opposite it was a mistake for him to be sitting here on this horse looking at her and thinking how much he wanted her. He'd wanted her from the start and had gone on wanting her throughout the two days of this drive as he'd watched her repeatedly riding after the heifer, braid bouncing, alluring backside lifted from her saddle. She was even more desirable like this in the moonlight, full mouth slightly parted as she eyed the herd, her breasts rising and falling with each breath she took.

Yeah, he wanted her. Wanted to drag her off her horse and place her in front of him on his saddle. Wanted to feel that backside squeezed against his groin while his hands wrapped around her and touched those soft breasts. Wanted to turn her face to his so that he could taste her sweet mouth.

Strong though it was, as frustrated as it left him, it was a temptation he resisted. Because it would end up being more than just sex, it would be an involvement bound to hurt both of them when they wanted entirely different things from life. A hopeless conflict. He wouldn't risk it.

But Roark wondered how long he could hold out.

They were silent for a long time, and then Samantha spoke, an edge of concern in her voice. "That's not heat lightning up there, is it?"

"No," he said, looking at the flashes that flared low in the sky above the distant peaks. "There's a storm in the mountains."

"Not headed our way, I hope. We've had our share of rain down here."

The sky above them was still clear, the moon bright. "It's a long way off."

But not so distant that they couldn't hear the dull rumbles of thunder that followed each flash.

"It's making the herd restless," she said.

"Yeah, they're a bit nervous about it."

"What do we do if—"

She got no further. The stillness around them was rent by a sudden, sharp crack that reverberated along the valley. The result of the blast was both immediate and startling. Like floodwaters bursting a levee, the longhorns bolted and took flight.

Roark heard himself shouting what every drover feared. "Stampede!"

Chapter Five

Roark followed up his first shout with another yell. This one was for Samantha. "Stay close behind me!" he ordered her as the cattle swept by them in a panicked stream. "I've got to go after them!"

He knew it wouldn't be necessary to go back and alert the others in the outfit. They would already have been roused by the unmistakable thundering of a herd in stampede.

"What are you—"

"Samantha, don't ask questions! Just keep safely behind me!"

His horse, sensitive to the urgency of the situation even before his heels dug into its flanks, sprang forward and raced after the fleeing herd. He had to get in front of the cattle, try to turn them. Otherwise, they would either run until they dropped or end up being so scattered it could take the drovers days to round them up again.

Bent low and strained forward in the saddle, Roark urged his mount to greater speed, making every effort to overtake the longhorns. The terrain was in his favor. A hillock lay directly in the path of the herd. It didn't stop the cattle, but its steep sides forced a division in the herd, resulting in two branches that were slowed in their struggle to pour around the ends of the hillock. The delay was just long enough to permit Roark to catch up with the herd.

He'd need help to turn them. He knew the others would have leaped on their horses at the first sign of trouble. They couldn't be far behind him. He swung his head around to look for them and to check on Samantha, and that's when he saw it, a sight that brought his heart into his throat.

Samantha had sped after him, but she hadn't stayed behind him. She was now opposite him on the other side of the herd, her horse wading into the ranks of the shoving cattle. What in sweet heaven did she think she was doing? And then he understood. That damn heifer!

Fearing the smaller animal would be crushed in the melee, she was striving to rescue Irma, to cut the heifer out of the herd. The little fool!

Standing in his stirrups, Roark roared a warning. "Samantha, no! Go back!"

Either she didn't hear him above the bellowing of cattle and the pounding of hooves that shook the ground, or she was too determined to commit suicide to listen to him.

Her horse had better sense than she did. The animal was trying to turn back, trying to carry her to safety as it had been trained to do. Samantha made the mistake of fighting the mare. Reacting with fear and confusion, it reared back. Its inexperienced rider, unable to hold on, was thrown to the ground into the midst of maddened cattle. Cattle with hooves that could trample. Horns that could gore. She would be cut to pieces.

Roark didn't hesitate. Spurring his mount, he plunged into the mass of surging beasts, battling to reach her before it was too late. It was like swimming across a river against a powerful current that wanted to drag horse and rider downstream. And all the while his desperate gaze searched the area where Samantha had gone down. He couldn't find her. Where was she?

There! She was just yards away, on her feet now. And as yet miraculously untouched by the longhorns that raged past her on all sides. But how long could she remain a safe island in that deadly sea?

He was close enough now to read the terror on her face. Close enough to count in seconds the time it took him and his horse to squeeze through the swarm to her side. Seconds that felt like light-years.

Understanding his intention to pluck her from danger, Samantha was ready for him, body tensed, arms upraised. His horse managed to slide past her as Roark leaned out from the saddle, intending a rescue that would have thrilled a rodeo crowd.

But this wasn't a competition. It was a life-or-death necessity, which was probably why he was able to successfully execute it even though he was on the move. Arm catching her around the waist, he scooped her up in front of him, recovered his balance in the saddle, and hung on to her tightly while his horse led them to safety.

As they broke free from the herd, Roark had a vague awareness of the last of the cattle vanishing around the hillock, followed within seconds by the other drovers giving chase. Then there was silence. He could feel Samantha trembling against him.

"Are you all right?"

"Irma—"

"Forget about the heifer. She'll survive. I want to know if you're okay?"

"All in one piece, thanks to you and your horse. That was some feat, cowboy. You can let me go now." He released her, and she slithered to the ground. She looked around, concern still in her voice. "But my own horse seems to have disappeared."

"She'll come back." He climbed down, drawing the reins of his mount over its head and dropping them to the ground to hold the animal in place. Then he faced Samantha, his hands closing around her shoulders, his tone anxious as he scrutinized her in the moonlight. "You're sure you're not hurt?"

"No, I'm fine. Well, a little dazed maybe and still trying

to catch my breath, but otherwise fine. And, like I say, very grateful.''

Roark couldn't remember when he had ever experienced such relief. Or pure anger, which he couldn't keep himself from expressing now that he knew she hadn't been injured.

''What in hell possessed you to try something as reckless as that? Why didn't you listen to me? Why didn't you stay behind me? Do you realize you could have been killed?''

That I could have lost you?

That's what he actually meant. Which was why, with the shock of his anger still registering on her face, he obeyed another unexpected impulse. He abruptly stopped lecturing her, hauled her protectively against his chest, and did what he had promised himself earlier he would not do. Crushing his mouth over hers, he kissed her. Kissed her fiercely, possessively.

It was a wild business, all hot and hard and demanding. At first, that is. But once Samantha stopped resisting him, understood he wasn't punishing her, that his kiss was a demonstration of how much she had already come to mean to him and how scared he had been, the kiss became something else.

Her mouth, which had opened under his in a struggle to voice an objection, now welcomed him. He answered her invitation with his tongue, and she responded to his invasion with her own compliant tongue. A molten fusion of tasting, cherishing, needing. A need that neither one of them could any longer deny.

As their kiss deepened, escalating into a passion that was in turns both rough and gentle but always intense, Roark found himself yearning to bury more than his tongue inside her. He could feel himself swelling, aching with his desire, as he strained against her. Could feel her breasts pressed against his chest, warm and heavy with her own desire.

Oblivious to all reason, he might have sunk to the

ground with her, taken her then and there had she permitted it, if sanity hadn't returned in the form of approaching hoofbeats. They parted, Roark with great reluctance and, by the expression on her face, Samantha with guilt. But not regret, he hoped.

Unhappy with the interruption, Roark scowled at the rider who arrived on the scene leading another horse behind him. Alex McKenzie gazed down at them with his boyish, engaging grin. Either the moonlight was that bright or what they had been doing was that obvious because the grin slowly sagged on Alex's face. Poor puppy, Roark thought. The young drover was devoted to Samantha, maybe even had expectations, and now he was disillusioned.

Embarrassed, Alex cleared his throat. "Brought your runaway back to you, Sam."

"Thank you, Alex," she said kindly.

"What about the other runaways?" Roark asked, referring to the herd.

"Managed to turn them. They're driving them back now. No more fight in them. They're docile as sheep. How about you guys? You okay?"

"Fine," Samantha assured him. "Did you see Irma? Is Irma all right?"

"Safe along with the rest." Alex cleared his throat again. "Well, I'll see you back at camp. Gotta let Ramona know to put the coffee on. Man oh man, what a night."

He left the mare with them and rode off. Roark didn't wait until he was out of sight to address Samantha, his voice husky with emotion. "About what just happened between us…"

"I know what happened," she said, making an effort to smile about it. "You were branding me. Or trying to. That's what cowboys do, isn't it?"

Knowing how she felt about cowboys, he wasn't sure whether it was a teasing observation or an accusation. "Is

that how you saw it? I thought it was a kiss between two
people who've come to care about each other.''

"Let's not discuss it. Come on," she said, turning away
and mounting the mare. "I could use some of that coffee."

She thought that what had happened between them was
a mistake. Hell, she was probably right. Except his acknowledgment saddened him.

"WHAT HAPPENED OUT THERE?" the irritated trail boss
asked them as everyone sat around the campfire drinking
coffee. All of them, that is, except Dick and Cappy, who
were watching over the herd.

Roark knew that Shep was referring to the stampede and
not Samantha and him. "The cattle were spooked." Before
he could continue, Ramona spoke up.

"There was lightning and thunder," she said quickly.
"It woke me up. You must have all heard it yourselves."

Roark eyed the woman. She looked tired, worried…and
anxious for them to believe that the stampede had to be
the result of a natural cause. He felt sorry for the cook,
wished he didn't have to contradict her.

"It wasn't lightning or thunder," he said. "That storm
was too far away to set them off, though I grant you it did
make the herd restless. Ripe for an opportunity, you might
say."

"What are you telling us?" Shep demanded.

"The stampede happened because of something much
closer than a storm up in the mountains. Right on the spot,
in fact. Wouldn't you agree, Samantha?"

Roark looked to her for confirmation. She had seated
herself well away from him on the other side of the fire.
She was nervous herself, though not for the same reason
as Ramona. He could tell by the way the lobe of her ear
was squeezed between forefinger and middle finger as she
pulled at it slowly.

She looked so much younger in those jeans and with
that braid hanging down her back, nothing at all like the

businesswoman back in San Antonio with her self-assured, sleek image. This was another Samantha, a vulnerable one who tugged at his gut, making him all the more determined to defend her against any threat.

Her eyes met his, and he knew she was remembering their kiss and wishing it hadn't happened. "Roark is right," she said quietly. "It wasn't lightning, and it wasn't thunder. It was another sound."

"Gunfire," Roark informed them. "Probably the crack of a rifle over their heads."

The trail boss leaned toward him earnestly. "Are you sure of this? Did you see someone out there?"

"I'm sure, and I didn't see anyone. It came from out of sight over on the other side of the herd. Samantha?"

She shook her head. "I didn't spot anyone either."

Alex was perplexed. "Somebody out there hunting at this time of night?"

"It wasn't a hunter," Roark said. "And it wasn't an accident. It was someone taking advantage of the storm, because I'd swear that shot was deliberate." *Meant to sabotage the drive, because if the cattle are somehow prevented from reaching Alamo Junction in time, Samantha will fail to qualify for her grandfather's inheritance.* But he couldn't voice this part of the explanation, not when there was no way to be certain of it. Yet.

"But why?" Alex wondered. "And who?"

Roark glanced at Ramona. She was looking more distraught by the moment. "Ramona," he said easily, "I know it's too early for breakfast, but this puzzle has got me all hollow inside. Do you suppose you could scare up something for me from that pantry of yours? Anything will do."

Ramona wasn't a fool. She had to realize his request was an excuse, that he was sending her away because he didn't want her to hear his answer to Alex McKenzie's question. That he suspected she was somehow connected to this whole business. But the cook offered no objection.

Tight-lipped and silent, she got to her feet and reluctantly moved off in the direction of her pickup.

Once Ramona was out of earshot, Roark started to quickly explain his intention to the others. "I don't know the *why,* but there is a good candidate for the *who.* Our shadow on the ridge. Which means—"

Shep interrupted him. "Why are we still worrying about this guy when you and I found no evidence of him evening before last? Plus, all yesterday there was no sign of him up there. I thought we'd agreed he left the area."

"I think we were wrong. I think he's still with us. And there *was* a sign of his presence. Samantha spotted the smoke from a campfire just before sundown last evening. Okay, that's not proof it was *his* campfire, but after what happened here tonight, I don't think we can afford not to deal with him."

"*If* he's still around," Shep said. The trail boss paused, and Roark knew he was thinking of the cattle and his responsibility to prevent any further danger to them. "What do you have in mind?"

"Surprise. It'll start to get light in another couple of hours. If we can find where he's bedded down, sneak up on him before sunup has him on the move again, there's a chance we can take him."

"All right," Shep agreed. "I suggest we try to get what sleep we can before then."

It was decided that Roark and the trail boss would handle the confrontation while Alex and the others remained with the herd where they were needed. Ramona returned and handed around a container of sourdough biscuits. She continued to wear an unhappy expression, but she kept her thoughts to herself.

Before they turned in, Samantha drew Roark off to one side. "What about me? Am I staying behind?"

He'd been thinking about that. There was no way to be positive their man on the ridge had crept down here and fired that shot. For all he knew, it could have been some-

one from their own outfit. Maybe the same someone who
had allegedly fired on Joe Walker in the ravine back in
Texas. In which case Samantha would be at less risk sticking close to him where he could exercise every caution to
keep her safe.

"Are you up to coming along?" he asked.

She hesitated and then nodded. "I'm in."

THE FIRST GLIMMER OF DAY WAS just beginning to streak
the eastern sky when the three of them slipped away from
camp. Though it lit the higher elevations, it was still dark
down in the valley. The moon had set, so they didn't have
the benefit of its glow, but the surefooted horses were able
to find their way.

It was also cold. Roark was glad of his denim jacket
and hoped that Samantha beside him was warm enough in
her own coat. And that he wasn't making a mistake by
bringing her with them.

The light had strengthened to a gray twilight by the time
they ascended the slope of the ridge. It was possible in its
pallor to fix their course on the spot that had been the
source of the smoke. Or at least in the approximate direction.

They lost that advantage when they entered the trees,
where the shadows were so heavy it was difficult to know
if they were still on target. They moved in absolute silence
now, the thick carpet of pine needles muffling any sound
of the horses that might alert their man.

Providing, Roark thought, he was even in the vicinity.
If he had been responsible for the stampede, there was the
possibility he had already moved on. Or, for that matter,
that he'd never been here at all.

They might have wandered forever through the pine forest without finding their man if it hadn't been for his horse.
Sensing the presence of other horses, the animal nickered
softly, betraying his position less than a hundred yards
away. They came to a standstill, with Roark praying that

none of their own mounts answered him. Thankfully, they didn't.

Shep raised his arm and pointed in the direction from which the whinny had originated. Roark nodded, and the three of them quietly dismounted. Not wanting to leave Samantha on her own, which could leave her vulnerable to an ambush from behind, he motioned for Shep to stay with her while he checked out their objective.

His gun is his hand, Roark stole silently through the trees. The light from an opening in the pines drew him to the edge of a small, grassy clearing where a chestnut was staked out to graze. Satisfied by what else occupied the clearing, Roark retreated to the place where he'd left Samantha and the trail boss.

"He's there," he whispered to them. "Fast asleep on the ground. Samantha, stay with the horses and do what you can to keep them quiet. Shep?"

The trail boss nodded, drew his own gun and accompanied Roark back to the clearing. The chestnut lifted his head as they came through the trees, noted their arrival in the clearing, then lowered his muzzle again to the grass. On the other side of a dead campfire, wrapped in a blanket and with his back to them, lay a motionless figure.

Neither Roark nor Shep nor the chestnut made a sound. But the man on the ground must have somehow realized he was no longer alone. Jerking awake, he twisted around to face them, a startled expression on his blunt features. For a second he gazed at them, then his hand started to reach for a rifle nearby.

"I wouldn't," Roark warned him.

Thinking better of his action, he withdrew his hand.

"Get up," Roark instructed him. "Carefully."

Eyeing the guns in their hands, he stumbled to his feet, the folds of the blanket twisted around his legs hindering him. When he was finally free of the blanket and standing, Roark could see he was short and stocky. There was something else he observed. The guy was young, probably in his early twenties. The surprised expression on his broad face had become a surly one.

"What the hell is this?" he demanded. "Who are you?"

"Oh, I think you know who we are," Roark said. "The thing is, we don't know who you are or why you've been shadowing us."

"Or why you stampeded our cattle last night," Shep said.

"That's bull, man. I never came anywhere near your herd."

"By firing that rifle there over their heads," the trail boss added.

"I never fired a shot from my gun. Check it if you don't believe me."

"Rifles can be cleaned," Roark said. "And you still haven't told us who you are."

"Why should I? This isn't private land. I got a right to be here when I ain't botherin' you or nobody else. Which means I don't have to answer your questions."

Roark and Shep communicated with quick glances that told Roark the trail boss was thinking the same thing— that it was time this young man and Ramona were confronted with each other.

"Maybe," Roark said, "you'll be in a friendlier mood about those questions back at our camp."

"I don't have to go with you."

"This says you do." Roark wagged the gun in his hand. "Now, get your things together."

The young man eyed first the pistol trained on him, then the gun in Shep's hand. "And who made you cops?" he muttered. But he obeyed the order and began to collect his gear while Shep saddled the chestnut for him. When he started to reach for his rifle, Roark stopped him.

"Uh-uh, that goes with me." Taking possession of the rifle, he gestured in the direction of the chestnut that Shep had waiting. "Now, get on your horse, and if you're a good boy and don't give us any trouble, we might even feed you breakfast.''

Sullen and silent now, he accompanied them to where Samantha was waiting with their own mounts. If he was surprised by her presence, he didn't indicate it. Nor was he any more communicative on the trip back to the valley, remaining stubbornly silent when Shep, who rode beside him, tried again to question him.

After a few minutes, the trail boss dropped back to Samantha and Roark, who were bringing up the rear. "He still refuses to tell me his name," Shep confided in a low voice, "but I've seen him before."

"You remember where and when?"

Shep nodded. "I do now. It was back at the Walking W, about six months ago. I only caught a glimpse of him storming away from the ranch house and roaring off in an old jalopy. Joe was on the porch glaring after him."

"You ask Joe what it was all about?"

"I tried, but you know what the old man was like. He told me in so many words to mind my own business, but if I ever saw that jalopy around the ranch again I was to throw its driver off the property."

Roark turned questioningly to Samantha. "You have any clue?"

She shook her head. "You forget I haven't been anywhere near the Walking W in a long time. I'm sure I've never seen him before, but…"

"What?"

She gazed at the rider in front of them, frowning in puzzlement. "There's something familiar about him."

Roark knew what she meant. He, too, had an impression of being reminded of something. Or someone.

The sun had risen by the time they reached camp. Cappy was still with the herd, but Alex McKenzie and Dick Brewster were having their breakfasts when they rode in and dismounted. Alex's eyes widened in surprise as he looked up from his plate and caught sight of the chunky

young man who was with them. Along with that surprise
was recognition.

Before Roark had a chance to question Alex, Ramona
came around the side of her cook wagon with a skillet in
her hand. She stopped when she caught sight of the new
arrival.

The young man met her anxious gaze and nodded.
"Hello, Ma," he greeted her matter-of-factly.

Samantha and Roark traded astonished glances. No
wonder he had seemed familiar. Although it wasn't an obvious likeness, mother and son resembled each other, sharing the same Hispanic heritage.

Ramona set the skillet on a tripod and moved toward
her son, this time expressing her anxiety in words. "Are
you all right?"

"Yeah, Ma, I'm okay."

She reached out to him with both hands. Roark, watching her, expected to see a loving embrace. What he and
the others witnessed was Ramona cuffing her son swiftly
on both cheeks.

"You should have listened to me!" she railed. "Why
didn't you listen to me?" And before he could answer her,
Ramona rounded angrily on the others. "What have you
done to him? If you've gone and hurt him—"

"Whoa, Ramona," Shep strove to pacify her, "take it
easy. No one's done a thing to him."

"Except drag him down here like he'd gone and com-
mitted some crime!"

"Maybe he did," Roark said. "Or have you forgotten
last night's stampede?"

"I told you, man," her son insisted, "I didn't have a
thing to do with that."

"Then why have you been following us the last two
days? What was that all about if you're so in—" Roark
broke off. "What is your name, anyway? Or are you still
refusing to tell us even that much?"

"Ernie," Ramona said. "His name is Ernie Chacon."

"Don't tell them anything, Ma. We don't have to answer their questions."

"No," Roark said, "we could leave them for the nearest sheriff to ask. There ought to be one somewhere in the area. What about it, Ernie?"

For the first time Ernie looked uneasy, his dark eyes shifting from face to face. He'd been in trouble with the law before, Roark guessed. The threat worked. Ernie caved.

"I heard things back in Texas," he mumbled. "They worried me."

"What things?" the trail boss demanded.

"Guys in the bars talking. Saying this cattle drive had trouble brewing for it. It worried me, you know."

"Because of your mother?" a perceptive Samantha gently prompted him.

"I told him that was all a lot of nonsense," Ramona said. "That he had absolutely no reason to think I wouldn't be safe."

"And that's why you've been following us," Samantha said. "You wanted to be there for your mother in case there was any danger."

"I didn't want her to come on this drive. I had a bad feeling about it. Then when she says she wasn't staying behind, and she wouldn't let me come with her..." Ernie shrugged. "Well, sons are supposed to look out for their mothers, ain't they?"

Roark could see that Samantha was touched by his explanation, as well as prepared to accept it. But he wasn't ready yet to buy it. It was altogether too innocent, besides leaving several unanswered questions.

"If that's the case," he said, "then why didn't you just ride down here and tell us who you were and what you were doing?"

"Yeah? And would you have let me join up with you?"

"Probably not," Shep replied honestly.

"See, I knew it," Ernie said defiantly, and then he

abruptly turned to his mother. "I'm famished, Ma. You got anything for me to eat?"

"Come on around to the back of the cook wagon, and I'll fix you a plate."

"Not yet," Shep said. "There are a few more questions we'd like to ask."

"You've heard enough," Ramona said swiftly. "He's explained everything to you. There isn't any more to tell. Let's go, Ernie."

Mother and son disappeared around the side of the truck.

"In a hurry to get him away, wasn't she?" the trail boss said after they'd gone.

"Oh, yeah," Roark agreed. "Like she was afraid of what he might say next."

"You don't think she's hiding something?" Samantha asked, sounding as though she couldn't believe Ramona was capable of being devious.

"Why not? She must have realized from the beginning it was Ernie up there on the ridge, and yet she denied knowing anything about him. Why keep it from us?" Roark turned to Shep as something else occurred to him. "There must be a father somewhere. You know anything about Ernie's father?"

"Hell, I didn't even know Ramona had a son. I never heard her mention anything about either a husband or a boyfriend, past or present."

No explanation there then, Roark thought. But he suddenly remembered something. Looking around, he saw that Dick Brewster had finished his breakfast and left the campsite to help Cappy Davis with the herd. But Alex McKenzie was still with them. Alex, who, along with his surprise when Ernie Chacon first arrived on the scene, had worn a look of recognition.

"You hear all that, Alex?"

"I heard."

"You know Ernie, don't you?"

The young drover hesitated. Then he put down his plate,

got to his feet and came to join then. "I don't know him, but I know about him," he admitted. "I used to see him sometimes hanging out in this bar."

"Back in Purgatory?" Shep wondered.

Alex shook his head. "I don't guess he ever spent much time in Purgatory. This was up in Austin when I was going to the university. He worked construction there, I think. When he had a job at all, that is. The thing is..." He stopped, an expression of reluctance on his boyish, good-looking face.

"We have a potential problem here," Roark urged. "You need to tell us what you know."

Alex nodded. "It's not what I know, just what I heard from other guys. That Ernie had this hot temper, and it would get him into trouble sometimes. Fights, and that kind of thing. Anyway, I steered clear of him."

Alex's disclosure had him looking increasingly uneasy, as if he hated being an informer. Shep took pity on him. "Thanks, Alex. You'd better go out and relieve Cappy now."

With a sheepish look in Samantha's direction, which she answered with a smile, Alex hurried away.

"Useful?" Shep asked when he was gone.

"Maybe," Roark said. "If Ernie has a bad reputation, it could explain why Ramona was afraid for us to know about him."

"And why Joe didn't want him hanging around the Walking W, even if it was to visit his mother."

"That doesn't make him responsible for the stampede," Samantha said.

"It could if he figured it was a way to prevent his mother from going on with the drive." Or, Roark wondered to himself, did Ernie Chacon have a more sinister agenda than that? Something that had his mother very nervous?

"What do we do about him?" the trail boss asked.

"Add him to the outfit. We could use another drover."

"Is that wise?"

"I don't think we have a choice. If we let him go, he could be a threat all the way to Alamo Junction. And no sheriff is going to hold him when we don't have evidence he sabotaged the drive. But if he rides with us, providing he's willing, we can keep a close eye on him." And Ernie bears watching, Roark thought. "Well, it's your call, Shep."

"I'll go talk to him." He went off to the back of the cook truck, leaving Samantha and Roark alone.

"This drive is getting awfully complicated," she said, her tone registering her regret.

In more ways than she meant, Roark thought, remembering the blistering kiss they had shared last night and how much he wanted her. Not just physically either, but emotionally as well. With each passing day, his feelings for her grew more intense. He didn't know if it could be defined as love, not yet anyway, but whatever it was, it was hell. Because in tandem with his longing for Samantha was his growing desire to live the kind of life she despised.

He had yet to make a decision to abandon PI work to be a full-time rancher, but the cattle drive was pulling him in that direction. All its hardships and difficulties aside, he found himself savoring the experience, feeling as if he belonged to it. It was a powerful argument, and a frustrating one when it made the gulf between Samantha and him all the wider.

Shep returned to report that Ernie had agreed to join the drive. "Let's hope he'll be of use to us. You two had better grab some breakfast. It's long past time we were underway."

Roark knew that the trail boss was right and that every delay was costly to the drive, which made him feel guilty when he and Samantha went off away from the others so that he could steal several more minutes of precious time. It was necessary.

Wendell's voice was so sleepy when he answered his

call that Roark knew he had gotten his young trainee out of bed. He had forgotten how early it was.

"You phoning from Lost Springs?" Wendell asked, referring to the town that was scheduled to be the cattle drive's first stop along the trail.

"Still ahead of us," Roark said, cell phone tight against his ear.

"Then you couldn't have picked up the photographs I e-mailed to the copy center there. Or my two reports."

"What reports would those be?"

"The outcomes of the interviews I had with the director of the Western Museum in Purgatory and the abbot of St. James Monastery." Wendell sounded grieved that Roark hadn't seemed to remember his assignments.

"Any luck?"

"Well, the good part is neither one of them was suspicious. They accepted my story I'm a freelance writer wanting to do articles on their operations, so they willingly answered all my questions. The bad part is they didn't seem to be hiding a thing. I mean, they both freely admitted funds are always a problem, but nothing sounded like there was any critical need."

"Doesn't mean there isn't one somewhere," Roark soothed his conscientious trainee. "We'll keep on digging, but this time we'll try another direction. I have a new assignment for you." He went on to explain about Ernie Chacon. "Try Purgatory first. Go back there and see if you can find out whether he has any kind of record. Do the same in Austin. Find out all you can about him, even if it means asking in the bars. This could be important, Wendell."

HE WAS DISAPPOINTED. The stampede had failed to achieve his intention. Samantha had emerged from it unharmed. Nor had it succeeded in halting the cattle drive. They would go on toward Alamo Junction and those waiting stock cars.

But they wouldn't get there. He'd see to that. There would be other chances to sabotage the drive, other methods to prevent her from qualifying for the inheritance. He just needed to be patient, ready for them. That's right, plenty of time to take care of her. All he had to do was make certain they didn't learn the secret he was guarding.

Chapter Six

Samantha was convinced of it. The cattle drive was cursed.

You would think, she told herself wearily, that after forcing two hundred reluctant longhorns into leaving their home range, dealing with a mysterious rider on the ridge and then suffering an even more mysterious stampede in the night, they'd had more than their fair share of trouble. Yes, and that they'd earned themselves a nice peaceful interval free of problems.

But whatever god was in charge of cattle drives, or maybe it was a demon, didn't see it that way. Because all that day, and throughout most of the day that followed, they encountered hazards in one form or another.

There was, to begin with, the weather. It rained. Not just a persistent all-day drizzle this time, which had been miserable enough yesterday, but a downpour. A hard, driving torrent that roared down from the mountains and soaked drovers and cattle alike. Mercifully, the cloudburst came and went. Not so merciful was what it produced.

Up to that point, the streams they had crossed had been lazy affairs, shallow at this season and easy to ford. This time they came to the banks of a course swollen from the storm and whose current was anything but gentle. No choice. They had to swim cattle and horses alike through the swift waters. By some miracle they gained the other side without losing a single cow, though at one point Irma was in danger of being swept downstream. Roark's quick action with a lariat saved the heifer.

The sun should have been a blessing when it finally came out. Yet it felt more like a desert sun in mid-July than a Colorado sun in autumn. It beat down on them, unseasonably hot, baking what had been mud into dust that hundreds of hooves raised into choking clouds.

And then there was the underpass. It was the only route beneath an interstate highway. The cattle weren't happy about that narrow tunnel, resisting determined efforts to drive them through it. It took almost two hours to squeeze the last of the bawling herd into the bottleneck and out into the open on the far side.

The raw, spectacular beauty of the mountains, their lower slopes ablaze now with a climax of fall colors, should have consoled Samantha. But by then she was too exhausted and exasperated to be anything but immune to the wonders of nature.

All of it justified her certainty that the drive was cursed and that the spirit of her grandfather was looking down on her every ordeal and cackling in glee. She confided as much to Roark riding close beside her on his big roan. Samantha was on Dolly again, for which she was supremely grateful. The little mare never gave her any difficulty. She couldn't say the same for some of the other horses in the remuda that the drovers, including her, had to use when their favorite mounts needed to be relieved.

Tugging at the brim of his Stetson, Roark turned those breath-robbing blue eyes of his on her and favored her with a teasing smile. "That's why you're here, remember? Joe Walker's dying wish to test his granddaughter."

"Yes, but I don't think I'm being tested as much as I'm being punished."

"What are you telling me? That, wherever he is, Joe is sending down stampedes, floods, and maybe, before it's all over, even a cattle rustler or two just to discipline you?"

"I wouldn't go that far, but I wouldn't put *her* past him. In fact, there are moments when I'd swear she's my grandfather reincarnated."

Roark looked in the direction she indicated, his smile broadening into a grin at the sight of the heifer romping in front of them. "Sweet little Irma? And here I thought you were so fond of her."

"I am when she isn't giving me grief, which lately is most of the time. I don't know. Every time I think she's starting to behave herself, she goes and acts up. It's my grandfather all over again."

"Now what did I tell you? If you'd let me teach you how to use a lariat, all your troubles with Irma would be over."

"Funny man," she said, surprised at how much she was enjoying their banter. "I'm having enough problems just staying in the saddle, never mind all the rest, and here you want me to learn how to lasso naughty cows."

His grin developed into a chuckle. "It's a thought. And, anyway, if Joe Walker did come back, it would be as a bull, not a heifer."

The blue eyes were laughing at her now. "You're enjoying this, aren't you?"

"Am I?"

"Oh, I don't mean just giving me a hard time. It's all the rest of it. Being out here like this with the cattle and horses, working with them every day and not minding how tough it is or any of the hardships."

"I guess you're right," he admitted.

"Then why are you a PI at all? Why aren't you a full-time rancher?"

"As a matter of fact…"

"What?" she urged him.

He hesitated again, and then he told her. "There's no reason you shouldn't know. I've promised myself that by the end of the drive I've got to decide one way or another whether to give up the PI work altogether."

"Is all this that much of a lure for you?"

"Yeah, I'm afraid it is."

"That's too bad. From what I've observed you make an excellent private investigator."

"I appreciate the vote of confidence." He gazed at her, a teasing glint in his eyes. "Or could it be that my family has somehow enlisted you in a campaign to keep me at the agency?"

"My testimonial comes unsolicited," she assured him, remembering how her grandfather's lawyer had mentioned to her that Roark's entire family was engaged in investigative work. "So what progress have you made with your decision? *Are* the Hawkes going to lose you?"

"Haven't made up my mind. I'm still working on it."

There was something about the way he said it that made Samantha realize this was more than just a straightforward decision for him. That it went beyond a simple question of whether he preferred cattle over clients who needed his PI skills. Whatever it was, she had the idea it was gnawing at him. But she felt no more entitled to ask him about it than to question any of the others in the outfit about the problems that were worrying them.

Watching them, Samantha was ready to believe they were as cursed by this cattle drive as she was. Nearly everyone seemed troubled by something. Except for Dick Brewster, of course. The horse wrangler remained perpetually cheerful. As for the others…well, they were a different story.

Ramona, for instance, continued to be uncharacteristically subdued. Still worried about her son, Samantha guessed. And maybe with good reason. Ernie Chacon was a moody young man, and although he behaved and kept to himself, it was evident he and Alex McKenzie didn't like each other. Alex, too, seemed unhappy, and had been since he'd caught Roark kissing Samantha. She felt sorry for Alex, though she wasn't prepared to regard his interest in her as anything serious.

"Puppy love," Cappy Davis pronounced in disgust. "He'll get over it."

It was hard to tell if Cappy himself was bothered by anything. The old man had always been impassive to the point of gloom.

There was no mistaking Shep Thomas's concern. The trail boss had the sad eyes of a man who wasn't sleeping well. And although this was understandable, since the burden of a cattle drive, which grew more difficult with each passing day, was his responsibility, Samantha wondered. Was it something more than just the drive and its delays that had Shep looking increasingly harried?

Secrets.

Nearly all of them seemed to be guarding secrets, Samantha decided. And each of those secrets added to the daily stresses of the drive. She could feel her own strain mounting, though to be honest about it Roark Hawke was more to blame for that than anything else. He was nearly always at her side, ready to deal with any further threat to her. There was none, unless you counted Roark himself. And she did.

Samantha was constantly aware of him riding close beside her. Of his tall, lean body and how cowboy-sexy it looked in the saddle. Of those big hands stroking the neck of his horse or capably handling the reins. Of his long, smoldering glances and how she knew whenever they were directed at her, which was far too often, that he too was remembering the explosive kiss they had shared the night of the stampede.

The kiss hadn't been repeated, but it was a temptation—always there reminding her of the heat of his hard body strained against her, contributing to the tension between them. Which it wouldn't have if Samantha hadn't found herself longing to feel his mouth on hers again.

It was a conflict she didn't need, not when she was struggling to survive all the rigors of this damnable cattle drive.

"I know what I'm doing when it comes to selling real estate," she confessed to Roark. "Even with my agency facing hard times, I can be self-assured when I'm handling properties and clients. But out here I feel lost."

"I don't know why you're worrying about it," he said with a reassuring ease. "Sure, the challenges are there, but you're making progress. You've come a long way since that first morning."

Thinking about it, she realized he was right. She no longer trembled before she mounted a horse, no longer backed hastily away from a longhorn that looked like it might charge her. Slowly, and in spite of all her doubts, she found herself being tempered into a tougher material, one that was resilient enough to meet and endure the trials of the trail. And though she was a long way from being skillful with horses and cattle, her confidence was growing. One way or another, she promised herself, she would conquer this drive, and, yes, her fears along with it.

But none of this was enough to soften her ultimate intention to keep far away from ranching and all that was associated with it. And that meant not risking a relationship with a man who was on his way to becoming a full-time cowboy.

She had to resist the allure of Roark Hawke, and that wasn't easy. Not just because of his sensual appeal, either. There were so many other facets of the man that were being revealed to her layer by layer, attractive qualities like his humor and the way he cared about people, which made her enjoy his company and even think of him as a friend.

But you are not going to fall in love with him. When all this is done with, you're going to put distance between you. A safe distance.

It was with this fierce resolve that Samantha and the others arrived at Lost Springs late in the afternoon of their fifth day on the trail.

"WHAT DO YOU SAY?" Dick pleaded with the trail boss. "After all we've been through, haven't we earned a little fun?"

"This was scheduled to be a one-night stopover, Brewster, not a party."

"Hell, Shep, it's not like I'm suggesting we all troop off to the nearest bar and tie one on. I just want to relax for a couple of hours tonight. You know, a few drinks, music, maybe some dancing. We can manage that right here, can't we?"

The horse wrangler indicated the broad meadows out on the edge of town where the herd was placidly grazing. Samantha, watching Shep as he considered the request, thought how worn he looked, how much older than his years.

"Dick has a point," Roark urged. "We could all use a bit of entertainment."

He's right, Samantha thought. Maybe a party would ease tempers. They'd gotten a little frayed on the trail, especially Alex and Ernie's. She wondered again why Ernie resented Alex. Had he managed to overhear Alex telling them of his unsavory reputation in Austin? It seemed the likeliest explanation.

"All right," Shep agreed, "but there's to be no liquor at this shindig."

"Aw, come on, we got to have beer at least. How can we celebrate the halfway point in the drive without beer?"

"You can have your beer, but I don't want any hangovers in the morning. We've still got cows to move. And as far as celebrating goes, I intend doing that with a hot shower."

Amen, Samantha thought, longing for a shower of her own. She had five days of grime to wash away, which her quick sponge baths on the trail had not adequately accomplished.

Leaving Cappy to mind the herd, they headed for the row of log cabins on the far side of the field. Shep had arranged in advance for the overnight rental of three of the cabins, one of which was equipped with laundry facilities.

The outfit separated outside the cabins. Ramona was driving into town to stock up on fresh supplies. Dick elected to ride with her to buy the beer and snacks for their party. Ernie disappeared into the cabin he and his mother would share. Shep and Alex took the largest cabin, which Dick and Cappy would also use when it came time for their own turns under the shower. That left the third cabin for Samantha and Roark.

Unlocking the door with the key Shep had obtained for them from the office, Roark glanced inside to make certain the place was secure. Then he moved aside in the doorway, waiting for her to precede him into the cabin.

Samantha hesitated on the stoop. She couldn't imagine why she should be nervous about going in there with him. It wasn't as if any of the others were watching them with knowing smirks on their faces. Their own cabin doors were already closed behind them. Even Alex had accepted the arrangement without comment, realizing along with the rest of the outfit that Roark's job was to safeguard her, and that meant they weren't to be parted.

And, anyway, it hadn't been decided that any of them would sleep in these cabins. They probably wouldn't, Samantha thought. They'd spend the night out near the herd, just as they'd spent every night since the start of the drive. Maybe.

So why was she stalling? Because the thought of being alone with Roark Hawke inside a cozy log cabin, even if only for a few hours, conjured up intimate possibilities that put butterflies in her stomach?

"Problem?" Roark asked.

She glanced at him. The glint in his eyes told her he was amused by her sudden reluctance. She looked away, gazing in the direction of Lost Springs whose rooftops peeked through a belt of trees. "Just wondering about the town,'' she said in a hasty effort to cover her discomfort. ''It must be pretty small.''

''Uh-huh.'' Roark wasn't deceived.

''Well, it's so quiet.''

''Come back in the winter. I hear it comes to life then.'' He pointed in the direction of lifts on the mountainside above the town, indicating that Lost Springs was a ski resort. ''If we're finished now with the local scene, can we go inside and strip for action?''

Samantha shot him a startled look.

''Showers, Samantha, remember?''

''Right.'' She scooted past him, unable to avoid a brief though warm contact with his hard body in the doorway. She wondered if this, too, amused him.

By the time she turned around—after admiring a stone fireplace and trying not to mind that the room was furnished with only one bed—Roark had the door locked behind them and a security chain in place.

She needn't have worried. He was all business. ''You first,'' he said, nodding toward the bathroom. ''I've got a couple of calls to make.''

He was already on his way to the phone on the bedside table as Samantha, bag in hand, headed for the bathroom. She had never thought of plumbing as a luxury, but that's exactly what it felt like as she stood under an invigorating spray, promising herself she would never take hot water for granted again.

When she emerged from the bathroom with a towel wrapped around her head and wearing a fresh change of clothes, Roark was just putting the phone down.

''I talked to Wendell,'' he reported, referring to his trainee back in San Antonio. ''Nothing new. He's still trying to find out about Ernie Chacon. Also called the copy center here. They have the material Wendell e-mailed me.'' He glanced at his watch. ''But the place is on the other side of town, which means I've got to hurry if I want to get there before they close.'' He collected his gear and moved toward the bathroom. "I hope you left me some hot water."

Samantha was tempted to tell him that, at this point, maybe what they both needed were cold showers. What she said instead was very ordinary. "There's plenty of hot water. In fact, there was so much of it that I opened the window in there to let out the steam."

When the door had closed behind him, she remembered she had a blow dryer in her hand and a head of wet hair that needed her attention. There was a mirror above a chest of drawers, with a plug beside it. Within seconds, she was in business.

Samantha was in the final stages of drying her hair when her attention was captured by a movement outside the window reflected in the mirror. She swung around in time to see a figure slipping past the window. Brief though her glimpse was, it left her with an impression of stealth.

Switching off the dryer, she hurried across the room. By the time she reached the window and peered through the glass, the figure had reached the belt of trees that masked the town of Lost Springs. The light had dimmed into the early twilight of fall, but it was still possible to recognize that lanky figure.

It was Shep Thomas, and he wasn't alone. Another shorter man joined him under the trees where they engaged in an earnest conversation. Even from this distance, Samantha could tell by the way Shep's shoulders were slumped, his head lowered, that his mood was a morose one. He seemed to be pleading with the other man, who listened to him for a moment and then shook his head emphatically.

Samantha felt there was something furtive about their rapid exchange, something that the trail boss didn't want his outfit to know about. Otherwise, why would Shep meet this stranger away from the cabins where they weren't apt to be overheard or observed?

Her last glimpse of Shep before he strolled away

through the trees with his visitor, and the shadows swallowed them, was of a man who looked absolutely defeated.

Roark would certainly be interested in what she had just witnessed, Samantha thought, returning to the mirror to finish her hair. But her intention to share that scene with him was delayed by other events.

She was putting the last touches to her hair when she heard something outside the cabin. Or thought she heard it. She couldn't be sure with the hum of the dryer in her ear. Not until she turned off the instrument was she certain of it. A roaring came from the other side of the front door. What in the—

Laying down the dryer, Samantha started toward the window to investigate. Before she could get there, the noise abruptly ended, and there was silence. Except, of course, for the uninterrupted rush of the shower inside the bathroom, which meant Roark wouldn't have detected the roar. Nor, she presumed, did he hear the sudden banging on the cabin door. Samantha went to answer it.

Several minutes later the shower was turned off. The roaring sound had resumed by then. Roark couldn't have missed it this time. And been alerted by it. Which would explain why the bathroom door burst open, followed by a wet body charging out into the main room.

A body, Samantha breathlessly observed, that was naked except for a towel snagged around its waist. The towel barely covered its wearer's vital areas. The rest left nothing to the imagination.

Roark Hawke was an unsettling sight with his dark hair in wet spikes and drops of moisture clinging to his broad shoulders and chest. Water ran in rivulets on his muscular thighs, trickling down his long legs, as though he were some magnificent sea god emerging from the surf.

Now, why did she have to go and think something as wild as that? And why was he forever flying to her rescue in a state of undress? she wondered, remembering that night at the Morning Star Ranch. Remembering, too, how woozy the sight of his sleek body had made her.

"Would you please go and put some clothes on?"

"Not until you tell me what the heck is going on. What is that out there?"

By now the roar was receding into the distance, and the front door against which Samantha was leaning had been closed and relocked. "Relax. It's just a motorcycle. A *noisy* one. I think he needs a new muffler. Do motorcycles have mufflers?"

"Who?"

"The young man who delivered this." She held up the brown envelope in her hand.

"You went and opened the door to a stranger?"

"I was cautious. I kept it on the chain." She waved the envelope at him. "It's the stuff from the copy center. They were afraid you wouldn't get there before they closed and were nice enough to send it over with—I think he said his name was Nick—who was coming in this direction, anyway."

Roark relaxed. "Great. Let's have it."

He started toward her, one hand reaching for the envelope and the other doing nothing to hang on to the towel. Samantha could see it was in danger of sliding off him. She held the envelope behind her back.

"Not until you put some clothes on."

He stopped and grinned at her. "I bother you like this, huh?"

"Just get dressed."

He did, much to her relief, and a few minutes later they stood looking down at the contents of the large envelope, which Roark had spread out on the surface of the desk just outside the bathroom. Those contents seemed to consist mostly of photographs. There were a number of them, Samantha realized.

"What are they?" she asked, puzzled by the collection. "They look like—well, just a lot of rocks."

"They are rocks. Or, to be more accurate about it, shots of the rock walls in the ravine where your grandfather claimed someone fired at him."

"I don't mean to be critical, but they don't seem to make sense. Can any of them be useful to us?"

"Maybe, maybe not," Roark said, sifting through the pile. His finger tapped at a photo of striated rock. "This one, I'm afraid, is just an example of Wendell being conscientious to a fault. These gouges here could have been cut by bullets, except they're not fresh enough. They were probably worn in the stone by wind and water."

The collection was accompanied by two lengthy, detailed reports of Wendell's visits to the monastery and the Western Museum. Roark rapidly scanned them, apologizing for his trainee. "There isn't anything worthwhile here, either, but I guess I can't blame the kid for being thorough, when that's what a good PI is supposed to be." Indicating his intention to read them more carefully later on, he put the reports aside and picked up the last two items contained in the envelope. "Now these look a little more promising."

"Photographs again," Samantha said. "But I have to admit faces are more interesting than rocks. Who are they?"

Roark peered at the labels Wendell had attached to the bottoms of the photos to identify them. "This one is the abbot at St. James Monastery, and this other is the director of the Western Museum in Purgatory."

"The people who will inherit my grandfather's estate if I fail to complete the cattle drive," she said.

"Not directly," he corrected her. "It's what they represent that will benefit. You know either of these two men?" Roark held the photographs toward her.

"I did meet the abbot when I was a little girl," she said, glancing at the tall, smiling figure in his cassock. "I remember he was very kind. But this one…" She gazed at the mature, more sober face of the museum's director. "I don't know. I'm sure I never met the man, though it's hard to tell. The resolution isn't the best, but maybe…''

"The face is vaguely familiar? Yeah, I wondered about that myself, except as you say the photograph isn't—''

Roark broke off, listening. Samantha had heard it, too. A sudden rustling noise from the direction of the bathroom.

"The window we left open!'' he said. "There's someone out there!''

Slapping the photos down on the desk, he tore into the bathroom. He was back before she could follow him.

"Did you see him?''

"Just a glimpse of someone taking off into the woods back there, not enough to tell anything. I'm going after him. Stay close behind me, Samantha.''

She had learned the wisdom of that from the stampede and gave him no argument as they raced out of the cabin. Her mind, thinking about what had just happened, was as active as her legs that carried her in Roark's wake around the side of the building.

Whoever had stationed himself by the open window had been there for a purpose, an obvious one. He must have been eavesdropping on their conversation. How much had he heard, and how vital had any of it been to him? Enough to constitute a threat in their pursuit of him?

That pursuit was hampered by the rapidly failing light. The woods into which the intruder had fled behind the cabin were almost as dark as full night. That didn't stop Roark from following him. Samantha, at his heels, hoped his night vision was better than hers. She could barely see where they were going and almost smacked into him when he came to an abrupt halt.

"Listen,'' he whispered. "Hear it?''

Samantha strained her ears. She could detect nothing but the eerie silence all around them. And then off to their left came the snapping of a twig. Someone was moving over there.

Roark launched himself in that direction. Samantha tried to follow and bumped blindly into a tree, where she decided to stay put. Hugging the trunk, she waited. Seconds later came the sounds of curses and two bodies locked in combat. The darkness was so total now that she couldn't make out the struggle.

A minute later there was the crashing noise of someone taking off through the underbrush, then the sound of swiftly receding footsteps. A tall shadow emerged from the trees and joined her.

"He got away," Roark reported. "There's no point in going after him. There's no light left now."

"Could you tell who it was?"

"I wasn't able to hang on to him long enough for that. He was like an eel. Come on, let's find our way back to the cabin."

"Wait. There's something I didn't get the chance to tell you." She went on to describe Shep's encounter with the stranger out under the cover of the trees. "It struck me there was something funny about their meeting. Do you think it's anything to worry about?"

Roark was thoughtful for a moment. "Probably not. Shep mentioned something about needing to get permission to water the longhorns at a private pond on the next section of the trail."

"You think that's all it was?"

"I'll ask Shep about it. Let's hope his explanation is an innocent one. But either way," he said grimly, "we remain cautious, because anybody in this outfit could be the enemy. It's even possible Shep's visitor was our eavesdropper at the window. Right now there's only one thing I know for sure. Before this drive is finished, I mean to find out just who our enemy is and why."

It took them a few minutes to find their way through the black woods and back to the cabin. Once there, Samantha was relieved to be inside again and with the lights on.

"I don't know about you," she said, "but I could use those laundry facilities in the other cabin."

"Good plan."

They began to collect their things. Samantha couldn't find a pair of socks she had discarded before her shower and wondered if she had left them on the desk, maybe buried under the contents of the envelope. She started to gather up the photographs and Wendell's reports, and that's when she noticed that two of the items were missing.

"Roark, they're not here!"

He joined her at the desk. "What aren't?"

"The pictures of the abbot and the museum's director."

"Are you sure? Let me see." He took the stack from her and went through it. "You're right. They're gone. Did you check the floor? Maybe they slipped down behind the desk."

Together they searched the room. Roark even moved the desk away from the wall. There was no sign of the photographs.

"What happened to them?" Samantha asked. "Do you suppose…"

"Yeah," Roark said, understanding what she was saying, "I think that's exactly where they went. Whoever got away from me managed to double back here, sneak inside while we were still up in the woods, and grab the photos. And he didn't have to waste a second searching for what he wanted. He knew just what those photos were and where they were."

Samantha nodded. "From having overheard us talking about them while we stood right here. The mystery is, why? What is there about those two pictures that would compel him to steal them and not take either of the reports that accompanied them? Or to bother with the other photographs. Unless—"

"No, the rest are all still here. I counted them when I went through the stack."

"Then why?"

"You tell me. Which maybe you can. Sit down, Samantha. It's time we talk again about who benefits from Joe Walker's will in the event that you don't."

She perched on the edge of the bed. "Are you thinking this theft is connected with that?"

"It's a strong possibility." He turned the desk chair around and straddled it facing her. "Let's start with the St. James Monastery. Why would your grandfather leave half of his estate to a monastery? Was he that devout?"

"Hardly. I think it must be because of what happened during the Great Depression. Times were so bad that my great-grandfather would have lost the ranch if the monastery hadn't helped the family to survive. Joe was just a boy then, but he never forgot it. After he inherited the Walking W, he made an annual generous donation to St. James."

"So, gratitude. That's understandable. What about the Western Museum in Purgatory?"

"I should think that's fairly obvious. The museum is dedicated to displays of everything connected with Texas and ranching, and since that was my grandfather's whole world…"

"Right. It's all pretty straightforward then, nothing out of the ordinary about either of these two institutions dividing his estate if you fail to qualify."

"None of this is getting us anywhere, is it? We'd agreed back in San Antonio that St. James and the museum are probably above suspicion, and that in any case neither one of them is desperate for funds."

"There's got to be a motive somewhere. And my job is to learn it."

"How?"

"Don't know, but I will before I'm through."

They were both silent, and then Samantha remembered something. "Dick Brewster's party tonight. I don't know about you, but I'm in no mood to celebrate. I suppose, though, we have to be there."

"I wouldn't mind sharing a dance with you," Roark said with one of his wicked smiles. "And who knows. Maybe tonight will turn up something worthwhile, because I intend to have my eyes on every member of the outfit. People at a party can be damn interesting. And sometimes revealing."

Chapter Seven

Depending upon your point of view, Samantha thought, this party was either as interesting as Roark wanted it to be or an absolute washout.

She was personally inclined to favor the latter opinion, although she couldn't argue with the setting. With the sky above them spangled by stars, an orange moon just beginning to peek over the distant mountaintops and the campfire around which they were gathered providing a comforting glow, she supposed the mood was as ideal as any greenhorn yearning for the romance of the old West could want.

She couldn't say the same about the moods of the company. With a few exceptions, they could be defined as dismal. Cappy Davis, his normally uncommunicative tongue loosened by beer, was one of those exceptions.

"Nasty business, castrating. Bet we castrated and branded two hundred head that day. By the time I got back to the bunkhouse…"

Samantha wished that Dick Brewster hadn't suggested they swap stories. Cappy's ranch tales about the old days before mechanization were much too graphic, as well as being exaggerations. She much preferred the old man entertaining them with his mouth organ, which he had earlier been persuaded to do. Cappy's harmonica had blended with Dick's smooth voice singing Western favorites that even Samantha had enjoyed.

"Sure you won't have one, Sam?" the horse wrangler urged, offering her a can of beer as Cappy wrapped up his story.

"No, thanks. I'm fine with my soda."

Poor Dick. He was genuinely enjoying himself…or trying to.

Ramona, making an effort to support him, kept pressing snacks on the company that no one really wanted. Her manner was as hearty as Dick's, but far less genuine. Samantha could see she was still worried about her son.

And with good reason. Ernie, along with Alex, was consuming far too much beer. The two of them sat there and glared at each other. Shep was in no better condition on the other side of the campfire. He remained silent and gloomy, though he hadn't touched the beer himself, leaving Samantha with the impression that he didn't approve of alcohol. The trail boss's problem was obviously something else, possibly connected with that meeting she had witnessed this afternoon.

As for Roark settled beside her…well, he was as quiet as Shep. From time to time, Samantha cast her gaze in his direction, watching him watch the others while he slowly, unconsciously flexed the fingers of the hand he had injured in the rodeo competition. She knew Roark was observing them, waiting for an interesting development that had yet to occur. It was a rare opportunity with the entire outfit assembled in one spot, a situation made possible by the two young men from town who'd been hired to take care of the herd for the evening.

But Samantha no longer cared about that opportunity. At the moment, as tired and dispirited as the others, all she longed for was the end of this dreary affair. But Dick wasn't about to let his party die a quiet death.

"Hey," he said, surging to his feet, "this is getting dull. It's time to make happy."

Producing a battery-powered radio from his saddlebag, he tuned into a station playing golden oldies. A loud and lively "Rocky Mountain High" issued from the speaker.

"Ah, this is more like it." Leaning over, the good-natured horse wrangler extended a hand to Samantha. "Come on, Sam, dance with me."

He was so enthusiastic about it that she didn't have the heart to disappoint him. She permitted him to raise her to her feet and lead her onto the floor. In this case, the floor was the hard-packed earth of the level area out in front of the cabins.

"You having fun, Sam?" Dick asked her as he spun her around the clearing. "I'm having fun."

"I'm having a fine time," she lied.

Unruly blond hair swinging over his eyes, he turned his head to call out to the others. "Come on, the rest of you dance, too."

Alex needed no further invitation. Springing to his feet, he hurried over to claim his own turn with Samantha. Dick surrendered her and went off to dance with Ramona.

Samantha didn't like the eager flush on Alex's face as he danced with her. Made bold by all the beer he'd consumed, he leaned toward her with a confession that was slightly slurred. "You are so beautiful, Sam. Do you know how beautiful you are?"

Samantha sent a look of desperation in Roark's direction, hoping for a timely rescue. All she got back was an amused expression that told her she was on her own. Damn him, why wasn't he asking for that dance he had earlier promised he wanted to share with her? On the other hand, maybe it was just as well she wasn't in his arms.

In the end, it was Ernie who saved her from needing to respond to Alex's embarrassing admiration. He swaggered forward with the determined intention to cut in on his rival.

"My turn."

Alex swung his head, scowling at him. "Go away. Sam doesn't want to dance with you."

"Who says?"

Afraid of a scene, Samantha swiftly intervened. "It's all right, Alex. I'd like to dance with Ernie."

Alex hesitated and then reluctantly left the field.

"He thinks I ain't good enough to dance with you," Ernie bitterly complained as he guided her in an awkward waltz around the clearing.

It was hard to argue with that when an impatient Alex hovered nearby, glowering at Ernie. In less than two minutes, he was back.

"You've had her long enough, Chacon."

Ernie laughed, a sneer on his broad face. "Go away, college boy. She's dancing with a man now."

Oh, great, Samantha thought. They were both smashed on beer and ready to start shoving each other. If that happened, it would end up in some stupid slugging contest.

"Now look, you two, I don't appreciate—"

"You're asking for it, Chacon."

"I am, huh?"

Samantha tensed, waiting for the fists to fly. But before that could happen, help arrived. The voice that addressed them was deep, calm, and meant business. "I don't think you gentlemen want to take this any further. Do you?"

Alex and Ernie exchanged fierce glances before prudently deciding not to challenge the tall figure who confronted them so forcefully.

"Why don't you boys go off to your corners for a little while?" Roark suggested. "Better still, help yourselves to that coffee Ramona brewed. *Lots* of it."

The two men separated and obediently retreated. Roark, casual but authoritative, called over to the horse wrangler. "Dick, what do you say we trade the radio for some live music? Cappy, how about giving us 'Shenandoah' on that mouth organ of yours?"

Meant to soothe the savage beasts, Samantha thought as Dick turned off the radio and Cappy delivered a poignant but lulling "Shenandoah." She could see the others at the party visibly relax, relieved that Roark had so smoothly dealt with a tricky situation.

"I could have handled them, you know," she said.

Eyebrows quirked, Roark looked offended. "What? You're not going to tell me how grateful you are that the cavalry arrived in the nick of time?"

"Actually, I am glad you stepped in."

"Then I think I deserve a dance as a reward."

It was about time he got around to that. "I suppose it would be a shame to waste what Cappy is doing with that harmonica."

"A damn shame."

He held out his arms. She stepped into them willingly if not wisely. The sweet strains of "Shenandoah" wooed them as they moved slowly around the floor. Roark was silent while they waltzed. He didn't have to talk. His body molded to hers said it all. And what it told her with its searing hardness was that she was making a mistake being in intimate contact again with this tall figure in boots, tight jeans that emphasized the muscles in his legs, and an open-neck Western shirt that revealed the pulse beating so tantalizingly in the hollow of his deeply tanned throat.

The garb of a cowboy. It reminded her of another cowboy she had once danced with this closely. Hank, whom she had loved and lost.

Needing to distract herself from the painful memories, to defuse all the unsettling emotions that Roark's arms around her generated, Samantha eased the tightness of his embrace by drawing back far enough to permit conversation. It created a safe space between them while giving her an excuse to learn what she wanted to know, anyway.

"Were you able to talk to Shep?" she asked, keeping her voice low. "Did you learn what that meeting this afternoon was all about?"

If Roark guessed her interest had more than one motive, he gave no sign of it. "I asked him. His explanation was what I figured it would be. He told me he was getting permission from a local rancher to water the herd and cross private land.''

''But wasn't all that kind of thing secured in advance? Isn't that what he told us back at the Morning Star Ranch?''

''He said this particular consent wasn't clear. That he needed to make certain of it in person. Maybe he was lying, maybe not.''

Samantha glanced in the direction of the trail boss, unable to believe that the burdens of the drive would have him looking this unhappy. ''And the others in the outfit?''

''What about them?''

''You've spent most of your time tonight just sitting there observing them. What were you looking for?''

''For one of them to be less cunning than he has been all along. To make some kind of slip that will tell us exactly who he is.''

Samantha stared at him. ''Do you know what you're saying?''

''I know just what I'm saying,'' he said softly. ''I've thought about it enough to be convinced that our man is right here in this outfit. And whoever it is, he's determined the drive will fail. One way or another, he'll prevent you from reaching the end of the trail.''

Samantha was startled by his grim certainty. Until now, she had been reluctant to seriously believe anyone in the outfit could be her enemy. It had to be some unknown person or persons who wanted her out of the way. A menace who'd managed so far to keep himself hidden from them. But if Roark was right...

Shuddering, she looked around, her gaze searching out each member of the company. A carefree Dick Brewster danced again with Ramona, who giggled over one of his jokes. Shep still looked preoccupied with whatever problem troubled him while Cappy, beside him, swayed happily from side to side, keeping time with the notes he coaxed from his mouth organ. On the other side of the fire, standing safely apart from each other, Alex and Ernie sipped the coffee Roark had urged and idly watched the dancers.

It was incredible to suppose that any one of them wanted to harm her. Even the surly Ernie who, after all, was still the likeliest candidate.

Her lingering doubt must have been evident to Roark. Plain enough, anyway, for him to tell her earnestly, "They're not all your friends, Samantha. One of them is ruthless, and sooner or later he's going to strike again. The worst of it is, we can't know when, where or how. But I'll tell you one thing. I'm not going to sit by and just wait for it. I plan to use every opportunity I can to learn who this guy is and to defeat him."

That wouldn't be easy, Samantha thought. Not when Roark already had his hands full moving the cattle while protecting her throughout every hour of each day. He was so determined, though, that she believed he *would* conquer their enemy. But it frightened her that she could no longer deny the source of the danger, pretend it originated from a stranger.

"There is another choice," he said, reading her fear. "You can still quit the drive, pull out now and save yourself from any further risk. No one would think any less of you."

"*I* would think less of me." She shook her head. "No, I wouldn't do it back in San Antonio when you suggested it, and I won't do it now. I *can't.*"

He said nothing, but his arms tightened around her, bringing her close again to his solid length. She offered no resistance this time, knowing his action was a silent promise to safeguard her. His arms were a welcome refuge.

"I WAS A DAMN FOOL last night," Alex apologized sheepishly to Samantha early the next morning. "Sorry for being out of line like that, Sam."

The puppy was not only anxious to be forgiven, Roark

thought, he looked like he was suffering one enormous hangover in the bargain. Poor McKenzie.

If Ernie Chacon regretted his own performance, he made no effort to express it. He was as surly as ever as the outfit mounted up for their sixth day of the cattle drive.

Roark spared a last glance at the cabins as they headed out on the trail. No one, except Ramona, had spent the night in them. He had mixed emotions about that. He'd certainly entertained all the enticing possibilities of sleeping there with Samantha. On the other hand, that very tempting arrangement was something he was better off putting behind him.

He had to keep his libido under wraps, his mind clear, in order to focus on guarding Samantha. Admittedly, that was a problem. Whenever he checked on her, which was probably more often than necessary, he was immediately aware of how she looked as they rode side by side in their customary position at the rear of the herd.

Samantha might have no fondness for anything connected with ranching, but she was a vision in the saddle. He couldn't keep himself from admiring all the little things about her that appealed to him so strongly. Like the wisps of warm-toned chestnut hair that escaped from her braid, the way she pushed her Stetson back when she lifted her face to the sun, the curve of her breasts in her denim shirt. Oh, yeah, especially her breasts. He wondered about those all the time, imagining them full and heavy in his hands.

It was much safer, though, if somewhat less satisfying, to admire what couldn't get him into difficulty. Like all her inner qualities that, with each day, he found himself appreciating more and more. Especially the courage of her resolve to go on with the drive. Okay, so that wasn't so wise. He would have preferred her safely back in Texas, but since that wasn't going to happen, he had to remain alert and ready for trouble.

There was something else he had promised both himself and Samantha he was going to do: solve this damn puzzle.

To that end, he called Wendell again in Texas. He told his trainee about the theft of the photographs in the cabin and asked him to probe further into the backgrounds of the two men they'd pictured, as well as to send him copies of the photos that had been taken. There had to be a connection and an explanation somewhere.

Something else gnawed at him, demanding answers: the ravine back at the Walking W. The more he thought about it, the more he was convinced it played a major role in the mystery. It frustrated him that he couldn't visit the place himself. But he could do the next best thing and ask Samantha about it.

"Tell me about the ravine where Joe had his accident," Roark urged her as they rode in the wake of the herd. "How familiar are you with the spot?"

"Enough to know there was nothing there to interest me. It's just a dry, barren ravine. I seldom had occasion to visit it, not as remote as it is. Why do you keep focusing on it, Roark?"

"Because I'm convinced now that somebody *was* firing on your grandfather that day, and I think there had to be a good reason for that. There's something about that ravine. I can feel it in my gut."

"Like what? Roark, there are no hidden treasures there. You must know that part of Texas has no precious mineral deposits, no gold or oil. Nothing valuable like that."

"All the same…"

Roark made a mental note to himself. The next time he spoke to Wendell, he was going to ask him to go back to the ravine. Request that he examine it again from end to end, take further photographs to send him. There had to be something there besides just rocks.

"I'M WORRIED," Samantha confided to him during the midday break.

Roark was immediately attentive. "Something happen?"

"That's just it. Nothing has. Haven't you noticed? The sun is shining, we're making good time on a level trail, and there hasn't been a single problem with the longhorns, including Irma. It's downright unnatural."

"Are you telling me you miss them? All those calamities we dealt with?"

"It's just making me nervous, that's all. I keep wondering where the thunderstorms are and the stampedes or even a swarm or two of gnats."

Roark chuckled, but he knew what she meant. There hadn't been a single delay all morning. Their progress had been steady and easy. Maybe deceptively so.

It didn't last. Trouble surfaced late that afternoon. It was nothing serious. Or at least it didn't seem to be serious. At first.

He and Samantha had gotten temporarily separated when he dashed off on his roan to check on a steer lagging behind the others. But though she'd been left on the far side of the herd, he made sure he kept her in sight.

Roark was on his way back to her after seeing the steer rejoin the herd when she shouted to him across the tableland over which the drive was currently traveling.

"Irma is missing again! I'm going after her!"

"Samantha, no! Wait for me!"

She either didn't hear him or chose to ignore his command. Wheeling on Dolly, she trotted away, disappearing down a slope. He was going to strangle her! With a possible killer in the outfit, she should know better than to go off like this on her own. And all for the sake of that damn precious heifer of hers! Angry and alarmed, Roark urged his mount into a gallop.

He expected to see her below him when he reached the top of the slope, but she was nowhere in sight. There was a path of sorts, probably a deer trail, that descended in easy stages through the shrubby growth. He followed it on horseback, searching for Samantha ahead of him, but he caught no glimpse of her.

So gently did the path sink into the floor of the mesa, and so anxious was he about Samantha's welfare, that Roark paid only scant attention to his surroundings. Not until there were walls that embraced him on either side to shoulder height did he realize the path had gradually become a narrow defile.

Irma or no Irma, what was she doing in this place? Or had she not come this far? Maybe he had missed her. He started to swing his horse around, intending to go back, when he saw the fresh droppings left by either the heifer or Dolly, evidence that she must have come this way.

"Samantha!" he yelled. There was no answer to his call, no sound of either her or her horse ahead of him. Where the hell was she?

Wherever she was, he had to find her. Taking off again in pursuit of her, he followed the winding route, his concern deepening with the crevasse. He was submerged within the very fabric of the mesa now. Close on either side of him, perhaps seventy feet or more in height, rose the sheer, solid walls of the passage.

The stone was ruptured everywhere by fissures. Stunted junipers and stubby pines sprang from them. In other places the vertical faces were so fractured that narrow shelves supported layer upon layer of broken rock reaching toward the rim of the mesa. The stacks were so precariously balanced they looked like they were in danger of collapsing if the slightest movement disturbed them.

"Samantha, where are you?"

Again there was no answer except for his own voice bouncing hollowly off the walls of the trench. The sunlight was far above him now, his only companions his horse and the silent shadows. The roan didn't seem to like the place, moving at a nervous pace.

Roark didn't call out for Samantha again, fearing the reverberations of his shouts would be enough to bring those lofty piles of rock tumbling down on them. There were already scattered rocks on the ground, evidence of

earlier falls. Spurring the roan, he went on along the tor-
tuous route.

*Come on, Samantha, show me where you are so we can
both get out of this damn hole.*

He was sick with worry by the time he came to a spot
where the walls met each other above him, forming a stone
arch that spanned the defile clear to the top of the mesa.
The passage beneath it was so deep it was more like a
tunnel than an archway. Without hesitation, Roark urged
his mount into the gap. Its ceiling was low and he had to
bend almost double in the saddle to avoid scraping his
head.

It wasn't until he emerged on the other side that he was
able to hear it, the sound of a female voice calling for
help. His gut tightening with fear, Roark hurried the roan
forward. Rounding a corner, he came upon them suddenly.
There they were in front of him, two obstinate creatures
locked in a battle of wills.

He took in the situation at a glance, his rigid body sagging with relief. It was all right. She was in no danger,
though how she and the blasted Irma had gotten down
inside that wide cavity, where she was swatting the heifer's
rump with her Stetson in an effort to urge her out of it, he
couldn't imagine.

For a few seconds he just sat there, amused by her frustrated performance. Then his anger kicked in. "I ought to
take that hat away from you and spank *your* bottom with
it!"

The thunder of his voice startled her into a squeak of
alarm. She whirled around to face him. "You scared the
wits out of me!"

"You didn't have any to scare, or you wouldn't have
chased after the fool cow. Or come all this way to get her
back."

Samantha looked around in surprise, as though just now
realizing how far she had traveled in pursuit of the heifer.
"I guess the distance sneaked up on me, and by the time

I realized I'd come too far and ought to turn back, I heard Irma bawling so pitifully I knew she was in trouble. I couldn't just leave her. I had to go on and try to help her.''

''You should have waited for me.''

''Oh, but if I'd done that, it might have been too late to save her.''

Her logic exasperated him, but he guessed he could understand it, even if he didn't approve of it. The heifer was Samantha's responsibility on the drive, her one and only way to prove herself, and she had no intention of abandoning that responsibility, even if meant risking herself. Sensible or not, he liked her for that.

''Anyway, I knew you'd find me if I kept hollering. And don't ask me how Irma landed in this trap. Nothing she ever does makes sense. How are we going to get her out?''

''Climb out of there, and I'll show you.'' Dismounting from the roan with lariat in hand, Roark stepped down into the hollow, approached the heifer and dropped the loop over her head.

''I don't know how you do it,'' Samantha said, clambering out of the hole. ''All *you* have to do is look at her, and she stands there and lets you rope her.''

''Charm,'' he said. ''Come on, Irma, if you managed to get down in here, you can get yourself out.'' He made quick work of the rescue, tugging at the heifer until she obediently scrambled up and out of the depression.

''Is she okay?''

''She's fine. Mount up and let's get out of here.''

Roark led the way. The heifer, docile now at the end of her lead, trotted willingly behind him. Samantha brought up the rear on Dolly.

Did he imagine it, he wondered as he started out of the other side of the arch, or had he heard the sharp crack of something high over his head? Drawing rein, he listened.

''What is it?'' Samantha demanded. ''Why are we stopped?''

She was behind him under the wide arch, where she had

apparently heard nothing. In any case, there was silence now. He was ready to move on again when the first tiny grains rained down on him, settling like sand on his head and shoulders. They were followed by pebbles the size of hailstones striking the floor of the trench. Larger stones tumbled after them, signaling disaster.

"Back!" Roark bellowed a warning. "Get back! The whole thing is coming down!"

Horses and riders, together with the heifer, retreated through the arch, scrambling for safety. Above the panicked cries of the animals came the ominous splitting noise of tons of rock parting from the high face of the wall. The ripping sound became a rumble that grew to a roar as the avalanche descended, crashing to the floor of the defile with such force that the earth trembled beneath them.

In the aftermath came the rattle of a last few stones falling, and then there was silence again. A cloud of dust rose like thick smoke from the mouth of the arch. When it cleared, they could see from where they huddled under an overhang that the opening on the other side was buried by massive boulders from ceiling to floor.

Roark cursed. "Blocked! Not so much as a gap!"

Samantha voiced her own frustration. "Nature has lousy timing."

But Roark wasn't so sure it was an accident. That crack he'd heard just before the landslide had sounded very much like the one that had stampeded the cattle the other night. Could the blast of a firearm trigger a rock fall of that magnitude? If so—

He didn't get to finish his thought. Samantha interrupted him anxiously. "Even if we wanted to leave the horses, the walls in here are much too steep for us to climb, aren't they? But there *must* be a way out." Before he could stop her, she goaded her mare out from under the shelter of the overhang to investigate the possibilities for herself.

"Samantha, no! Keep back!"

He didn't hear the bark of gunfire, not this time, but the

ping of a bullet biting into the sandstone within inches of
Samantha's exposed body was unmistakable. Leaping
from his horse, Roark dashed forward and dragged her
from the saddle, throwing his own body in front of her to
shield her.

Another bullet struck, missing them again but so close
he felt the bit of rock it chipped hit his shoulder. He didn't
wait for a third bullet. Gathering Samantha into his arms,
he flew with her back under the protective overhang.

Dolly had the good sense to join them, but neither the
horses nor the heifer liked being targets any more than
Samantha and Roark did. They were snorting in fear and
threatening to bolt. As soon as he'd released Samantha,
Roark dealt with them. They shied away from him, dancing nervously, but he was able to catch their reins.

When he'd managed to calm them, including the heifer,
he turned back to a bemused Samantha. Her eyes were
wide with fear and disbelief. "Who?" she whispered.

"Couldn't tell." But whoever it was, he'd wager it was
the same someone who had fired on Joe Walker in a similar situation back in Texas. *And none of us believed the
old man,* he thought wryly. Not then. "Maybe I can find
out. Stay here and try to keep the animals quiet."

"You're not going out there again!"

"I'll be careful."

Sliding his gun from its holster and hugging the wall,
he sprinted a few yards along the passage, trying to keep
under the overhang as he searched for a place to get a look
at whoever was up there on the rim above them. His move-
ments must have been detected because they drew a rapid
fire. Bullets ricocheted all around him, but none of them
came close to touching him.

Sounds like a rifle, Roark thought, though he couldn't
be certain of that. Ernie Chacon had a rifle, but then so
did the others in the outfit, including Ramona.

Roark returned the fire. The angle and height were impossible, both for him and their assailant. But one of

Roark's bullets must have found his target. He could swear
he heard a yelp from the rim. Either he had wounded the
enemy or come so close that he'd scared him into a retreat.
A long silence followed. The bastard had gone. He must
have realized how useless it was to try to keep them pinned
down. He hoped.

In any case, Roark had been unable to identify him.
Only briefly had he caught glimpses of a figure up there,
no more than a shapeless shadow against the blinding glare
of the sunlight on the mesa above him.

Roark waited, and when the silence remained unbroken,
he turned and made his way back to Samantha's side.
"Couldn't recognize him," he reported, returning his gun
to its holster. "I think he's gone, though."

"What now?" she asked. "Do we stay here?" She
glanced up nervously at the rock hanging over their heads.
"Maybe it isn't safe. Maybe this will come down, too."

He shook his head. "This section looks solid enough."

"The others must have missed us by now. They're probably out searching for us."

And one of them found us, Roark thought grimly. *And
at this moment he's hoping we never find our way out of
this place, that we die down here trying.* But he didn't say
that to Samantha. She was upset enough as it was.

"Roark, I'm so sorry. It's my fault we're in this mess.
If I had been thinking at all—"

"Don't," he interrupted. "You did what you felt you
had to do. Beating yourself up over it is just a waste of
time. We need to figure out what we're going to do."

Her gaze strayed to the cell phone clipped to his belt.
"Do you suppose we could call out for help?"

He looked up at the towering walls that surrounded them
on all sides. "Not much chance of any reception in here,
but it's worth a try."

Roark paused with his hand on the instrument. Shep had
a cell phone of his own, which made him the logical

choice. Providing he wasn't the enemy himself, and he could be. Well, he would have to risk it.

Samantha watched him tensely as he turned on the phone's power and checked the display. It informed him there was no signal.

"No good?" she asked.

He shook his head and returned the phone to his belt.

"Then we're trapped down here!"

"Not necessarily. Just because we can't go back the way we came in doesn't mean there isn't some other way out. We'll try the other direction."

"Do you think it's safe to move? What if you're wrong and he's still up there just waiting for us to show ourselves again?"

"My instincts say he isn't, but let me go first." Leading the roan out from under the overhang, he lifted himself into the saddle and waited. Silence. "All right, let's risk it."

There was no further threat from the enemy when Samantha emerged with Dolly, mounted up, and with the heifer trailing behind, followed him along the twisting defile. But he knew she was nervous about another sudden burst of gunfire. Hell, he was nervous himself. They were vulnerable down here.

The possibility of another ambush lessened as they proceeded along the winding trench, only to be replaced by other concerns. The loss of daylight, for one. This blasted gorge had already been as dim as a cavern, but Roark judged by the slowly fading light that the sun was low in the sky now. It would go down in another half hour or so, leaving them caught here in the darkness.

Bad enough, but what if there was no way out? That was also a possibility, as they discovered when the channel divided. Roark chose the left branch. They had traveled along it for a hundred yards or so when it abruptly dead-ended in sheer rock.

"We have to go back to the fork," he said.

"Yes," Samantha said hopefully, turning the mare. "Maybe we'll have better luck with the other branch."

But he could detect the first threads of panic in her voice, and he knew he had to distract her, to occupy her mind with something other than the gravity of their situation. And, anyway, he wanted the knowledge she could provide him.

"Tell me about them, Samantha," he said as they arrived at the fork and made their way along the right branch. "The members of our outfit. All I know about them as individuals is what I've been able to observe on the drive. But you grew up on the Walking W. You must have a lot more than just impressions."

"Not really. Not when you consider I left the ranch not long after my mother died and never went back, except for a single visit, and by then the staff had changed."

"Like who, for instance?"

"Shep Thomas, for one. The foreman before him had quit, and my grandfather replaced him with Shep. He and his wife occupy a cottage on the ranch. I think they came from somewhere near Dallas, but I'm not sure of that. In fact, I'm not really sure of anything about Shep, except I get the feeling he's a lot deeper than he seems. Another fork! Which one this time?"

They took the wider of the two passages.

"Go on with what you were telling me," Roark encouraged her.

"Why do you want to know? Is it that useful, or are you just trying to keep me busy?"

She was no fool. "Both," he said honestly.

"You think my information is going to bring you closer to learning who wants me out of the way?"

"It's possible. What about Dick Brewster?"

"In his case, he was hired on a few months before I left the ranch. Long enough for me to learn that, where Dick is concerned, what you see is what you get."

Maybe, Roark thought, and maybe not.

"This is no good, is it?" Samantha said.

She was referring to their route. It had narrowed, was so tight in places that it barely accommodated horse and rider. But it hadn't dead-ended. Yet.

"Let's give it a chance."

They continued to pursue it, claustrophobic though it was.

"And Cappy?" he prompted.

"There isn't much to know about Cappy. He's been on the Walking W forever. He and my grandfather went way back. Cappy gave me my first riding lesson. Roark, we're losing the light."

The shadows had thickened in the gorge.

"I know. How about Ramona?"

"She was hired as housekeeper to replace my mother. That happened after I was gone. She was there when I came back for the one visit, which wasn't long enough to learn anything about her history. We did get to be on friendly terms, though, and I could see how efficient she was. I suspect that's all that mattered to my grandfather."

"So Ramona is something of a mystery."

"Not as much as her son is. Roark, what are we going to do if it gets completely dark before we find our way out of here? *If* we ever do."

"We still have time, and we will."

But he was less confident about that than he wanted her to think, particularly when the route divided again. There were three galleries this time, and the first two they tried turned out to be impassable after a few yards.

The third artery allowed them to proceed, but Roark realized by now that this entire section of the mesa was seamed with deep rifts. A network nature had carved into a bewildering maze of fissures. For all he knew, they were riding in circles, crossing routes they had already traveled.

"It's hopeless, isn't it?" Samantha said in a small, bleak voice. "We're lost."

"Don't give up. We still have enough light left to guide us. Come on, you haven't told me about Alex yet."

"Yes, Alex. Well, his father's ranch adjoins the Walking W. They've always been good neighbors. But you know that already. After all, the McKenzies are your neighbors, too."

"What with keeping my own spread going, along with the agency in San Antonio, I never had the time to learn much of anything about my neighbors. Like, just how serious is this crush Alex McKenzie has on you?"

Samantha laughed softly. "It's a leftover from our high school days. He used to leave notes for me in my locker, but since he was a freshman and I was a senior…well, you know what it's like at that age. We were light-years apart. Satisfied?"

"For now."

There was a pause, and then she said quietly, "Thank you."

"For what?"

"Keeping me from going hysterical on you. But maybe I should have been screaming my head off. Do you think the others would have heard us if we'd hollered?"

"Not much chance of that down here."

There was another silence between them, no sound but the steady clopping of the horses' hooves on the hard bed of the defile. The precious light continued to fade. The silence lengthened.

"Roark, stop!"

He drew rein. "What is it?"

"Don't you hear it?" she asked, her voice excited.

He listened, and now he could hear it, too. The murmur of water over stone. It came from somewhere in front of them.

"Do you think…"

But Roark was afraid to count on anything. Snapping the reins, he moved forward again, leading the way toward the source of the water. It was louder now, identifying itself as a stream tumbling over rocks.

There was something else. The deepening gloom had lessened. He was puzzled about that until he realized that the walls on either side had diminished considerably in height, permitting the last light of day to enter the trench. The channel had also widened. He and Samantha could ride comfortably now side by side.

Smelling the water, the animals quickened their pace without urging. They rounded a last bend, emerging from the mouth of the defile into a low canyon. And there in the gray, lingering twilight, situated above the stream that had beckoned them, was a sight that astonished them.

Chapter Eight

"Look at them, Samantha! They're incredible!"

She *was* looking, and she was impressed, though her interest couldn't begin to match Roark's excitement over the spectacle of the tumbled sandstone walls. In fact, she found more pleasure in his enthusiasm than in the reason for it.

"I've seen the cliff dwellings at Mesa Verde," he said, "and they're more extensive than these. Probably in a better state of preservation, too, but it's not the same as stumbling onto our very own ruins like this!"

She knew he realized, just as she did, that they couldn't possibly be the first to discover these crumbling structures, isolated though they were in a remote region. But it was fun to claim them as their own.

They went on standing there, feasting their gazes on the mass of finely crafted masonry above them in a deep alcove under the overhanging rim of the mesa. From what Samantha could tell in the rapidly dwindling light, the compound consisted of a series of connected rooms and towers, some square, others round, all of them positioned on terraces at various levels.

Roark, who could scarcely control himself, started to climb down from his roan. "I've got to have a better look at this while we still have a glimmer of light."

"Do you think we should?" she said, hating to temper

his exhilaration. "I mean, while we have any light left at all, shouldn't we be concerning ourselves first with a few practical matters? Like how we're supposed to find our way back to the outfit when we're still lost in the wilderness? And, if we can't manage that, where we're going to spend the night and what we're going to eat?"

"Samantha, we're looking at prehistory here. This stuff has got to be centuries old."

"I know, but I'm hungry, and I'm thirsty. I imagine the animals are, too."

"You're right." Muttering something about the joyless necessity of reality, Roark directed a last, regretful glance at the roofless ruins before turning his attention to their more immediate needs. "I don't see any point in our trying to go on in the dark." He looked around. "We couldn't ask for a better spot to camp. There's the stream here and grass for the horses and Irma."

Which didn't solve the problem of what she and Roark were going to eat, Samantha thought, but she had to agree that spending the night here was the wisest plan. "There's another advantage," she pointed out to him. "If we're here when the sun comes up, we'll have some real light to explore the ruins."

She anticipated the chance to share an interval like that with him and hoped that he felt the same. It pleased her when he responded warmly, "You and me playing archaeologists together sounds good."

Unsaddling the horses, they watered them and the heifer. There was no risk in turning the animals loose afterward. They were too exhausted to wander, including Irma, and were content to graze in the immediate area.

It was completely dark by then, but the moon had risen. Its pale glow shed sufficient light for their other chores. There were cottonwoods along the stream and the ever-present quaking aspens elsewhere in the canyon, providing a supply of fuel.

Samantha gathered wood and built a fire in a level spot

beside the stream while Roark tried his hand at fishing in one of the pools. Or his version of it, anyway. This amounted to whittling the end of a long stick into a sharp point. It was hard to have faith in his intention, especially when he was operating by moonlight. But, miracle of miracles, he actually managed to spear and land a fat trout.

Impressed, she watched him as he cleaned the fish with his knife before crouching beside the fire to toast his catch on a makeshift spit. "Survival skills you learned in cowboy class, I suppose."

"Actually, it was the Boy Scouts, and not out on the open range either. It was back in Illinois where I grew up."

Samantha knew very little about his history, only that he came from a big family and that all of them were PIs like him, including his parents, who operated the home office of the Hawke Detective Agency in Chicago. She wondered if they were a close, loving family.

For a moment she was tempted to ask him about that, suddenly longing to know more about him. But then she decided her interest wasn't smart. Not when he looked the way he did hunkered down by the fire, the flames lighting his strong face shadowed by a day's growth of whiskers, his black hair tousled from his Stetson. The image was a sexy one, all male. It also reminded her of how much Roark had in common with her rugged grandfather, and this was a subject that always made her uneasy.

"It's ready," he said, dividing the trout and handing her her portion on a plate. Or what passed for one in the shape of a hunk of birch bark. "Careful, it's hot."

The fish was charred and flavored with smoke, but no meal had ever tasted better to her. And no dinner setting had ever been more—well, with the moonlight on the ruins above them, she supposed *romantic* would be the appropriate word, though *mysterious* might be more accurate, even *ghostly*. Contributing to this mood was the soft rattle of dry aspen leaves that had drifted to the ground where a faint breeze scattered them. That, and a sudden, sharp yelping off in the canyon. Startled, Samantha huddled closer to Roark on the horse blanket they shared.

"Relax," he said. "It's just a coyote."

"I know."

But it was a nervous sound, reminding her of the danger they had faced today and of an enemy that could still be lurking out there in the darkness, even concealed in the ruins. Not that this was likely. Whoever it was would have returned long ago to the outfit in order to preserve his mask of innocence.

"The others must be worried about us," she said.

"There's nothing we can do about that until tomorrow."

Roark had tried again just after their arrival in the canyon to raise Shep on his cell phone, but his effort had been as unsuccessful as his first attempt.

The fish eaten and the fire replenished, they sat there without talking, listening to the popping of the blazing wood, Irma and the horses stirring nearby, and the babble of the stream. She watched Roark as he stared into the flames. He was working the fingers of that hand again, a restless action that told her he was troubled.

"You're thinking about the decision you have to make, aren't you?" she guessed.

He turned his head to look at her. "As a matter of fact, that's just what I was doing."

It was uncanny the way she could read him, and even more unsettling that he had the ability to read her as well. Just as though they had been together for years, instead of a few days. "What's so difficult about it? You obviously prefer ranching to investigative work."

"It's not that simple. There's—" He hesitated, and for a moment Samantha thought he wasn't going to tell her. But then, apparently deciding he wanted her to know, he finished what he'd started to say. "—an issue involved."

"Oh?"

Her response didn't sound very concerned, she realized.

But she sensed he wasn't ready for either encouragement or sympathy, that he had yet to determine whether he wanted her to hear the rest. So she waited quietly, prepared to listen to him if he chose to continue.

Was it the mood of this place? Samantha wondered. Did it have a kind of magic at work, inviting confidences that otherwise wouldn't get expressed? Or was it simply the intimacy of their situation which, in the end, had Roark sharing his secret with her? Not that it made any difference either way. His explanation was all that mattered.

"It's not that I dislike being a private investigator," he said. "Or that ranching is more important to me. It's that I don't trust myself in the role anymore. There's a reason for that. A damn painful one."

This is difficult for him, she thought, understanding his struggle even before she knew the cause of it. And why not, when she was no stranger to personal despair and the scars that resulted from it.

"What happened?" she urged him gently.

"A case that went wrong. *Very* wrong." He went on exercising his fingers, this time with an unconscious rapidity. Evidence of his inner agitation. "I've always considered myself a good judge of my clients. Able to read their characters. Whether they're telling me the truth or withholding information. That's vital in PI work. But with this guy I missed. Never saw what was coming until it was too late."

"He hired you for…?"

"To find his wife. That kind of thing makes up a big chunk of PI cases. There are so many missing persons reported each year the police can't handle the loads. That's when desperate friends or family turn to private investigators."

"Like this man who came to you."

"A few months ago, yeah. He seemed to be all he claimed. A sad little guy who was deeply worried about his wife. Couldn't understand why she'd walked out on him when they had a happy marriage. He'd tried to trace her, but she had simply disappeared. It's a familiar story.''

''And that's where you came in.''

''I made the mistake of accepting his case after cautioning him his wife might not want to be found. He didn't argue with that. If she didn't want to see him, he'd live with it. But he had to know if she was all right.''

''Roark—''

''Don't say it. I know what you're thinking, but a good PI is always careful about that kind of thing. I did my homework and checked into the records. There was no history there of spousal abuse. Absolutely none.''

''So you went ahead and found her?''

''A week later. Client was so anxious I made the further mistake of telling him I'd located his wife, but he couldn't have the address until I'd talked to her and gotten her okay. He agreed to that. Only the little bastard was not only crafty but a whiz when it came to computers. He broke into my office that night and managed to get her address from my records.'' Roark's fingers went still, his hand slowly closing into a tight, angry fist. ''He killed her, Samantha. Pulled a gun and shot her when she opened her door.''

''Dear God.''

''Yeah, she never had a chance, and all because I was careless. Because I failed to examine his motive and made it possible for him to get to her.'' Roark frowned, his gaze straying in the direction of the broken walls of the cliff dwellings. For a moment he looked at them in silence, as though he'd forgotten her presence.

He's been holding it all inside, Samantha thought. Living with this awful thing for weeks now. How hard that must have been for a strong, self-contained man like Roark Hawke. And how difficult it must have been for him to tell her, to admit his vulnerability.

She suddenly understood there was no magic at work here. Not anything external, anyway. He'd shared his anguish with her simply because he had trusted her, cared enough about her to want her to know. The realization of this warmed her, made her long to comfort him, even though she recognized the peril in the fierce compassion she was feeling.

"So now you can't forgive yourself," she said, reaching out to him. "But that's all wrong. You weren't in any way to blame for this woman's death. There's only one man to blame, and that's the husband who killed her."

There was a crooked, humorless smile on his mouth when he looked at her again. "That's what I've been telling myself. Funny thing is, it doesn't seem to be working. I'm still carrying around this baggage of guilt, still thinking that if a PI screws up as big time as I did, then maybe it's time he gets out of the business."

"Because you feel you can no longer be effective? How can you possibly think that when, all through this case of mine, you've been demonstrating just how responsible a PI you are? People make errors in every business, Roark, even the best of them. Come on, you know that."

"My error involved the loss of a life. But thank you for your vote of confidence."

She hadn't helped him, Samantha thought sadly. He was still suffering from a crisis of faith in himself. She could only hope that, whatever decision he ultimately made, it would be for the right reasons.

Roark got up from the blanket to feed more wood to the fire. Not that they needed its heat. The night was thankfully a mild one. But it was pleasant to sit here, hands clasped around her knees, looking into the flames.

"It's ironic, you know," she said in a dreamy voice.

"What is?" Dropping back down onto the blanket, he stretched out beside her.

"That you should want to turn to ranching because of a tragedy in your world while I turned away from it because of a tragedy in mine."

She was in such a mellow state in that moment it didn't

really register with her what she'd just said. Not until he lifted his head and stared at her intently did she realize, startled, that she had just opened an old wound.

"Are you going to tell me about it?" he said quietly.

She'd not only opened it, Samantha thought, but now he was asking her to shine a light on it so that he could examine it. "You knew, didn't you?" she said softly.

"That you've been holding back on me? Yeah, I figured there was more to your hatred of your grandfather's world than what you were sharing with me."

She had kept that particular heartache private for so long she didn't know if she could bear now to discuss it. Or if she even wanted him to know. But, then, why shouldn't she be willing to trust him with it when he had trusted her with his own grief?

Taking a long, slow breath, as if preparing herself for a difficult dive into deep waters, Samantha took him back to her last year on the Walking W. That bittersweet time when, as a young woman just emerging from her teens, she had so unexpectedly found love and then just as suddenly lost it.

"He was one of my grandfather's hands on the ranch, not a whole lot older than me. We were probably all wrong for each other, too young for one thing, and our backgrounds were so different. He came from a family where education wasn't important. He'd dropped out of school and was, well, a bit rough around the edges."

"Everything that's supposed to matter," Roark said perceptively, "and none of which means a damn when two people want each other."

"Exactly. It shouldn't have happened, but it did happen."

"And Joe?"

"I didn't think he'd mind about us. I thought he'd be pleased. I mean, here was his granddaughter who disliked horses and cattle falling for a guy who loved everything he valued himself. What match could be more perfect?"

"And you were wrong."

"Oh, yes," she said, unable to help the bitterness that crept into her voice. "But I was so starry-eyed I forgot just how cunning my grandfather could be when he wanted something his own way and realized that his usual fireworks wouldn't get it for him. He knew he couldn't put an end to our relationship by ordering me not to see Hank or firing him, that I would just—"

"Hank?"

"That was his name, yes. Hank Barrie. Didn't I say?"

"No," Roark said, and she wondered if the taut look on his face meant something or whether it was only an illusion, a shadow cast by the flickering of the firelight.

"Anything wrong?"

He shook his head. "I just may have heard the name before."

"You probably did. He was on the rodeo circuit. That's what my grandfather used to separate us. Hank may have known very little about the things that come between the covers of books, but he was a walking wonder when it came to horses and cattle."

"And Joe took advantage of that to destroy a love affair he didn't approve of."

"Hank wasn't good enough for a Walker, so my grandfather went to work on him, flattered him, told him he was too talented not to be a success on the rodeo scene, even offered to back him financially. Oh, I knew just what that sly old devil was up to, and I tried to make Hank see that, begged him not to go. 'He's trying to part us,' I said. 'And if he succeeds, it will change everything between us.' Hank wouldn't listen. 'Honey,' he kept saying, 'there's big prizes to be won from those competitions, and if I can make us some real money, we can start a spread of our own.'"

"So your Hank Barrie left you and the ranch behind."

"I never saw him again," Samantha said, her voice dull,

lifeless. "He was killed three months later. Thrown from a bull in a rodeo contest in Wyoming."

Roark sat up and looked down sharply at the fingers of the hand he had been exercising earlier. "No wonder you went wild that night I told you I'd injured this hand when I was tossed from a rodeo bronc."

Samantha shuddered over the memory. "Now you know."

"Yeah," he said slowly, "now I know. You blamed your grandfather for Hank's death. Still do, I suppose. That, along with everything else, is why you wanted no part of either him or his world ever again."

"I left the Walking W the day after I heard about Hank, and except for that one visit to settle my mother's affairs and collect some of her personal things, I never went back."

She gazed at Roark, wanting his understanding. Hoping for it.

"You've had your own load to bear, haven't you?" he said. "A heavier one than mine, too."

His words of compassion released her anxiety. She felt it drain out of her. She was glad she had told him everything. That's what people did when they cared about someone, and why she had confided in Roark. Because he mattered to her, mattered so greatly that she was shaken by the full realization of it.

She looked at him, saw the stubble on his jaw. It gave him a slightly dangerous look, like a desperado. But it was an exciting look as well, one that made her tremble in anticipation when he moved closer to her on the blanket.

"You need holding," he said, his voice a deep rumble as he reached for her. "Hell, we both need to be held."

He was right, which was why she didn't resist him. Why she welcomed his arms when they slid around her waist, hauling her snugly against him. And why her own arms wrapped around him in return.

They clung to each other, and it felt right being nestled

against his chest. Not just comforting but familiar, too, as if she belonged there. The rightness of it made her forget all her earlier resolves not to involve herself intimately with this man. They had no meaning in this time and place. She wanted him, and that was all that mattered.

Samantha assumed Roark wanted her as well, that his strong hands stroking her back so sensuously, along with his warm breath at her ear, signaled his desire for her. Why, then, was this not more than just an embrace? What made him hesitate to fasten his mouth on her own?

Drawing her head back, she searched his face in the firelight. She read uncertainty in his eyes. "What?" she whispered, puzzled by his reluctance.

"Maybe we shouldn't," he said, his voice low and raspy, fighting for self-control.

That should have halted her right there, stopped her cold. But she could see him swallowing with difficulty, as if trying to relieve a tightness deep inside him. And when he did that, when she watched his Adam's apple bob slowly in his throat, she found the action so incredibly sexy it robbed her of all reason. She was lost.

"Oh, but I think we should," she informed him softly.

Surprising herself with her boldness, and probably Roark as well, Samantha lifted her hands and placed them on either side of his head, framing his face.

"Hold steady now," she instructed him, "and this shouldn't hurt."

Leaning into him, she placed her lips against his mouth. He stiffened, as if jolted by a charge, but was otherwise unresponsive. Not permitting herself to be discouraged, she applied an insistent pressure. Nothing, though she may have detected an anguished groan.

She had better results when she used her tongue, seducing his mouth from side to side with a series of slow, swirling caresses. He withstood her assault for less than thirty seconds, and then all restraint was shattered. With a primal growl, and a fiercely possessive tightening of his arms around her, he began to kiss her.

It was an eager, hungry business, as if his mouth was desperate, needing to recover what it had wasted. Her own responses to his marauding tongue were just as wild, just as deep and demanding.

"Clothes," he muttered between their kisses, his voice husky and impatient. "What are we doing with our clothes on? They're in the way."

She couldn't argue with that. They *were* in the way. They took care of that, shedding each article in a feverish, almost comically awkward haste. There was nothing amusing about the hard body that emerged in front of her on the blanket when he had stripped away his last garment.

Roark Hawke, fully exposed, was a superb specimen of manhood, all powerful muscle and ruddy flesh in the glow of the fire. Samantha was entranced. Not just by his awesome arousal but by the heat of his gaze riveted on her own body.

"Sweetheart," he said, his voice gruff with his need, "you are one hell of a woman."

To be regarded as desirable by him was pleasure in itself. To be made love to by him was absolute rapture. He demonstrated just how intense a rapture when he folded her in his arms again, his mouth covering hers with searing kisses that stole the air from her lungs.

There was no relief either when that relentless, wicked mouth of his traveled down the length of her, tugging in turn at the nipples of her breasts, branding her stomach, scalding her parted thighs before settling at last at the core of her womanhood where his clever tongue proceeded to destroy her.

"This," she whispered, barely able to get the words out, "is what heaven must be like. Or hell."

"If I'm a devil," he rasped, lifting himself above her, "then I'm a devil in far more torment than the little witch I've captured."

"Let me go then."

"Do you really want that?" he challenged her.

"No, I guess I don't."

And she didn't. She wanted more of him. All of him. He complied, his body joining with hers there on the scratchy blanket that smelled faintly of horse. Between his swollen kisses, his hands filling themselves with her breasts, he crooned words of endearment while the light from the twisting flames licked at them. And overhead, in concert with their raw, primitive rhythms, the moon wheeled out of control.

In the end, blaze and moon merged, flared and were consumed in a blinding, white-hot radiance.

Limp from her release, Samantha felt herself sinking back to earth, aware of the popping of the fire that was just a campfire, after all. But what she and Roark had shared was not ordinary. It had been so sublime she couldn't find words to express it.

"Are you all right?" he asked, elevating himself to gaze down at her in concern.

"Yes."

Dipping his head, he kissed her. Slowly this time, very tenderly. Then, rolling to her side, he reached for the other blanket and drew it over them. Snuggled against her protectively, he drifted off.

Are you all right? She had lied. She wasn't all right. She would never be the same again. Because as wonderful as it had been, as secure in his embrace though she had felt, she had done the unthinkable. What she had promised herself she wouldn't do. She had been intimate with a man cut out of the same material as her grandfather. Roark Hawke, a man as dedicated to ranching as Joe Walker had been.

There was something more serious than that. She was falling in love with Roark. And *that,* she knew, could result in a heartache far worse than anything she had experienced with Hank Barrie.

ROARK CAME AWAKE and was instantly alert.

Trouble?

Realizing it must have been some sudden noise that had awakened him, he lifted his head from the blanket and listened. Except for the snorting of the horses nearby and the sound of Irma munching peacefully on a bit of vegetation, the night was silent.

Seconds later, the sound came again. Recognizing it as the sharp bark of a fox farther down the canyon, Roark relaxed. There was no enemy on the scene. Even so, he was reluctant to go back to sleep, and he made sure his gun was within easy reach.

What time was it? He tried to check his watch, but it wasn't the digital kind and he couldn't manage to read its face in the darkness. It had to be late, though. The moon had set, and the fire had died to a few glowing embers.

Undisturbed, Samantha slept soundly beside him. Her naked body pressed warmly against his side roused memories of their lovemaking. The recollections had his own body stirring painfully. But he didn't try to act on his fresh arousal.

Bad enough, he thought, that he had taken advantage of her last night when he had known how vulnerable she was. When her tale of her young cowboy had been a warning he had failed to obey.

Hank Barrie. Hearing the name like that had startled Roark, leaving him unprepared. Was that why he had missed an opportunity to tell her then and there all about her cherished Hank Barrie? Or was it because he'd been unwilling to hurt her with the truth, destroy her illusion of the man she'd loved?

Or, he wondered, guilt gnawing at him, had there been a more selfish motive for his omission? Samantha already had a strong dislike for everything connected with ranching, and if she were to learn how her young cowboy had betrayed her, that dislike could easily escalate. And Roark didn't want to risk that. Didn't want her unable to forgive him. Not now when she was beginning to trust him.

So, instead, unable to withstand her allure, he had gone and made love to her. Which probably made him as much of a bastard as Hank Barrie. So, what now? Should he remain silent on the subject of Barrie? Would that be kinder in the end? He didn't know. All he knew for certain was that his feelings for Samantha were intensifying and that, given all the issues, this whole thing was a real mess.

Roark didn't expect to go back to sleep, but that's just what he did. When he awakened again, the first gray light of morning was stealing into the canyon. And Samantha was gone!

Alarmed, he jerked up to a sitting position on the blanket. That's when he heard it. A sudden splashing followed by a sharp cry. His head twisted around in the direction of the stream. Finding the source of the noise, he stopped breathing. It was a sight he expected never to forget.

She stood knee-deep in one of the pools, looking exactly as nature had made her. And nature had done one hell of a job. Her naked body gleamed with the beads of water she had splashed over herself, a lushness in the flesh of her rose-tipped breasts, rounded hips and tantalizing thighs.

When he could breathe again, Roark found himself immediately hard and unable to resist what he regarded as an invitation. Samantha had her back to him by the time he rose and waded into the pool. The water was damn cold, which explained her cry. But he sure wasn't going to let that stop him.

Hearing his approach, she swung around, almost losing her balance in the swiftness of her action. Her eyes widened at the sight of his arousal, but she offered no objection as he joined her.

"It's not smart bathing in this frigid stuff, but I just had to get clean." He could hear the effort she was making to sound casual.

"Yeah, me, too," he said, his voice husky.

They both knew he was lying, that he was interested in only one thing. His throbbing arousal was clear evidence of that. And yet they hesitated, watching each other in a long silence. Roark could sense her uncertainty. Was she regretting last night? Wondering if it had been a mistake?

Well, hadn't he been wondering the same thing himself only a few hours ago? And wasn't he thinking at this very moment that, considering how much she disliked and feared everything he stood for and wanted, they were about to commit another mistake?

But it was already too late. He knew that when, unable to help himself, he reached for her. And Samantha must have known it herself when she came willingly into his arms.

They were both lost as he kissed her deeply, his hardness already probing for an entry in his eagerness to be joined with her. She moaned, clutching at him for support. He steadied her, his hands cupping her soft bottom.

They made love standing there in the pool, her legs wound around him as he lifted her and held her against him. It was a frenzied, urgent business, surging to a powerful conclusion.

There was no question of either of them being cold now. Their heated bodies accepted, even welcomed, a full immersion in the pool. But afterward, back on shore where the morning air chilled them, they hurried into their clothes after drying themselves as best they could.

He caught Samantha glancing back at the pool, an anxious expression on her face that tugged at his gut. "Are you sorry about what just happened? Tell me you're not sorry."

"What I'm sorry about is not having any breakfast. I'm famished. I don't suppose you'd like to try spearing another trout out there?"

Roark chuckled. "Sorry, love. I imagine our, uh, activity had the fish flying in all directions to get out of the way.

No time, anyway. We've got to try to find our way back to the outfit.''

"Not until we investigate the ruins up there, remember?''

"No, we're not going to cheat ourselves out of that. We'll grab a few minutes for that much.''

His few minutes stretched into something closer to twenty as they climbed from level to level on crude ladders. Roark was fascinated by the site. He examined curious T-shaped doorways, peered through yawning window openings, admired the faint traces of decorations that remained on patches of pinkish plaster. And all the while he wondered about the people who had built and abandoned these structures ages ago.

"What are these?'' Samantha asked, examining a row of round pits that had been sunk into the floor of the lowest terrace.

"Storage for things like grain, I imagine. But not this larger one over here. It's a kiva.''

"Of course it is,'' she said, looking at him blankly.

He explained it to her. "I saw one like it at Mesa Verde. Kivas were underground ceremonial chambers. Only the males were allowed to enter them to participate in the rituals.''

"I can think of a few men I'd like to drop down there.'' She laughed, then lifted her head, sharing the wonder of the site with him as she surveyed the alcove from one end to the other. "It is all pretty marvelous, even if there isn't any buried treasure to be found here.''

"No. Even though the place is too isolated for tourists, it would have been excavated long ago and any valuable artifacts removed.''

She nodded. "Just like at the Walking W.''

Roark stared at her. "Are you telling me…''

"It's not so unusual. There are pueblo remains all over the Southwest. You must know that.''

"But at the Walking W?''

"Well, nothing like this. Not cliff dwellings."

"What?" he demanded. "And where exactly?"

"Just caves. Up in the sides of the ravine."

"The ravine where your grandfather had his accident that probably was not an accident?"

"Not in that spot. Farther along the ravine, so if you're thinking there's any connection—"

"Samantha, why didn't you tell me when I was asking you about the ravine?"

Damn! He couldn't believe it! How could she be so matter-of-fact about a possibility that had him burning with excitement?

Chapter Nine

Samantha fortified herself with a deep breath before patiently repeating what she had been trying to make him understand for the past several minutes.

"Roark, I'm telling you there is nothing important about those caves. Don't you think I would have mentioned them before this if there had been? Yes, there is, or was, evidence in them of some ancient occupation. But there are no relics now. And if there ever were, they were picked clean long ago. So no secrets, no buried treasure."

Roark wasn't satisfied. "How can you be certain of that? Have you ever personally visited them?"

"Once, as a little girl in the company of my grandfather and Cappy, who were out looking for a stray cow."

"And since then?"

"No. Why would I, with them being so far away from the ranch house? Anyway, I was forbidden from ever trying to explore the caves. Both my mother and grandfather cautioned me about them being dangerous places. Inhabited by rattlers, I think is what they said." Samantha shuddered over the memory of her last encounter with a diamondback. "Believe me, I would never have gone there on my own, even if I had been interested, which I wasn't."

"No recent visit to the caves then?" he persisted.

She shook her head. "Why do you keep asking? What are you thinking?"

"That maybe there is something of value in them. Something that could have been overlooked until recently. Do you know what Native American artifacts are worth, Samantha? There's a hot market for them, buyers both eager and capable of paying huge sums to acquire them."

He had her attention now. "Are you saying…"

"Yeah, that someone has learned there are things in those caves to be mined. Stuff so priceless he's prepared to kill to protect his discovery."

"And," she said slowly, beginning at last to appreciate his theory, "willing to go to any lengths to prevent me from inheriting the property."

"I'm not saying this is the explanation for Joe's death and the threat to you, but it could be, Samantha. There are still a lot of unanswered questions, but this is the first lead we've had that makes any kind of sense."

"So what do we do now?"

Roark lifted his head, squinting into the sun that was just beginning to rise over the rim of the canyon. "Find our way back to the outfit. The rest can wait."

Considering they were lost, Samantha wondered just how they were going to achieve this as they left the ruins, saddled their horses and collected their gear. But Roark seemed confident of managing it, now that they had full daylight and the position of the sun could provide them with a clear direction.

With Irma in tow, they traveled upstream and within minutes found an easy trail that took them up through thickets of juniper and out onto the open mesa that stretched away on all sides.

"Which way now?" Samantha asked.

"Let's stop here a minute."

She figured he meant to get his bearings before they rode on. Instead, he removed his cell phone from his belt.

"Now that we're out of the canyon," he said, flipping open the phone and extending the antenna, "maybe—ah, got a signal."

Watching him punch in the numbers, she prayed that the signal would be strong enough.

"Reception's good," he reported, "I can hear it ringing. Let's hope that Shep—"

He broke off, the grin on his face telling Samantha the trail boss had answered. In fact, she could hear Shep's yell of relief as Roark identified himself. She waited anxiously while the two men discussed the problem.

"What?" she demanded the instant Roark rang off.

"They were just about to spread out to start looking for us again. They spent the night camped near the spot where we went missing."

"How do we find our way back to them?"

"Shep and I reckoned we need to ride due east into the sun. They're going to build up their campfire. It's a still morning. We should be able to spot their column of smoke a long way off."

"Sounds good."

Breakfast sounded even better to her as they headed across the mesa, scanning the horizon for the first sign of the smoke that would lead them back to the outfit. Roark was silent on their ride. She supposed he was busy examining his theory about the caves back at the Walking W. Since there was nothing more she could contribute, she left him to his thoughts and turned to her own reflections.

But dwelling on her empty stomach brought her no great pleasure; nor did the unavoidable necessity of resuming this hellish cattle drive. Memories of what she and Roark had shared in the canyon were far sweeter, potent images that she was convinced would have made a courtesan blush. Her skin continued to feel his touch, the flavor of him was still in her mouth, the masculine scent of him lingered in her nostrils. They were sensations that made her squirm in the saddle. And they worried her.

As wild and wonderful as their lovemaking had been, as strong as both the physical and emotional bond between them now was, she feared their relationship. Feared all the unhappy things she associated with falling in love with a cattleman. The despair of loving Hank Barrie was still with her.

"It's out there in front of us," Roark said. "Can you see it?"

Startled from her reverie, Samantha searched the horizon. Looking straight into the sun made it difficult, but she could finally make out the plume of smoke signaling the location of the outfit.

They were all there waiting for them, eager for explanations when they rode into camp. Samantha, claiming responsibility for the whole thing, offered an apology. Roark cheerfully related their misadventure with the rockfall that had trapped them in the gorge. She knew by the way he looked at the face of each member of the company that he was testing them, hoping for some reaction that would betray the culprit. The concern came from all sides.

"You could have been killed, man!"

"We were worried sick when you didn't turn up."

"Just about to look up the nearest sheriff and have him organize a posse."

"Someone shooting at you? No! Who could it have been? Are you sure?"

Sympathy and outrage were expressed by all of them. Except Ernie Chacon. He stood apart from the others, silent, the familiar little sneer on his mouth. Did it mean anything? Samantha wondered. Alex must have thought so. He turned to Ernie speculatively. "We all split up to look for them, went off in separate directions. You were gone the longest, Ernie. Which way did *you* go?"

Ernie rounded on him furiously. "What are you suggesting, college boy?"

"You had your rifle with you, didn't you?"

"Why, you little bas—"

"Stop it!" Ramona came hotly to her son's defense, flying between them to prevent a fight. "Both of you stop this right now! I won't have Ernie blamed, because *all* of us had our guns with us on that search, including me."

"Ramona is right," Roark said calmly. "No one is accusing anyone of anything. The rockfall was probably just an accident, and whoever was taking potshots at us might have been someone trying to warn us off his land. We weren't hurt, so let's just forget it and move on."

Samantha was surprised, knowing that Roark didn't believe what he was saying. Then she realized he had simply decided to be practical. What good would it do to provoke a scene when they had no proof that the culprit *was* someone in the outfit, including Ernie? Because, even though it was beginning to seem more and more unlikely, the enemy could still be a stranger.

One thing was for certain. If Roark *had* winged their sniper yesterday, and that individual was one of the outfit, he had no visible wound. None of them evidenced any sign of an injury, though it was possible clothing concealed a flesh wound.

"You two better grab some breakfast," the trail boss said. "And then we need to pack up and head out. We've had enough delays on this drive, and those stock cars in Alamo Junction aren't going to wait for us."

This was the seventh day of the drive, and Samantha knew that they still had a long way to go. Was that why Shep looked even more unhappy than usual, a bleak expression on his tired face? Or was there another explanation?

Samantha was so busy pondering this, as she tucked into the eggs and biscuits Ramona had waiting for them at the cook wagon, that for a moment she didn't realize Roark was gone. He had taken his own plate and disappeared. Several more minutes passed before he arrived back at her side to explain the mystery of his absence.

"I went off where I couldn't be overheard to phone Wendell," he confided to her in an undertone. "I didn't want to waste any time getting him back out to the Walking W to take a close look at those caves. And while he's there, I asked him to take more photographs of the ravine. Not just in the area where Joe went down but all of the ravine. I don't want to overlook anything.''

''I hope you warned him about the possibility of snakes.''

''I didn't forget.''

''Did he have any news for us?''

''He's still digging into the backgrounds of the abbot and the museum director. Nothing useful so far, and Ernie Chacon is proving to be almost as elusive. He was arrested in Austin on a disorderly charge, but all anyone in Purgatory seems willing to admit is that our Ernie has a bad temper.''

''Which we already know. Is that it?''

''For now. You finished with those eggs? We need to mount up. The others are already out waiting with the herd.''

Samantha, knowing she was about to undergo another siege of assorted miseries on the long trail, suppressed a groan.

IF HE'D BEEN A VILLAIN in a melodrama, this would have been the place to say, ''Curses! Foiled again!''

But he was no villain, old-fashioned or otherwise. Not by his definition. He was simply someone going after what he wanted. What he *deserved* to have. And Samantha Howard was in his way.

Damn that PI! Hawke was forever at her side. He made it tough to get at her when he was always there to rescue her. Like yesterday, when he'd spoiled another opportunity.

What made it so difficult was the necessity of being careful not to reveal himself. Never lowering his guard, continuing to play his role. That was essential.

So, all right, he'd need to find some way of separating

Hawke from Samantha. He would have to wait for that, because the moment had to be right. He still had time, but he was growing impatient.

"THIS TIME I MEAN IT," Samantha informed the heifer. "You get into trouble, and you're on your own. I'm not making a fool of myself again and chasing you into another gorge. No, sir, I turn my back and I ride away."

This drive has affected my brain. Listen to me talking to a cow.

Worse than that, she was convinced that Irma, who was trotting beside her, actually heard and understood. Insanity couldn't be far away.

Of course, there was no reason for the heifer to believe her. They both knew Samantha wouldn't keep her word. Nor did she when that same afternoon Irma was cornered by a rattlesnake. Backed up against a boulder, the heifer rolled her eyes with terror and bawled pitifully.

Samantha looked around. There was no help available. Roark had dashed off to the other side of the herd to deal with a pair of reluctant longhorns.

It would be a snake, she thought. Refusing to give in to her horror, she dismounted, found a rock and launched it in the direction of the threat. To her satisfaction, the rattler slithered away. Irma scooted back to the safety of the herd.

Samantha was back in the saddle when Roark arrived at her side. "Problem?"

"Nope," she said. "Just routine stuff."

She supposed it was a measure of her progress that she could be so matter-of-fact about a thing that once would have had her trembling in panic. Was Joe Walker getting his wish?

All right, maybe the drive was tempering her into a tougher material. Maybe she could even be proud of herself. It didn't mean she had softened in her resolve to have no part of ranching. Roark's presence was a constant reminder of that.

After yesterday's menace, he seldom left her alone for

more than a moment or two at a time, and then he always kept her in sight. Otherwise he rode so close beside her that his nearness inflamed her senses. She knew that he was every bit as aware of her as she was of him. But never once did he try to touch her. Nor did he refer to their blissful interlude in the canyon. And though she ached for him, she understood his restraint, knew he was right. Considering the issues that still loomed between them, it was better to let it all go now before either one or both of them was hurt beyond recovery. Or was it already too late for that?

"LET'S STOP IN HERE for a few minutes," Roark said, halting them on the sidewalk.

Samantha looked at the shop he indicated. "A bookstore? Why? Is there something you want?"

"Maybe just to browse," he said, offering no further explanation.

The drive was laying over for the night near another town. There would be no cabins this time, nor a party around the campfire. But several members of the outfit had strolled into town to shop for essentials.

Edgerton, once a thriving mining center and now a quiet community, was tucked between the mountains, its business district a single street that wound through the narrow valley.

Samantha followed Roark into the store. He went off toward the back, leaving her at the front to examine a window display of volumes featuring old Colorado mansions. Houses of all eras were her business, and she never failed to be fascinated by their stories.

She was returning one of the books to the pile when she caught sight of Shep through the window. He was on the other side of the street, and he wasn't alone. He and another man had just emerged from a café. Even from this distance, she could tell they were arguing. Samantha watched them for a moment. When the trail boss started to glance around, as if suddenly worried he was being observed, she quickly pulled back from the window.

Roark found her hugging the wall at the side of the window when he joined her a few seconds later. "What are you doing?" he asked, one of his thick eyebrows lifted in bemusement.

"Hiding."

"Why?"

"Shep is out there, and I didn't want him to spot me." Roark leaned over and looked out the window. "Get back before he sees you."

"There's no out there but an old lady on the corner."

"Well, they were there a minute ago, he and this man he was talking to."

"What man?"

"The one he met back in Lost Springs."

"You sure?"

"Positive. I recognized his hard face. Roark, what's he doing here in Edgerton? And don't tell me Shep was meeting him to secure permission for the drive to cross private lands. That might have been true in Lost Springs, but the explanation doesn't work twice. Not with the distance we've covered since Lost Springs."

"You're right, it doesn't. On the other hand, if our trail boss has a reason to keep this guy a secret, then why did he risk being seen with him out on a public street?"

"Will you ask Shep about it?"

Roark shook his head. "Not much use in that. If he lied to me before, then he won't hesitate to lie again."

"So all we can do is watch and wait," Samantha said, discouraged by their inability to find answers. She was so caught up in her frustration that she didn't notice the plastic sack Roark had under his arm until they came away from the bookstore. She stopped him out on the street to ask him about it.

"You bought books?"

"I'm not going to just watch and wait, Samantha."

"I don't understand. Aside from the fact that we barely have space as it is to carry the necessities, what with the outfit's gear squeezed into the truck and on two of Dick's packhorses, just when do you expect to find time to read between here and Alamo Junction?"

"I don't. Look." He opened the sack, inviting Samantha to inspect its contents.

She glanced at the titles of the three volumes inside, was puzzled for a moment, and then she understood. "You're going to use these to smoke out the enemy."

"As bait, they may be a little too obvious, but it's worth a try. Let's get back to camp and see what happens."

ROARK WAITED until they were all collected around the fire after supper to set his trap.

"Anyone know anything about Native American artifacts?" he asked, beaming at them around the circle.

Dick laughed. "Not me, that's for sure."

"Me, either," Roark said, withdrawing his purchases from the sack at his feet and, with deliberate carelessness, displaying their titles. "That's why I picked these up at the bookstore. Supposed to be a whole education in them on the subject. Not that I'll get the opportunity for that until after the drive." He tossed the books back into the sack. "They'll end up in the bottom of one of my saddlebags until then, but at least I have them."

"What brought all this on?" Ramona wondered.

"My interest? Oh, it's because of the canyon. I told you there are cliff dwellings there, didn't I? I got to thinking about that. What if there are valuable relics in those ruins? Stuff that somebody could be looting, and maybe that's why Samantha and I were shot at. You know, to warn us off."

"That's not very likely," Alex said. "I mean, if the place is being looted, you'd have seen signs of digging, wouldn't you?"

"You're probably right. Anyway, when I get the chance

I want to learn more about the subject. There are ancient sites all over the Southwest, and some of them could still be rich with artifacts.'' He chuckled. ''Who knows, maybe there are even Native American relics buried on my own spread back in Texas. Or my neighbors'. It's worth looking into.''

All the while that Roark so casually explained about the books, Samantha watched the faces in the firelight, looking for some indication that one of the company was worried about his fascination for ancient sites. After this afternoon, she was particularly careful to observe Shep's reaction. He'd remained silent throughout the conversation, his expression even more glum than usual. But was it her imagination that, when Texas was mentioned, the trail boss scowled grimly in Roark's direction?

As for the others…well, none of them revealed by word or action that Roark might be a threat to a desperate scheme. Ernie looked bored, Dick and Cappy equally disinterested, and Alex and Ramona only politely interested. No one made any mention of the caves at the Walking W.

Dick got to his feet and stretched. ''Time for my shift with the herd.''

''You oughta been out there with them already,'' Cappy complained.

The others indicated their readiness to turn in for the night. The subject of ancient relics was forgotten.

Samantha was disappointed. Roark's experiment had produced no results. Nor had he made the effort she'd been anticipating. She'd looked for him to follow her example and sharply examine each face around the campfire, but he had seemed almost indifferent to their responses, barely glancing at them. Then why had he made them aware of the books he'd purchased?

Samantha had no chance to ask him about it. Nor, as it turned out, did she have to. Her question was answered early the following morning when she rolled out of her sleeping bag to the sounds of a scuffle behind the cook truck. Alerted by the commotion, Roark was already on his feet. She didn't wait for him to order her to stay behind but hurried after him as he strode around the side of the truck to investigate.

They found Alex and Ernie engaged in a struggle for possession of a battered canvas bag.

"Take your hands off of it, college boy, before I smash your face!"

Alex, hanging on with determination, called out to them. "He's got something he's hiding in here! I open my eyes to find him snooping through our belongings! Then I catch him sneaking back here and stuffing whatever he took into the bag!"

The books! Samantha thought. Ernie had raided Roark's saddlebags for the books. That's what Roark had intended, to lure the enemy into snatching material in order to prevent Roark from being enlightened and in consequence a threat to his schemes.

Both men were red-faced and huffing when Roark separated them. Ernie had the bag back in his keeping and was clutching it tightly.

"Let's have the bag, Ernie," Roark commanded him, holding out his hand.

"The hell I will!" Ernie growled. "It's my bag, and I didn't swipe anything that's in it. All I was looking for was to borrow a razor blade."

"Then you won't mind showing us what's inside," Alex said, reaching for the bag.

"Get away, all of you!"

Alex made a dive for the bag, seizing one end of it. In the renewed struggle for it, the bag landed on the ground, spilling its entire contents. To Samantha's surprise, there were no books. No sign of anything but what seemed to be Ernie's personal possessions, including a safety razor with a missing blade.

"Ernie," Roark said, his tone apologetic, "if you needed a blade, why didn't you just ask one of us?"

"You were all asleep," the stocky young man muttered.

Dick and Cappy were still in their sleeping bags, and Shep was out taking his shift with the herd. She assumed Ramona was off fetching water for her breakfast preparations. But then why, if he hadn't stolen anything, had Ernie so fiercely resisted having his bag examined? And why did he crouch down now on the ground and begin to swiftly throw his belongings back into the bag, as if fearful of a discovery?

That question, too, was answered when Roark leaned down and clamped his hand on Ernie's wrist, preventing him from shoving into the bag a tube of tightly rolled paper secured by a rubber band.

"Let go!" Ernie tried to snatch his hand away.

"Not until we've had a look at what's inside that roll. Samantha?"

While Roark continued to hang on to Ernie, she reached down and took possession of the roll. She slid the rubber band from the tube, which opened to reveal itself as two photographs. The same photographs Wendell had sent to his boss back in Lost Springs.

"Ah," Roark said, releasing Ernie to look over her shoulder at the likenesses of the abbot of St. James Monastery and the director of the Western Museum, "that's what happened to them. It was you who was listening outside the cabin window that evening, huh, Ernie? And the minute you got the chance, you helped yourself to the photos."

"So what?" he snarled, coming defiantly to his feet.

"Not *what*, Ernie, *why*. What is there about these two photos that could possibly interest you?"

"He only cares about one of them," said a calm voice from behind them. They swung around to find Ramona standing there bearing a bucket of water in each hand. Setting the buckets on the ground, she came forward and placed a finger on the likeness of the Western Museum's director. "This one."

"Ma, don't. It ain't none of their business."

"It's become their business, Ernie," she said, looking at Roark and not her son. "And if we don't explain it, they're going to think you're guilty of something criminal. Which you aren't, unless you count taking a photograph of your father as a crime."

Samantha's startled gaze went from the photo to Ernie's face. No wonder she and Roark had thought there was something vaguely familiar about the man in the photograph. She could see it now. Ernie bore a faint resemblance to the museum director.

Ramona nodded. "That's right. Frank Costello is Ernie's father. He was also very married when I had an affair with him."

Samantha's gaze went sympathetically to Ernie, but he met her look with a hard glare that told her he didn't want her sympathy. "Did he know about…"

"Ernie?" Ramona said. "Oh, yes, Frank knew all right. These days, of course, young women handle such situations differently. Things like paternity suits, I suppose. But back then all you thought about was avoiding a scandal. I didn't want to ruin Frank or hurt his family, so I did what he wanted. I accepted the money he gave me and went away to have my baby."

"And afterward?" Samantha pressed her.

"I let it go. I forgot about Frank Costello and concentrated on raising my son."

"But Ernie didn't let it go," Roark said perceptively.

"No, he didn't. I made the mistake of telling him who his father is, thinking that would satisfy him. It didn't. Ernie wants to be recognized by his father, but…" Ramona shrugged. "Even though Frank's wife died years ago, it doesn't seem to make any difference. He doesn't want to acknowledge his son."

"That's between me and him, Ma," Ernie said bitterly. "The whole world don't have to know about it. Damn it, why do you think I took the photograph in the first place?

It was to keep these two from poring over it and maybe finally seeing I have his nose and his eyes. I even grabbed the other picture so's to throw them off the scent, and now you go and spill your guts about stuff that's private and ought to have stayed that way.''

"Then why did you keep the photos, Ernie?" Roark asked him. "Why didn't you just destroy them?"

Ernie was silent, his face stubborn and proud.

"I guess I can understand that." Alex spoke up softly. "If it was my father, maybe I'd want to keep his picture, too. Just to look at, you know."

But Ernie didn't want Alex's understanding any more than he wanted Samantha's sympathy. Muttering an obscenity, he turned and stormed away.

Ramona gazed after him sorrowfully. "I'm sorry," she murmured. And Samantha didn't know whether she was apologizing to them or her son. Her heart went out to both Ramona and Ernie, but she said nothing. The woman wore an expression that plainly said she wanted to be alone. They left her behind the cook truck and moved silently away.

Alex went off to find the others. Roark, with Samantha trailing him, made straight for his saddlebags. "The books are still here," he reported after checking the contents. "Undisturbed."

He had a speculative look in his potent blue eyes when he got to his feet. "What are you thinking?" she questioned him.

"That maybe Ernie Chacon's motive is less innocent than it seems."

"What does that mean?"

"Frank Costello is the director of the Western Museum, and if his son is willing to go to any lengths to win his approval…"

Samantha understood him. "The museum gets the Walking W if I fail to qualify for my grandfather's estate. If I'm deliberately *made* to fail."

"It would be quite a gift to present a director. Say, an ambitious director who'd be very grateful for it."

It was an unpleasant thought, but a possibility that Samantha couldn't ignore.

"No proof for any of this," Roark said grimly, "but now more than ever, Ernie bears careful watching."

THE SUN WAS STILL a good hour away from setting when the drive stopped for the night. Samantha suspected that the other members of the outfit were as grateful as she was for Shep's decision to call an early halt. The trail boss had pushed them hard that day, insisting they had to make up for lost time.

"Don't know why he's so worried," Cappy had grumbled, his jaws working on his familiar tobacco chaw. "Alamo Junction can't be more'n a couple of days away now. Plenty of time to make those stock cars."

If only we could count on that, Samantha thought, sharing the trail boss's tension. After all, she had a lot to lose if they failed to meet the deadline. And with all that had been happening, it was certainly possible. Shep's concern, of course, could be explained by his responsibility for the progress of the drive. That and whatever private devil was riding him.

"I'm going to hug Shep for taking pity on us," Samantha confided to Roark when they arrived at the site for that night's camp.

Roark, chuckling, jerked his head in the direction of the nearby creek along whose banks the longhorns were already crowding. "I think his decision had more to do with the availability of water than any compassion for our backsides."

"Well, this backside is so exhausted I don't think it can take another minute in the saddle. On the other hand, I'm not sure I have enough strength left to get out of the saddle."

Roark had already dismounted with maddening ease.

''Here, let me help.'' He stood by her stirrup, offering his hand to her.

''I can manage,'' she insisted.

But her body, unsteady with fatigue, betrayed her as she started to climb down, threatening to tumble her from the mare's back. She would have collapsed on the ground if Roark hadn't caught her as she slid from the saddle. The next thing she knew she had been dragged to her feet and was solidly in his arms.

Samantha instantly forgot how stiff and sore she was. Forgot everything but her traitorous senses clamoring for the man who held her. For his long, lean body pressed tightly, securely against hers, searing her flesh even with the barrier of their clothing between them. For the scent of him, all male in its mixture of horse, sweat and musk. And for his bold, sensual mouth that hovered promisingly just above hers.

''Tell me you want this as much as I do,'' he said gruffly, his deep blue eyes pinned on her with the intensity of a hungry predator. ''That nothing else matters.''

In this moment nothing else did matter. She didn't care about the past or the future. All she knew was that she wanted more than the sight, scent and feel of him. She wanted his flavor as well. Wanted what she had missed since their night in the canyon. His mouth devouring hers.

It didn't happen. The cell phone clipped to his belt trilled sharply, demanding his attention. With a muttered oath, Roark released her and reached for the phone. Samantha didn't know whether to feel regret or relief. Both emotions were at war inside her, and had been from the start.

When he answered the call, she could hear an excited voice at the other end. ''Wendell?'' she asked, mouthing the name. Roark nodded and angled his head toward her, holding the instrument so that they could both listen. There was no risk of being overheard. Ramona was busy over at the cook truck getting supper underway. The rest of the

outfit was occupied with watering and settling the herd for
the night.

"What have you got for me, Wendell?"

"Something you're going to like," the young trainee
informed him triumphantly. "All my work in Purgatory
finally paid off. See, I got to talking to this woman in one
of the bars there. I swear there are more saloons in that
town than gas stations. Anyway, it turns out she's a friend
of Ramona Chacon. Amazing how a few beers oiled her
tongue. Guess what she told me about your Ernie?"

Wendell proceeded to gleefully tell them Ramona's secret, how she'd had an affair years ago with the director
of the Western Museum and that Ernie was his illegitimate
son. There was a silence when he breathlessly finished his
story.

"Hey, you still there?"

"Still here," Roark assured him. "It's just that, uh, we
learned all this from Ramona herself this morning."

"You already *know?*"

Samantha heard the disappointment in Wendell's voice
and felt sorry for him. Roark made an effort to soothe him.

"It's all right, Wendell. It's still good work. Did you
get into those caves yet?"

"Yeah, I went out there this morning. Creepy places.
No snakes, but I could feel the ghosts of all those Native
American ancestors that were supposed to have lived in
them. If they left anything behind, though, it's long gone."

"Any evidence of digging in them?"

"Not a sign. Hang on a minute. There's another call
coming in."

Roark turned to Samantha while they waited. "I still
say the answer is in that ravine. It must be there somewhere, and whatever it is, there's a chance it's connected
with Ernie Chacon."

"Why Ernie?"

"Have you forgotten that Shep told us your grandfather
sent Ernie packing? What if Joe found him messing around

that ravine and ordered him to keep away from the ranch?
And if Ernie did discover something, say in the caves
there, it could be another reason for wanting the Walking
W in his father's control. Because if Frank Costello *was*
grateful to his son for the property, there's every likelihood
he would permit him the freedom of—''

"I'm back," Wendell said. "It was just a question on
the billing for the Adams case last month. Oh, there is one
more thing I got from this woman in the bar, but, heck, I
suppose you already know that, too."

"Let's have it, Wendell."

"I guess the lady gets around, because she claimed to
also be a good friend of your trail boss's wife."

"And?"

"The wife told her she's worried about her husband. It
seems that the guy is in financial trouble. The serious
kind."

Samantha and Roark turned their heads to exchange
glances of sudden, eager interest. She knew Roark must
be thinking the same thing she was. *Shep Thomas.* Was it
possible?

Chapter Ten

Roark urged his trainee to explain. "Just how serious, Wendell? Did you get any details?"

"Oh, yeah. The guy is a gambler, and now he owes the wrong people. The sort that don't make idle threats."

Shep Thomas a gambler? Samantha thought. She found the information hard to believe. It just didn't belong with the straight-arrow image the trail boss had always projected. But then individuals seldom fitted the molds into which society was forever casting them.

"The wife told this friend," Wendell continued, "that Shep had asked his boss for a loan before his death but that Joe Walker had turned him down. Said her husband didn't know how he was going to cover his debt and that he's been plenty worried about it since. You sure you didn't hear this already?"

Roark assured him they hadn't.

"Well, I'm sorry I saved it for last, but I didn't see how it could be useful. I mean, it's not like Shep Thomas benefits from Walker's will if his granddaughter fails to inherit."

"Is that everything, Wendell? What about the new batch of photos?"

"I took a lot of them like you asked, shot those ravine walls from end to end. As soon as they're developed, I'll send them on. The results should be waiting for you at your next stop after this one. That would be Willow Creek, wouldn't it? You have anything more you want me to look into?''

"Keep checking into Ernie's background. And while you're at it, start asking around about the other members of our outfit. I'm not ruling out any of them.''

Roark made sure that Wendell had all of their names, thanked him and rang off. He turned to Samantha, a speculative look on his rugged face. "You thinking what I'm thinking?''

"About the stranger Shep met back in Lost Springs and again in Edgerton the other evening? Could it be?''

Roark nodded. "One of those good people pressuring him for the money he owes them, or someone who doesn't want to give him a loan he's trying to negotiate to pay the crowd he owes. Either way it explains the secret he's been hiding and why he's been looking so miserable.''

"Yes, but Wendell is right. This can't have any connection with my inheritance or all that's been happening on the drive. Anyway, we don't know for sure that what Wendell was told is true. It could have been just a lot of unfounded gossip from someone who'd had too many beers.''

"Anything is possible, Samantha, when a man is desperate. And that's something that will have to wait to be explored, because right now Cappy is over there giving us a look that says he's wondering why we're standing around doing nothing while he and the others are handling all the work. Come on, we've got some horses that need to be unsaddled.''

THEY WERE CAMPED that night in the vicinity of another town, Donovan, Colorado, this time. A county seat, according to Dick Brewster. None of them, including the horse wrangler, were interested in visiting the place, which in any case was several miles distant from their camp.

They were all too tired to do anything but lounge around the fire after an early supper of fajitas and fried rice.

All but Roark and Shep, that is. Leaving Samantha where she would be safe in the group by the fire, Roark had gone off toward the cook truck to treat himself to a sponge bath behind the blanket Ramona always strung on a line for that purpose. He and Samantha hadn't discussed the heated moment interrupted by Wendell's phone call. Nor had he tried to touch her since then. In order not to think about that, to save herself from anguishing about a situation that seemed to have no solution for them, she focused her mind on Shep.

She was worried about the trail boss. All through supper he had been silent and hollow-eyed. Afterward, he had taken his canteen of water and wandered off on his own. There was a long slope just below the campsite. It ended on the lip of a wide, deep canyon. She could see Shep down there now. He stood in the twilight on a ledge overhanging the canyon, sipping from the canteen and gazing vacantly into the abyss.

He was such a solitary, brooding figure that Samantha's heart ached for him. A gambler in debt or not, she liked Shep, had liked his wife, too, and she grieved for his torment. Her sorrow was so strong that when he turned away from the canyon and started back up the hill, moving as slowly as an old man, she could no longer stand it.

Getting to her feet, she glanced in the direction of the cook truck and decided that Roark had no reason to object. It wasn't as if she intended to be alone with Shep, only to speak to him privately within sight of the others. Perfectly safe.

Samantha met the trail boss on the brow of the hill. He looked up, surprised to find her there. She wasted no time in explaining her presence.

"Shep, if you're in trouble I'd like to help."

"What are you talking about?"

"You owe money, don't you? A lot of money. At least I think that's why you've been sick with worry."

Shep had always been polite to her, gentle even. It was a shock now to see the haunted look on his face turn to a mean scowl. "How do you know I'm in debt? Have you and Hawke been snooping?"

He could be forgiven his ugly anger. The stress of his plight was responsible. "It doesn't matter how I know. It's true then."

"What of it?"

"I know what it's like to owe money and not know which way to turn. There's nothing I can offer you now, but if you can hold out until the drive is ended and I inherit my grandfather's estate, then I can—"

"How?" he snarled. "By selling the Walking W to some developer who'll divide it into building lots? That's what ambitious Realtors like you do, isn't it?"

Under a strain or not, he wasn't being fair. Samantha had spent her first years in real estate with another agency, working hard, learning the business before she borrowed a sum to open her own agency. Not to destroy properties but to put them in the hands of people who would treasure them.

"I probably will have to sell the ranch, yes, but—"

"Yeah, that's all the Walking W means to you."

He thrust his face into hers as he said it, and that's when Samantha realized the canteen he carried didn't contain water. The fumes of a breath thick with alcohol blasted her. Shep Thomas, a man she'd had every reason to believe was a teetotaler, who hadn't touched the beer at Dick Brewster's party, was drunk on what smelled like cheap whiskey.

He was also in a dangerous mood. Samantha realized she'd made a mistake in approaching him. She started to back away, but his hand closed around her wrist, holding her in a tight grip. Shep Thomas had suddenly become a menacing stranger.

"You're not entitled to that ranch, Samantha. Not feeling the way you do about it."

Her mouth opened to demand her release, but Samantha never got the words out. Without warning, a voice as hard as granite coldly informed the trail boss, "I wouldn't like to hit a man when he looks like he's all liquored up, but if you don't let her go, Thomas, you're going to find yourself flat on your back. *Now.*"

Shep hesitated only a second, and then he dropped Samantha's arm. She spun around to find Roark looming above them, legs braced apart, a formidable expression on his lean face. He didn't look at her. His gaze remained locked on Shep. For a taut moment the trail boss met the challenge in Roark's eyes. Then he surrendered by dropping his own gaze.

"It wouldn't be a good idea for you to ever touch her again," Roark advised him with a lethal softness.

Shaking his head in an effort to clear it, Shep muttered an apology, though Samantha had the feeling he didn't really understand what he had said or done. He was still in a fog when he brushed past them and headed back to the campsite, hopefully to climb into his bag and sleep off the whiskey he'd consumed.

When they were alone on the path, Samantha started to thank Roark for another of his timely rescues. He never gave her the chance. Catching her by the same wrist that Shep had grabbed only a moment ago, he pulled her behind a tall fir at the side of the path. The thick tree screened them from the others in the outfit, although none of them seemed to be paying any attention to what was happening on the slope.

"That was a real smart thing you did," Roark said, lashing her with his anger. "Coming down here on your own to meet him like that."

She looked up into his face and then down at the fingers that encircled her wrist like a steel band. "Now, I wonder why," she asked him coolly, "you feel entitled to bruise the same wrist that you just warned Shep never to touch again?''

''Damn it, don't avoid the issue,'' he said, but his hand loosened its hold on her wrist and slid away.

''The issue is, you may be my protector, but you're not my jailer.''

''No, the issue is that the man was threatening you.''

''You saw yourself he'd been drinking and didn't know what he was saying. He wouldn't have hurt me,'' she insisted, refusing in her own anger to admit Shep had frightened her. ''Why would he, when I was offering to help him, and once he accepts that—''

''When are you going to realize that someone wants you out of the way?''

''Not Shep. Not when we agreed he has no motive.''

''That was your conviction, Samantha, not mine. And Shep Thomas, now that I've had time to think about it, *does* have a motive. A damn good one.''

''I can't imagine what since he doesn't benefit from my grandfather's will, except for that modest cash legacy which he must have already received.''

''And which probably doesn't begin to cover his gambling debt. But what if there's a way for him to make a lot of money, a fortune even? Those caves, Samantha. What if it's Thomas who's discovered there are treasures there?''

''Then why wouldn't he have already helped himself to them?''

''Time. Providing there are valuable relics buried there, whoever is after them would need both time and freedom to excavate them. Hell, you've made no secret of your decision to sell the Walking W as soon as you inherit it. And where would that leave Shep Thomas? Either out of a job or under the watchful eye of a new occupant. But if the Western Museum gets the property, there's every likelihood the ranch will continue to operate under the current foreman. At least for the present. And with an absentee owner, which the museum would be, Thomas would be free to mine those caves without outside knowledge or interference.''

Samantha thought about it. Roark's theory was certainly possible. It would even explain the trail boss's uncharacteristic rancor over what he regarded as her heartless intention to sell the ranch. But in the end she couldn't bring herself to believe Shep Thomas was capable of any desperate act, especially murder, to get what he wanted.

''All right, Shep is frustrated,'' she said, ''and, yes, liquor made him mean tempered, but I can't convince myself he isn't basically a decent man who would never intentionally hurt anyone.''

Roark's jaw tightened in an expression of impatience. ''You've said yourself you don't know him all that well. When are you going to understand that people aren't always what they appear to be?''

''And you would know all about that, wouldn't you?'' she said, referring to what he had confided to her the night they had spent below the cliff dwellings.

It was a thoughtless reminder of how Roark had misjudged the client who had murdered his wife, and the words were scarcely out of Samantha's mouth before she deeply regretted them. How could she have been so cruel?

No longer was it just his jaw that was tight with emotion. His whole face had hardened. Deeply ashamed, she was prepared to apologize. Before she could, his hands shot out and gripped both her arms just below her shoulders. She expected him to actually shake her and was startled when, instead, he pulled her up against his solid length.

''What are you—''

''Be quiet,'' he ordered her. ''You've said enough.''

She couldn't have managed to utter her challenge in any case. He was clasping her so strongly the breath was squeezed out of her. What air she had left in her lungs was

entirely robbed by his mouth when it swooped down and
captured her own.

There was something so entirely possessive in his kiss,
so punishing in its ferocity that Samantha was shocked.
She knew she ought to be livid. *Was* livid. No woman,
whatever anger she had invoked, deserved to have her
mouth ravished like this.

But if there was anything intentionally brutal in Roark's
kiss, it almost immediately vanished, becoming instead so
intimate and loving, so persuasive in its probing hunger
that she forgave him his initial assault. She even forgot
she was supposed to object to it when her senses rioted
under the intensity of the kiss.

Samantha was suddenly aware of everything about him.
The clean, fresh scent of the soap he had used only moments ago and which still clung to his skin. The virile taste
of him as his tongue mated passionately with hers. The
feel of his rigid arousal straining against her, summoning
memories of the incredible rapture they had shared in the
canyon that night.

It was all there, everything his mouth had silently promised and been unable to deliver when Wendell's phone call
had interrupted them earlier. Everything and more. And
then suddenly there was nothing. His mouth lifted from
hers, he released her.

She was instantly aware of a sharp sense of loss as she
stood there recovering her wind while she searched his
face, seeking an answer. But there were no answers for
them, not now, maybe never. She could see that much in
his eyes, which registered both regret and a hopelessness.
And she knew her own eyes must be reflecting a similar
despair.

Nothing had changed. There was still this barrier between them, keeping them apart, forever reminding them
that their needs and values were impossibly different. Her
growing love for him should have been enough, but there
was no use in pretending it was. Not when she couldn't

endure the lifestyle that was vital to Roark, and he couldn't be happy in her world far removed from his beloved horses and cattle. A conflict without a resolution.

Desolate, Samantha found herself longing for the completion of the cattle drive. Whatever its outcome, she needed to remove herself from the temptation of Roark Hawke, to get far away from the ache that his mere presence inflicted on her daily. But there were still many hard miles to cover with threats from an unknown enemy around every bend in the trail. Would it never end?

IT WAS LATE when Samantha awakened. She had the impression it was long after midnight but with daybreak still several hours away. The moon was overhead, though it had waned over the past few days and was a sickle now. But its pale gleam was sufficient for her to make out the contours of the terrain and the dark forms of the outfit scattered around the campsite in their sleeping bags.

For a moment she lay there, listening to the soft whickering of one of the horses and what sounded like Cappy snoring on the other side of a fire that was now only ashes. There was no other noise. Nothing to disturb the peaceful stillness of the night.

In the end, Samantha couldn't deny the urge that had awakened her. She had to visit that juniper thicket up on a nearby knoll she and Ramona had been using for their needs. But, oh, how she hated to leave the snug warmth of her sleeping bag. The nights were colder now with the advance of autumn, the aspens on the mountainsides rapidly shedding their leaves.

It couldn't be helped. She had to go. But she didn't dare venture off to the thicket on her own. She had learned that lesson back at the Morning Star Ranch and again when she had pursued Irma into the narrow gorge. Nor had Roark forgiven her for seeking out Shep last evening, even though she'd pointed out to him that she had remained within sight and sound of the others.

"I don't care," he had instructed her on their way back to camp after their emotional scene behind the fir. "From now on, you're never to be alone with any of them. And if for any reason I have to be away from your side, you stay with the group."

Fine. If he insisted on accompanying her everywhere, even on so basic an errand as this one, then he could just sacrifice his sleep to escort her. Still, she experienced a moment of guilty hesitation after removing herself from her sleeping bag and leaning over him where he was stretched out close to her side. She could tell by his even breathing he was sound asleep.

Not so soundly, however, that he wasn't instantly awake and fully alert when she lightly shook him. "What is it?" he demanded.

Samantha whispered a quick explanation. "And, no, I can't wait until morning. Sorry."

Rousing himself from his bag, he pulled on his boots and groped for the flashlight while she collected a roll of tissue and a package of premoistened wipes. Samantha shivered. There was a strong chill in the air, made clammy by a mist that had gathered since she had left her own sleeping bag.

None of the others stirred as they silently stole away from camp and headed up the slope to the juniper thicket on the crown of the knoll. Looking back, Samantha could see the longhorns drowsing peacefully in the broad hollow beyond the campsite.

Bands of mist drifted through the hollow. Through their ghostly layers, she could make out two figures on horseback watching over the herd. Too far away to recognize them, and she couldn't remember who had drawn this particular shift. Shep and Dick Brewster, she thought. Not that it mattered.

The beam of the flashlight in Roark's hand cut an eerie swath through the mist that swirled around them as they climbed the knoll. When they neared the thicket, which loomed out of the mist with all the substance of a wraith, Roark pressed the flashlight into her hand.

"I'll wait right here," he directed her. "If you have any problem, you call me."

"I'll only be a minute," she said, bearing the flashlight, tissue and wipes as she squeezed through an opening between the junipers and found her way to a tiny clearing at the heart of the thicket.

But what with juggling the flashlight and wipes, dropping the roll of tissue on the ground and having to retrieve it, then managing to snag her clothing on the prickly junipers, Samantha was longer than she'd promised.

Roark checked on her. "You all right in there?"

"Fine."

She wasn't fine. The flashlight quit on her, and she had no luck in restoring it. Damn, she would be so glad when she was back in civilization again. The wilderness was all right until nature called and you had to deal with its primitive conditions. Then she wanted plumbing, electric lights and a nice, cozy furnace to warm her on a cold, damp night like this.

Samantha was relieved after she'd finally completed the essentials, though finding her way back out of the junipers without a light was a bit of a challenge. Relief turned to dismay when she stepped into the open. In her absence, the mist had thickened into a heavy fog. The moonlight barely penetrated its gray mass.

Even more bewildering, there was no sign of Roark. Had she emerged on the wrong side of the thicket? That would have been an easy thing to happen without light and the thicket being the maze it was. She thought she detected a slight rustle off to her left.

"Roark," she called out softly, "are you there?"

There was no response. Straining to listen for any sound of movement that might offer her his location, she heard nothing. Where was he? What had become of him? He wouldn't just desert her. Not without telling her he was leaving. He must be on the other side of the thicket.

Unable to bear the eerie silence, Samantha opened her mouth to call out to him again, this time with sufficient volume. But the memory of that rustling sound, and Roark's failure to hear her first soft call, which he should have done if he was close by, had the words freezing on her tongue. Wisdom suddenly told her to keep quiet. A wisdom she neither liked nor fully understood, but she obeyed it. Because if there was someone else in the area, someone who was not Roark or a friend, then any loud call she made would betray her location.

What was she supposed to do? She couldn't go on just standing here like this. Quelling the urge to panic, she decided that her best course was to grope her way as silently as possible back to camp. Stumbling around in this fog in search of Roark would be useless. He could be anywhere. And if he was in trouble, then she needed to rouse the others to help her locate him.

However, finding her way back to the campsite proved to be far more of an undertaking than she'd anticipated. She hadn't traveled three yards from the thicket when the fog completely enveloped her, blotting out all landmarks, destroying any inner compass that might have provided her with a sense of direction.

Fumbling her way blindly forward, hands stretched out in front of her to avoid smacking into any invisible obstacle, Samantha crept on through the dense shroud. She paused after every few feet, struggling to get her bearings. But all she could tell for certain was that she was descending the incline.

That was a good sign, wasn't it? It meant she was headed in the right direction, that sooner or later she would encounter some evidence of their camp. Except the route seemed longer than she remembered, the slope steeper. An illusion created by the fog? She convinced herself this was the explanation.

Feeling her way with each careful step, she moved on. The fog licked at her from all sides. She could smell it, taste its wetness.

She stopped again. Surely, she was close enough now to the camp to shout a plea to the outfit. Should she risk it? Samantha was prepared to make that effort when she heard it…the whisper of a movement somewhere in her vicinity. Impossible to tell from where it came or exactly how far away it was. The fog confused all direction, muted sound.

Roark? It must be Roark. His name formed on her lips, but another inner warning prevented her from eagerly voicing it. It couldn't be Roark. If it were, he would have been calling out to her long before this.

It was then, with a chilling awareness, that Samantha knew for certain she was not alone here in the fog. That she didn't dare to reveal her position by crying out to either Roark or the others. Someone was with her. Someone who didn't want her to know he was seeking her.

An animal? It could be an animal. But her sense of danger told her it wasn't an animal. It was human, and it was hunting for her. Lifting her head like a frightened doe striving to detect the exact location of her enemy, Samantha could swear she heard a harsh breathing.

Stifling a sob that would have revealed her presence, fighting the alarm that had her trembling now, she started cautiously to move away. She must have stepped on a dry twig. Something snapped under her foot. Not a loud sound but treacherous in all this silence.

There was a rush of movement behind her, someone charging in her direction. Samantha bolted, plunging down the hill through the blank wall of the fog. A dark shape rose up in front of her, and for a horrified second she thought her stalker must have circled around and was waiting to ambush her.

The phantom turned out to be nothing more menacing than a fir tree. She had no memory of a fir along the route to the juniper thicket. Nor had the grade been this rough in places and in others dangerously slick. Slithering down one wet stretch, she lost her balance and fell to her hands and knees.

Picking herself up, knowing she was hopelessly lost now but too terrified to turn back, Samantha fled onward through the fog. Disoriented, worried sick about Roark, she failed in her mindless dread to realize just where she was going. And she paid the penalty of her error.

In one second there was solid earth in front of her. In the next there was nothing but empty space. Samantha suddenly found herself teetering precariously on the sharp lip of a precipice. Too late she understood that she had not been headed for the camp at all. She had come the wrong way!

Samantha knew where she was. Below the camp lay the deep canyon on whose brink Shep Thomas had earlier stood and where she was now trapped between a yawning void and a deadly pursuer.

Recovering her balance, she started to back away. Somewhere behind her sounded the crunch of a foot on gravel. He was here, close by! He had found her! Choking on both fog and fear, she altered the direction of her escape and began to edge along the rim of the canyon to her right. It was another fatal blunder.

With one wrong step the earth was crumbling beneath her, threatening to pitch her into a hideous oblivion. Throwing herself sideways, she landed on her knees where, in desperation, she fought to save herself, feet scrabbling for a purchase, hands clawing at ground that continued to disintegrate.

And then she was fighting another horror. A human one whose arms reached down and wrapped around her, snatched her back from the edge, and dragged her forcefully to her feet. Battling her enemy, her breathing quick and ragged, she struggled in his grip, tried to beat at him with her fists.

"Samantha, it's all right. It's me."

When the familiar deep voice finally penetrated her panic, she went limp in his arms. For a long moment, as Roark continued to hold her, she surrendered totally to the blessed relief of his solid body comforting her. Then, drawing her head back, she challenged him with an accusing "Where have you been? Why didn't you answer me when I called?"

"I didn't hear you. What did you do, come out on the wrong side of the thicket?"

"I guess that's exactly what I did. Roark, there's someone else out here with us. He was hunting for me." She looked around wildly, but the fog continued to veil everything.

"I know. When I finally realized something was wrong and came looking for you, I could hear the two of you playing cat and mouse in this damn mess. All I could think of was finding you before he did. Thank God I did."

"But if you had called out for me—"

"You would have answered, and it would have led him straight to you. So I kept quiet and used my ears. I could swear I heard him once whispering your name. I almost had him then, but he gave me the slip. Are you all right?"

"Yes, but if he's still here somewhere—"

"I think he's gone. Let's get away from this edge before one of us takes another wrong step. Looks like the fog may be breaking up. Let's see if we can find our way back to camp."

"What if we run into him?"

"I'll regard it as an opportunity to introduce him to my fists. But my guess is he isn't hanging around long enough to get himself identified. Not this time, anyway."

Roark was right. The fog was easing, leaving patches like smoke as it slowly drifted away. Between those patches, the moonlight revealed the route up the long hill. They were climbing it when Samantha realized that somewhere on her flight she'd abandoned the tissues, wipes and

useless flashlight. They weren't important. What mattered
was learning who had stalked her in the fog.

"If one of them back at camp is missing," she said,
"it's a good bet he's our culprit."

"He's much too cunning to be caught like that, Samantha."

She was still hopeful that one of their members would
be absent from camp, but Roark proved to be right. The
fog that had filled the air only moments ago had shrunk
to nothing by the time they reached camp. It was possible
to count occupied sleeping bags without approaching anyone. Everyone who was supposed to be there *was* there,
rolled in his bag on the ground. Ramona, Ernie, Alex,
Cappy.

"What about Shep and Dick?" she whispered.

It was a possibility that was easily checked. Roark drew
her off to the top of a rise where they could look down
into the hollow on the other side. A light mist still lingered
at its bottom, but the moonlight was enough to reveal the
figures of Shep Thomas and Dick Brewster on horseback
stationed on opposite sides of the quiet herd.

"All of them accounted for," Roark said as they turned
back to the campsite.

Yes, Samantha thought, but the fog must have been even
thicker in the hollow than on the knoll. That meant either
the trail boss or the horse wrangler could have slipped
away under its cover without his partner being conscious
of his action, then managed to return before he was missed.

One of them, she thought, focusing on the still figures
on the ground as they regained the campsite. One of them
either here or back in the hollow saw his opportunity and
came after me. And after he'd struck and failed to achieve
what he'd intended, the fog swallowed him again, permitting him to steal back to camp without detection.

Which one? she asked herself, wondering if one of them
there on the ground was only pretending to be asleep. The
rest of them remained undisturbed, not aware of the des-

perate drama that had been enacted out there in the fog just moments ago.

"Let's turn in," Roark whispered. "Get what rest we can before daylight."

Samantha was dismayed by his casual suggestion. "Aren't you going to wake them? Tell them what happened? Question everyone?"

"What for? If anyone saw one of the others sneaking off, he'd already be up and talking about it. And whoever did sneak off isn't going to admit it. Assuming it was one of our outfit, that is. We still don't know for certain our man is one of us."

That was true. They had no hard evidence yet to support the belief. Even so, she couldn't fall asleep again after she'd crawled back into her bag, though Roark was close beside her in his own bag, his gun within his reach.

She kept thinking about her fellow drovers. Thinking how she was almost certain one of them wanted her out of the way, while at the same time struggling with this probability. It still seemed incredible to her. Who? And why?

Equally disturbing was her awareness of the man at her side. Of the hopeless issues that continued to divide them. Where Roark Hawke was concerned, her emotions remained in turmoil. She wanted him while knowing that she shouldn't want him.

IT WAS MORNING and the camp was stirring when Samantha first noticed that something was wrong. She had managed to drift off an hour or so before daybreak just as the fog made another appearance, though it had burned off altogether by the time she emerged from her cocoon.

It wasn't surprising that her attention should be drawn to the saddlebag at Roark's feet. Since it was his saddlebag and she remembered watching him close it last night before turning in, its present condition was immediately no-

ticeable. The leather flap was unbuckled and lifted, the bag
gaping open, as if it had been invaded in haste.

Roark's eyes were still closed, his good-looking face
shadowed with an early morning beard when she crouched
down and placed a hand on his lean length. He was instantly awake and alert, his deep blue gaze searching her
face.

"What is it?" he asked, his voice raspy from sleep.

"Have you been inside your saddlebag since last
night?"

"No."

"Well, someone has."

In seconds he was out of his sleeping bag and hunkered
down beside his saddlebag to swiftly investigate its contents.

"They're gone," he reported.

Samantha didn't need to ask what he meant. She knew
he referred to the three books on the subject of ancient
Native American habitats and their rare artifacts. When
Roark had bought the volumes back in Edgerton, intending
them as bait to smoke out the enemy, she had privately
regarded his plan as ineffective. Why, she had thought,
would a smart culprit risk his identity by snatching those
books? And he *had* resisted the temptation. Until now.

The books were missing. Proof that Roark's trap had
not been so unlikely, after all.

"But it doesn't tell us who took them," she said.

"No," he agreed, "but it does tell us I must be on the
right track about the worth of those caves back at the
Walking W. Someone is worried about that. Worried
enough, I think, to try to keep me from gaining a knowledge about relics that could be dangerous to him."

"That still doesn't tell us who stole the—"

She broke off. Roark wasn't looking at her. His gaze,
narrow eyed now, was focused on something behind her.
Samantha swung around. Ernie Chacon was standing
nearby eyeing them uneasily.

Roark got slowly to his feet. "You hear all that, Ernie?"

The stocky young man frowned, his mouth turned down in the familiar surly expression. "I dunno what you're talking about."

"Yes, you do, Ernie." Roark approached him. "Did you help yourself to the books in my saddlebag?"

"I ain't touched your damn things."

"You did once before, Ernie. Remember the photographs you snatched?"

"That don't make me guilty this time."

"He's right, Roark." Alex, a towel slung around his neck, had come around the side of the cook truck in time to witness the whole exchange.

Samantha was surprised to hear Alex on the side of his rival. But Ernie didn't seem to appreciate Alex's defense. He rounded on him angrily. "I don't need you standing up for me, college boy."

Alex shrugged. "I'm not doing you any favors. I'm just trying to be fair about it, that's all."

Roark regarded him thoughtfully. "You seem pretty certain that Ernie was nowhere near my saddlebag. Does that mean you saw someone else messing with the bag?"

Alex was silent.

"It does, doesn't it?" Roark pressed him.

"I don't like to say," Alex mumbled, looking increasingly uncomfortable, as if he wished he'd never become involved.

"You'd better tell me."

"I'm not sure. I only had a glimpse, and I was still half-asleep in my bag."

"When?"

"Just as it was starting to get light. He was coming away carrying something from the place where your saddlebag is. Only, I guess I didn't think much about it at the time. Nothing like theft, anyway. Not *him*."

"Who, Alex?"

Alex hesitated. "Shep," he muttered unhappily.

Samantha remembered the grim look on the trail boss's face the night Roark had announced his purchase of the books. Was it true then? Had Shep learned those caves contained treasures he would go to any lengths to keep secret until he had the opportunity to excavate them? Including the prevention of Roark's knowledge on the subject of relics, a knowledge that might raise his suspicion.

"If Shep was back here in camp before sunup," Roark said, "that means he left his shift."

Samantha looked around. "He must have gone back to the herd because he isn't here now."

"No, but his belongings are."

His jaw tightening with determination, Roark strode in the direction of Shep's sleeping bag. A nervous Alex hurried after him.

"You're not going to search his stuff?" Alex objected. "I mean, it's Shep. He wouldn't have done anything wrong."

Roark ignored the young man. Crouching at the foot of the bag, he reached for a bulky canvas satchel that contained Shep's possessions. Samantha knelt beside him, watching intently as he dumped the contents on the cover of the bag. The missing books were not among them. Nor did Roark discover them when he patted the sleeping bag for any telltale lumps.

"He must have them with him in his saddlebags," he said. "Either that or he's destroyed them."

Alex, hovering over them, was still unable to believe his trail boss was guilty of any misdeed. "Or he never took them in the first place. I could have been wrong about what I saw. I probably was."

"No," Samantha said slowly, reaching for a slip of paper tucked among the articles that Roark had removed from the satchel, "he took the books all right. Look."

She handed the slip to Roark for his inspection. "The receipt from the store where I bought the books," he said.

Something occurred to Samantha. "Leaving this behind is a bit obvious, isn't it?"

"Or careless. He could have been just that if he'd been drinking again."

"This is crazy," Alex said. "He probably just borrowed the books. And, anyway, what does it matter? They were just books."

"Hey," an aggrieved voice hailed them, "have you guys forgotten about me? Somebody was supposed to have relieved me a half hour ago."

They looked up to see Dick Brewster riding into camp from the direction of the hollow. Alex was immediately contrite.

"That would be me and Cappy. Sorry, Dick. We got occupied here and I forgot it was our shift." He started for his horse. "I don't know where Cappy got to. Any of you see him, tell him I'm already on my way to the herd."

Roark and Samantha, on their feet now, approached the weary horse wrangler as he dismounted. "Where's Shep?" Roark asked him. "You leave him with the longhorns?"

"Hell, no. I sent him back to camp and told him to stay put. He looked so miserable with that hangover he was suffering, and what with the cows so peaceful, I told him I could manage fine on my own." Dick looked around, puzzled. "You mean he's not here?"

Roark and Samantha exchanged looks of concern. Had Shep Thomas run out on them? Alex, hearing their conversation, turned back.

"What's wrong? Is Shep missing?"

Roark shook his head, indicating he didn't know. Ernie, having lost interest in the scene once he'd been vindicated of any theft, had drifted away. They could hear him talking to his mother at the back of the cook truck where Ramona was rattling pans as she busied herself with breakfast preparations. Roark called to them.

"Either of you two seen Shep?"

They poked their heads around the side of the truck, their blank expressions signifying they hadn't.

Alex looked anxious. "He must be somewhere nearby. We should spread out and search for him."

"No call for that," Cappy said.

They turned to see the old man lumbering into camp from the direction of the canyon below the hill.

"You know where he is?" Roark asked him.

"Yeah, I do," Cappy informed them matter-of-factly. "He's lying at the bottom of the canyon, and don't look like he's in any state to get up and walk out of there. *Ever.*"

Chapter Eleven

Samantha stood on the rim of the canyon, gazing anxiously at the ghastly scene below her. Roark, together with Dick and Alex, had found a trail that had taken them into the bottom of the canyon. They were there now on its boulder-strewn floor, the two younger men hovering over Roark as he crouched down to examine the trail boss's broken body.

Emotions that collided with one another chased through Samantha's mind as she waited for Roark's verdict. Hope that he would find some evidence Shep was still alive. Horror over the sight of that spread-eagled body. And fear that came with the memory of last night when she had almost plunged into the canyon herself from this very spot.

That could be her down there, her body limp and life-less. Instead—and ironically as well if it had been the trail boss who had pursued her through the fog—it was Shep. How had it happened? Why?

Roark looked up, met her desperate eyes and slowly shook his head. He had obviously found no life signs. Shep was beyond their help. Ramona, Ernie and Cappy had been waiting with her on the rim for Roark's judgment. She heard now the cook's sharp intake of breath and the old man's grunt. From Ernie there was only a silence.

Sickened by the sad finality of the whole thing, Samantha had started to turn away when she saw Roark lean over one of the books by Shep's outstretched arm. Without touching it, he looked at it closely. She knew it had to be one of those missing volumes. A second book, standing on its spine between two rocks, was nearby.

The third book wasn't there, but they all knew by now what had become of it. Its pages had been shredded, ripped from their binding, and strewn along a path from the brow of the hill to the rim of the canyon. It was this trail that a mystified Cappy had followed, leading him to the discovery of Shep's body.

Those torn pages were still there, fluttering in the breeze on the side of the hill. It was a sight that shocked Samantha. The pointless destruction of the book was an act that must have been generated by a terrible rage.

She and the others were waiting back at camp when the three men returned from the canyon minutes later. No one questioned Roark's swift instructions. They were all ready to have him take charge, looking to him for direction.

"Dick, take your fastest horse and ride into Donovan. Since it's the county seat, there should be a sheriff there. Cappy and Alex, you'd better get out to the longhorns before they start wandering on us. Whatever happens, the herd is still our responsibility. And, all of you—" he paused to look grimly around the circle "—be prepared to answer questions, because when the sheriff arrives he'll have them."

"But it was an accident," Alex said. "Shep's death had to be an accident. Didn't it?"

No one answered him. It was then that Samantha noticed Ramona and Ernie. Mother and son were exchanging glances of some shared understanding.

When the others had moved off, Samantha anxiously sought Roark's opinion. "It *was* an accident, wasn't it?"

"No, Samantha, I don't think so. I think it was murder."

SHERIFF HARVEY WILKINS LOOKED more like an academic on some Ivy League campus than a Western lawman. Sa-

mantha thought this was because of his carefully mani-
cured beard and the horn-rims he wore.

Choosing not to question them separately, he'd collected
the entire outfit on the rise above the hollow. The position
permitted Alex and Cappy to be included in the meeting
while maintaining their watch on the herd. Samantha could
understand that. Unfortunately, the elevation also offered
them a clear view of Shep's removal from the canyon. The
sight of the black body bag being loaded into a van that
would bear his remains to the medical examiner was not
a sight she wanted to remember.

"So," the sheriff said, reviewing the information they
had given him, "let's see if I've got all of this straight.
Your trail boss was depressed over debts he owed."

"Gambling debts, we think," Roark specified.

"Right. And as a result, he'd been drinking."

"Not like him," Cappy said, "but he was boozing it up
pretty good, I'd say."

"And in this state," the sheriff continued, "he wandered off from camp sometime before sunup. We don't
know exactly when, because none of you saw him leave.
Is that correct?" Satisfied by their nods, he glanced down
at the open notebook in his hand. "But you're fairly certain the fog had rolled in again."

"Thick enough to lose your way in it," Dick added.
"At least it was out here where I was on duty with the
herd."

"Uh-huh. The man was distraught, drinking, and allegedly angry about—" Sheriff Wilkins looked up from his
notebook and surveyed the circle of faces "—these books
he'd taken. Funny thing for him to be mad about. Yeah, I
know. You explained how it upset him to think this Walking W Ranch could be violated, but to go and destroy
books just because…" He adjusted his glasses and looked
thoughtful. "Still, if a man is drinking like that, anything
is possible."

The sheriff was silent then. They waited for his decision.

"It seems fairly evident to me," he finally concluded, closing his notebook. "This was an accident. He was liquored up, there was the fog. Easy enough for a man in those circumstances to miss his way and fall into the canyon. I'm not ruling out suicide either, not if he'd been as depressed as you say he was. Nothing is for sure until I get the medical examiner's report."

"How long do you think that will take?" Roark asked him.

"Maybe by the end of the day, if I ask for a rush on it. In the meantime," he instructed them, his expression severe as he looked again around the circle, "you all stay put. I can appreciate your time line on this cattle drive, but until I release you, you don't move."

"Understood," Roark assured him.

Finished with this portion of his investigation, the sheriff started to turn away and then paused as something else occurred to him. "There is the matter of informing his next of kin."

"That would be his wife," Samantha said, "and that's already been taken care of."

While they'd waited for the arrival of the sheriff and his team, Ramona had volunteered to phone a friend of Mrs. Thomas back in Texas. The woman had agreed to break the news of Shep's death to her.

Roark and Samantha followed the sheriff back to his car after the others, looking strained and uneasy, had drifted away. "Something bothering you, son?" Sheriff Wilkins asked Roark.

"There could be another explanation for Shep Thomas's death, sheriff."

"Like?"

"Murder."

"You got any reason to believe it could have been that?"

"If you're asking whether I can prove it, no, I can't. But the circumstances make it a possibility." Roark filled the lawman in on what had been happening on the cattle drive and how they were convinced that someone was determined to prevent Samantha from qualifying for her grandfather's estate.

Sheriff Wilkins looked doubtful when Roark had finished, even a bit resentful that a PI might be telling him how to handle his investigation. "That's all a lot of conjecture, son, and nothing in it that provides a motive for the murder of your trail boss. But I'll keep it in mind."

"He's not going to seriously consider it, is he?" Samantha said when the sheriff had departed.

Roark shook his head. "Not unless the medical examiner turns up some evidence it wasn't an accident. The man's incompetent."

"I can see where this is headed. You're not going to ignore the possibility of murder, even if Sheriff Wilkins does."

"I can't, Samantha. All right, so Shep might have been in some way to blame for trying to put you out of the running. Maybe he had a partner, and they had a falling-out. I don't know. What I do know is that I have to make an effort to solve his death."

"How? What do you have to go on?"

"Nothing at the moment. But I had a word with the police photographer who shot the scene from all angles before Shep's body was removed. He isn't supposed to do it, of course, but he agreed to provide me with a set of prints. Maybe if I study them hard enough, I can learn something from those photographs."

Roark fell silent. She watched his angular features tighten into a tough mask. "What are you thinking?" she asked him.

"That, if the medical examiner does find something, Wilkins will have no choice but to conduct a thorough investigation. And if that happens, the drive will end here and now. We won't be permitted to go on, not in time to make those stock cars in Alamo Junction, anyway."

"You look like you want that to happen."

"Maybe I do," he said gruffly. "Because if we're forced to call a halt, our culprit will no longer have any reason to try to stop you. You'll be safe."

"*No!*" Samantha said, surprising herself with the fierceness of her determination. "I've come too far to quit now. It's all so close. I have to go on, Roark. I have to finish the drive."

His eyes turned hard. "Even though it puts you at more risk than ever before?"

"It's my decision," she said stubbornly. "Anyway, I trust you to protect me. I'll stick close to you from now on, I promise."

"Damn right you will. Not just in my sight, Samantha, but joined at the hip. If we've got a killer for certain now, and I'm thinking we have, then I've got to do whatever is necessary to keep him from getting his hands on you."

HE WASN'T EXAGGERATING. He kept her constantly at his side as the day dragged on, not even permitting her and Dolly to wade a few yards into the herd to check on Irma when she and Roark took their own shift with the cows after lunch.

Samantha was beginning to feel as though she was attached by handcuffs to an uncompromising jailer. And never mind he was a jailer whose backside in a pair of snug jeans was a decidedly appealing sight at close range. It was still a drain on her nerves.

But then she wasn't the only one under stress. She had noticed how restless the whole outfit was as they waited for the sheriff's release. They didn't talk about Shep, but Samantha knew his death had to be on all of their minds. Especially Roark's. The situation had him so short-tempered that he lost his patience with Dick when they rode in from the herd that afternoon and found the horse wrangler playing poker with Alex and Cappy.

"Remember how you complained when Alex and

Cappy forgot to relieve you?'' he said, his deep voice rumbling out of him. "Well, who's late now, Brewster?''

Alex and Cappy looked sheepish at being caught playing poker after this morning's tragedy. But, death or not, Dick was irrepressibly good-natured. "Sorry. I was on a winning streak here, so I guess the time got away from me.'' He must have realized he had a gloating look on his face as he collected those winnings and got to his feet, because he added quickly, "I'm not keeping the money. I'm going to turn it over to Shep's widow.''

Samantha had the feeling his intention was an inspiration of the moment. Nor did Cappy trust his sudden generosity, observing sourly, "That ain't no sacrifice, cowboy. Just about everybody knows you always been partial to her.''

"Shut up, old man.'' Jamming his Stetson on his head, Dick ambled off to saddle his horse and head out to the longhorns.

Since the meadows on the other side of the rise offered ample grazing, the drovers had determined that for now only one of them at a time needed to ride vigil with the contented herd. With the exception of Roark, Samantha thought. Like it or not, where he goes I go.

At the moment Roark was going nowhere. He stood there and watched Dick's departure with a frown on his face. When the horse wrangler was out of sight, he turned that frown in another direction, his gaze sweeping over the area of the camp.

"Where's Ernie?'' he demanded.

Alex and Cappy looked around, puzzled expressions on their faces. "Gee, I don't know,'' Alex said. "We were so busy losing to Dick we didn't notice. He must be around somewhere.''

"His things aren't over there where he had them by that tree,'' Samantha observed softly to Roark.

"I don't see his horse, either.'' They exchanged meaningful looks. Roark spoke again to Alex. "What about Ramona? Where is she?"

"She was here a minute ago asking us if we wanted coffee."

"Think she must have gone back to the chuck wagon," Cappy added with his usual lack of concern.

The back end of the cook truck faced them on the other side of the camp, its door wide-open. But there was no sign of Ramona there.

No longer hesitating, Roark strode across the camp and around the rear of the truck to its other side, Samantha close behind him. The ancient vehicle was parked with its nose in the direction of the canyon below the hill. They didn't see Ramona until they reached the gap where the driver's door should have been. Ramona had said she preferred the door missing. Open like that, it reminded her of a genuine, old-time chuck wagon.

She was seated behind the wheel of the pickup, an unfamiliar sight in her idleness as she gazed toward the canyon where Shep had lost his life. There was an expression on her face that made Samantha think immediately of her moody son. She paid no attention to their arrival.

"Ernie is missing," Roark announced. Ramona offered no comment. "He's gone, hasn't he? Taken his things and cleared out."

The woman turned her head then and considered them. "Has he?"

"You know he has. Damn it, Ramona, you should have stopped him."

"Why?" she said, her voice animated now with anger as she came swiftly to the defense of her son. "So he could hang around and wait to be arrested when that sheriff gets back?"

"No one has accused him of anything. Why should he be charged, unless— Ramona, do you know something you're not telling us? Maybe something connected with Shep's death?"

"Don't say that! I won't listen to you say it!"

"Then why did Ernie leave?"

"Because when anything goes wrong, he's everyone's favorite suspect. That's how it's always been. I don't want to talk about it anymore. Go away."

Roark looked like he wasn't going to give up, that he intended to question her further. But it was obvious to Samantha that Ramona was hurting and wanted to be alone with her grief. Samantha placed a hand on Roark's arm, signaling their need to retreat with an insistent squeeze of his hard muscles. Understanding her message, he held his tongue.

They left Ramona in the cook truck. Samantha waited until they were out of earshot before she expressed her concern. "Was she telling us the truth? Did Ernie run away because he was afraid he might end up being blamed for Shep's death? Or is Ramona unhappy because she knows her son *is* guilty of everything that's gone wrong on this drive?"

Samantha had a sudden memory of the understanding glances mother and son had shared this morning on the rim of the canyon. It was followed by another memory of a much earlier episode. An unpleasant recollection of that night back at the Morning Star Ranch when Ramona had wandered off in search of an elusive nightjar, leaving Samantha alone in the darkness. An innocent desertion? Or a deliberate action that had left Samantha vulnerable to the enemy?

It was an ugly thought, and she couldn't bring herself to voice it.

"Speculations," Roark answered her. "And none of them are worth a damn. But if Shep was innocent, that leaves only Ernie Chacon with a motive. Or at least the only motive we know of. No one else seems to have anything to gain by eliminating you from the race. And if Ramona is unwilling, or unable, to provide us with answers, then maybe…"

Samantha watched him decisively remove the cell phone from his belt. Seconds later she listened to him as he instructed his assistant back in Texas.

"Wendell, I know you're already working your tail off, but you've got to dig deeper. If there's anything more on Ernie Chacon, I need you to turn it up for me. Concentrate on Purgatory and that Western Museum. I think we're missing something there. And don't forget to keep asking around about the others in our outfit. Yeah, as soon as possible."

"What do you expect Wendell to learn about Ernie that we don't already know?" Samantha asked after Roark ended the call and restored the phone to its clip.

"Maybe exactly how dangerous he is. Or, for that matter, how dangerous any one of the others might be on this drive. And how desperate. Wendell's findings wouldn't be conclusive, but they could be one more piece in the puzzle. And we need those pieces, Samantha. We need to understand just what direction the trouble is coming from and why, because, come hell or high water, I mean to see you safe when I deliver you and those cattle to Alamo Junction."

There was a steely determination in his voice and direct blue eyes that heartened her. And twisted her insides as, not for the first time, she wished Roark Hawke was anything but a man linked so strongly in her mind with her grandfather and all he had represented...and all she despised.

LAZY AND PEACEFUL. That was the climate of the drovers' camp. Dick was still out with the herd, Cappy and Alex stretched flat and dozing, their hats over their faces to shield them from the sun. Ramona, though tight-lipped and silent, was occupied over at the cook truck with preparations for supper.

Roark knew this image was an illusion, that beneath the

relaxed attitudes was a tension as they waited for an outcome from the sheriff.

He was experiencing a tension of his own as he perched
on the enormous trunk of a fallen cottonwood, though he
was careful to conceal it with his long legs stretched out
casually in front of him, hands idle in his jeans pockets,
Stetson shoved to the back of his head. His tension had
nothing to do with the sheriff.

Samantha, hair freshly washed and rubbed dry with a
towel, was seated a few feet away from him on a camp
stool, dragging a brush through the chestnut masses. The
sight of her tumbled hair gleaming in the sun brought
memories of that night and morning in the canyon with
the ruins. Memories of how her hair had spilled loose from
her braid, permitting him to sift his fingers through its silky
length, to bury his face in its scented thickness.

There was another scent he recalled. A womanly scent
that had driven him wild with desire, and taunted him now
as the images of that night flooded his mind. His mouth
powerfully suckling her breasts while she mewed her pleasure. His finger circling through the nest of hair at the
juncture of her parted thighs, then dipping inside her hot,
moist center. And his own arousal, bigger and harder than
it had ever been before, sinking into her deeply and, with
long, frenzied strokes, bringing her to a shattering release.

Suppressing a groan, Roark felt his groin tighten as
those memories surged through him. All he could think
about, all he wanted was Samantha under him again, her
alluring body out of control.

*This is no good, Hawke. Your going crazy like this is
only going to make things worse.*

But how much tougher could they get? He had been
suffering every hell since their time in the canyon, knowing that what had happened between them couldn't happen
again. Knowing that when this blasted cattle drive was
over, he had to let her go. That there could be no future

for them, not when she hated everything he loved and valued.

After her encounter with Shep yesterday, he had dragged her behind the fir tree beside the path from the canyon and kissed her. Unable to help himself, he had kissed her with a ferocity that had shocked both of them. Whether Samantha knew it or not, that kiss hadn't been an expression of his anger but of his frustration. The same frustration he was experiencing now and had been experiencing ever since they had ridden away from that other canyon.

God Almighty, how could he go and fall for a woman who wanted no part of ranching?

Fall?

And that was when it struck him like a hard blow in the gut. He had been determined all along to keep her safe. But somewhere on the long drive that resolve had altered, becoming a fierce need to protect her with his life if necessary. Becoming vital because she was so vital to him now. He was in love with Samantha.

And where is that going to get you, Hawke? Because choosing private investigation over ranching just to win her is not fair to either of you. If it's not an honest choice, then both of you lose in the end.

But it didn't have to be that way. Did it? Hell, no. There had to be a solution. If she felt anything like what he was feeling, they ought to be able to sort it out. It was time to find out.

Drawing up his legs, he hunched forward with his arms braced on his spread knees. "Samantha, we have to talk." He'd meant to be gentle about it, yet somehow his voice came out harsh.

His abruptness startled her. The brush in her hand froze in midair. She stared at him for a moment before asking simply, "About?"

"Us. This thing between us. It isn't going to go away. We have to deal with it."

She lowered the hairbrush and laid it in her lap. "I'm

listening,'' she said quietly. But there was a sudden wariness in her soft brown eyes.

''What happened that night in the canyon meant something. For both of us, I'd say. And we should have talked about it then, but we didn't. I don't know, maybe the idea of us was something we both needed to get used to. Only now, with the cattle drive winding down, the time is running out. So what happens to us after Alamo Junction?''

That wary look had now become an expression approaching fear. ''Are you saying—'' She paused to run the tip of her tongue over her lower lip, an action that made him ache. ''What are you saying, Roark?''

This wasn't easy for him, either. He struggled with it. ''It's tearing us up inside, isn't it, Samantha? What we feel for each other is tearing us up.''

''I don't know what I feel for you,'' she said evasively.

''Damn it, I think you do.'' Removing his hat and tossing it to the ground, he plowed a hand through his hair and leaned toward her earnestly. ''I think we both know, like it or not, that we've fallen in love with each other. And if we haven't, we're a long way down the road to it.''

Her fear had become outright panic now. ''I can't do this,'' she said, looking as if she was ready to bolt.

But Roark wouldn't let her run away. ''Why?'' he demanded.

''You know why.'' She caught the lobe of her right ear between her fingers and began tugging at it furiously.

''I want to hear you say it. I want you to tell me you don't love me.''

''I can't be in love with you. I *won't* be. Not with a man who's ready to throw everything away to bury himself on a ranch with cattle and horses. And you are, aren't you?''

''Maybe. Probably.''

''Not with another cowboy,'' she said, the alarm growing in her voice.

''Hank Barrie,'' he said, unable to help his sudden anger. "That's what it's all about, isn't it? What it's been about all along, your hatred of your grandfather and everything connected with his world, the suffering you've lived with since Barrie's death."

"I thought you understood. I thought when I told you everything that night—"

"Oh, I understand all right." There was hurt in her eyes, but Roark didn't let that stop him. He had been holding back long enough. It was time she learned the truth about her Hank Barrie. "It's you who doesn't understand, Samantha. Who needs to hear she's been grieving for a man who wasn't entitled to her grief."

"You don't know—"

"What? That the guy was a bastard who never deserved you? Because he was, Samantha. That's right, your Hank Barrie was no stranger to me. Why should that surprise you? The rodeo circuit is a pretty tight scene. And if you're any part of that scene, even for a few months like I was, then sooner or later you encounter everyone else related to it. As I did, in a Wyoming bar the night before he died."

"Don't," she whispered, begging him not to go on.

Roark ignored her plea, his anger fueled by Samantha's image of her pure and innocent young cowboy. A lie that had been gnawing at him ever since their night in the canyon.

"Your Barrie was a lesson to me, Samantha. I saw what could happen to a man's ego after he won a few purses. The glory went right to his head. He was wallowing in it, swaggering over the attention all the rodeo groupies were lavishing on him. He had a redhead with him. His latest girl, they said, laughing because he had slept with all of them and boasted about it. You didn't know about that, did you, Samantha? You didn't know about all the drinking, either."

"It isn't true."

"Yeah, it is true. It was the drinking that cost him his life the next day in that competition. He died because he was no longer sure and steady. That was your Hank Barrie, Samantha. A drunk and a lecher who cheated on you. How many years have you been mourning him and blaming your grandfather—and all he stood for—for taking him away from you?''

Samantha was silent, staring at him with a stricken expression on her face. It was only then that Roark realized what he had done. And hated himself for it. He had wounded her. Wounded her cruelly by robbing her of the memory of a sweet and gentle lover. It didn't matter the man who was the focus of that memory had never really existed in this form, had in fact betrayed her without remorse. And though she might accept the reality of Hank Barrie now, she would never forgive Roark for confronting her with it.

He had risked a gamble and failed. Samantha could never be his, and he would have to live with that loss for the rest of his life.

IT WAS AFTER SUNDOWN before the outfit learned of the decision about Shep's death. Sheriff Wilkins sent one of his young deputies to their camp, an indication in itself that his office entertained no serious suspicions.

"Alcohol," the deputy informed them. "Medical examiner detected a high enough level in his bloodstream to determine that, in his opinion, the cause of death was an accident. No evidence of any injury other than the result of his fall into the canyon. There'll be the formality of a coroner's inquest sometime in the near future, but until then—"

"That mean we're free to go?" Cappy barked.

"No reason to detain you, not when you've got those cattle to move."

"What about this here inquest?"

"It probably won't be necessary for any of you to appear, but you should be available if you're called. I'll need addresses from all of you. Oh, and we should settle on arrangements for the body to be shipped back to Texas.''

He wrote their addresses in his notebook and never seemed aware that one of their company was missing. Anxious to be underway again, none of them mentioned Ernie Chacon's absence.

The deputy took Roark aside. ''Police photographer asked me to give you this,'' he said, handing Roark an envelope. ''I don't know what's inside, and I don't want to know.''

Which meant, Roark thought, that Sheriff Wilkins wouldn't have approved of this action. He accepted the photographs, hoping that when he had a chance to study them, they would offer him some truth about Shep's death. He and Samantha had revisited the scene this afternoon before their quarrel, and although he had searched the area carefully, he'd found nothing. All he could do now was move on with the cattle while making every effort to protect Samantha.

And that, he knew, meant keeping her at his side, which wasn't going to be easy considering how she felt about him now. Because, although physically she'd continued throughout the afternoon to stay as close to him as he had earlier commanded, emotionally she was as far away from him as it was possible to get.

Lost in his black mood, it took Roark a moment to realize that the others were gathered around and gazing at him expectantly. They were looking for direction from him, just as they had this morning. The outfit clearly regarded him as their new trail boss. Roark accepted this, realizing that safeguarding Samantha might be easier if he was in control. It was time to get practical.

''If any of you have decided you've had enough, now is the time to say it.''

Cappy sniffed in disdain. ''And do what? Just walk away and abandon the cows?''

The others were silent, but none of them indicated a desire to quit the drive.

"This isn't going to be easy, folks," Roark cautioned them. "We're two men short, we have to reach those stock cars the day after tomorrow, and we have another rough stretch of country between here and Alamo Junction." He had already ascertained this from having consulted the maps and detailed notes Shep had left behind. "But I think if we push hard enough, we can still make that deadline."

No one raised an objection.

"Good. Then in the morning at first light we move long-horns."

When he and Samantha were alone again, Roark snatched a few moments to look at the photos the police photographer had shot. None of them produced a result. He wasn't giving up. He would study them more carefully when he had better light and more time.

He and Samantha turned in early that night along with the others who anticipated tomorrow's challenges. But sleep eluded him. Among all his concerns, Samantha chief among them, was a nagging uneasiness about the ravine back at the Walking W.

He continued to sense the explanation to everything was somewhere in that ravine and that it must be connected with the caves there. At the same time, something didn't feel altogether right about it. But no matter what angle he examined it from, he couldn't imagine what it might be.

HE WAS DESPERATE. His every effort to destroy the cattle drive, to keep Samantha Howard from winning the Walker ranch, had been defeated by her and that damn Hawke. He could feel the time running out, the prize slipping away from him. *No.* He couldn't permit that. *Wouldn't* permit it. Not now, when he was so close. He had to stop her, needed to find another way. Two days. He had two days left, and somehow, somewhere between here and Alamo Junction...

Chapter Twelve

Roark was in a foul mood. He had every reason to be, didn't he? Damn right he did.

The beleaguered cattle drive alone entitled him to bad humor. What with a terrain even more rugged than he'd expected, the clock ticking on that deadline and a shrunken outfit that frayed tempers over the increased workload, the problems never seemed to quit. Starting with the cook truck.

"If my chuck wagon stays, then I stay with it," Ramona stubbornly insisted when Roark had suggested they temporarily abandon the pickup, arguing that the trail ahead of them was too difficult for it and that they could pack enough food supplies for two days on the horses.

Roark had relented in the end, not wanting to leave Ramona behind, especially with her son a loose cannon somewhere out there in the wilderness. In fact, he intended to keep both her and the rest of the outfit at close range at all times. So the battered cook truck with its missing driver's door—or, as Dick began to call it, the Doorless Wonder—went with them. But the vehicle was a pain in the backside, especially on the tough grades they frequently encountered.

And then there was the worry of Ernie Chacon himself. Was he gone for good or shadowing them again? Although Roark maintained a constant vigilance, he never spotted any sign of Ernie. But his concern intensified when Wendell reached him on his cell phone late in the afternoon of their first day back with the herd.

"Chacon may not have a record in Purgatory like he does in Austin," Wendell reported, "but that's only because charges weren't pressed. I found out from talking to the desk clerk at the Western Museum that Ernie assaulted the guy when he refused to let him in to see the director."

It was clear by now that Ernie had an obsession about his father. One sufficient enough, Roark wondered, to make him willing to go to any lengths to please the man? Even kill to win his recognition? It was a chilling possibility, especially since Roark had had another opportunity to examine those police photographs. This time something registered with him about one of the three books taken from his saddlebag.

The first book, of course, had been shredded along the path to the canyon rim. The second had landed on its spine several feet away from Shep's body. The third had ended up by Shep's arm. Or, to be exact about it, lying at an angle across the top of his arm. But if it had fallen with him into the canyon, maybe while he still clutched it, it should have landed *under* his arm. Even if he had released it in his fall, it should have ended up under him or beside him, not on top. To Roark, it was an indication the book had been thrown into the canyon after Shep. Nothing conclusive, certainly, but enough to go back to Sheriff Wilkins after the cattle were delivered and convince him to reopen his investigation.

Meanwhile, Roark knew he couldn't relax his guard for a millisecond. Maybe Ernie wasn't a murderer, but someone was, although Wendell had been unable so far to learn anything incriminating about the others in the outfit.

Roark had no better luck with the new batch of photographs he collected from Willow Creek's copy center that evening. Wendell had dutifully shot every wall throughout the length of the ravine, many of them at close range, including those in the caves, but Roark was unable to spot anything unusual. Either the ravine had no secret to reveal, or he wasn't seeing it. Still, there was something about the photos that bothered him, something that added to his frustration.

But who was he kidding? It wasn't the ravine, the tensions of the drive, a potentially explosive Ernie Chacon or his worries about the others in the outfit that had him in a vile mood on this morning of their second day back on the trail. The woman who rode close beside him at his insistence was responsible for that.

Samantha had barely spoken to him since he had told her the truth about Hank Barrie. She was unfailingly polite, responded whenever it was necessary, and remained as cool and detached as their proximity would permit, rejecting any of his efforts to discuss their conflict. And with the two of them practically joined at the hip, and her enticing presence bombarding his senses, Roark was miserable.

He didn't know whether to be relieved or reluctant when, soon after midday, they reached the high, stony ridge that put them within sight of their destination.

Just on its other side was a dry bowl into which the first of the cattle, led by Cappy, were already pouring. At its far end, the curving trail lost itself in an expanse of evergreen forest that blanketed the mountainside. They would climb that trail up through the pass that was their last barrier. Alamo Junction waited down on the other side. It was almost over. The cattle drive would end at the stock cars, and Samantha, having qualified for her inheritance, could walk away from him and never look back.

Knowing he would go crazy if he thought about that, Roark turned to more practical matters. "I wish we could stop long enough down there to find water for them," he said to Dick, who had joined him on the flank of the ridge, "but I don't want to risk it. The contract specifies that we have the herd at the rail line before five o'clock, and while we still have more than enough time to make it, that pass won't be—''

He was interrupted by the insistent blare of a horn several yards below them.

Dick grinned. ''The Doorless Wonder is calling you.''

Exasperated, Roark cursed under his breath. That damn truck again! Though Ramona had refused to leave it behind, she was nervous about the steeper slopes, and this one was no exception. Picking his way with care on his mount back down the gravelly surface of the incline, he joined Ramona, who had emerged from the truck midway on the side of the ridge.

''I'm sorry, Roark. She stalled on me, and I can't get her started again. I guess the grade is just too much of a challenge for her.''

''Leave the truck where it is. We'll take care of it after we get the rest of the cattle over the ridge.''

The herd was as resistant as the truck about crossing the rocky ridge. The next several minutes were a melee of scrambling, bawling cattle, clouds of dust and shouting drovers. Roark, along with the others, found himself dashing in and out of the turmoil, calling orders in an effort to urge the cows up and over the ridge.

When the last of them were streaming to the top and down the other side, Roark turned back to deal with the truck. And found his heart leaping out of his chest. The truck was on the move, rolling slowly backward down the incline. And directly in its path at the bottom was Samantha arguing with the obstinate Irma, who refused to climb the ridge with the others.

''Samantha!'' he yelled.

She didn't hear him in all the noise and confusion. Didn't even look up. His heart doing a somersault now, Roark raced for the runaway truck.

He didn't have time to wonder if Ramona had neglected to set the emergency brake, which seemed unlikely, or whether the cattle swarming around the truck, shoving against its sides, had somehow caused a release of the brake. All he knew was that he had to stop the truck.

The vehicle was beginning to gather speed on its descent when Roark reached it, flung himself from his horse, and managed to dive through the doorless opening and behind the wheel. But not in time. Just as his foot started to stomp on the brake, the pickup lurched sharply, its back wheel striking what must have been a large rock.

The jolt was so sudden and so hard that Roark felt the top-heavy truck begin to topple over in the direction of the driver's side. Without a door or a seat belt, he knew he faced serious injury by remaining at the wheel. Dimly aware of a woman's alarmed cry, he threw himself out of the cab in an effort to save himself.

His body twisted, landing him on his backside. Scrabbling frantically, he managed to get clear of the rapidly descending truck. All but his right leg. There was the sound of metal grinding against rock, a spasm of pain somewhere above his knee, and then a silence.

When his shock ebbed, Roark realized that the truck was on its side, roof facing him and his leg pinned beneath the stout door frame at the top of the cab. By this time he could hear the shouts of Samantha and Ramona as they clambered up the hill.

Samantha was the first to reach him, a sob in her voice as she knelt beside him. "Dear God, your leg! It's—"

"Not crushed," he assured her quickly. "At least I don't think it's that bad. There's a dip in this band of rock where it's caught, and that saved me."

Alex, arriving on the scene, crouched down on the other side of him. "Can you move it?" he asked.

Roark tried to withdraw the leg trapped down in the narrow depression across which the top of the pickup had squarely landed, sucking in his breath at the pain his exertion cost him. "It's no use. I'm locked in here good and tight."

"What if we tried to dig you out?"

"It's solid rock, man. We'd need tools we don't have. Look, go get Dick. Maybe the four of you heaving together can raise the damn thing just high enough for me to scramble out of here."

Alex rose to his feet and ran to his horse. Within seconds, he was in the saddle and urging his mount toward the top of the ridge.

"Ramona," Roark instructed her, "see what you can do about clearing out your pantry. Lightening the load should help."

Ramona hurried around the fallen pickup where Roark heard her tugging at the door of the camper unit. Samantha continued to huddle beside him, her eyes registering her concern.

"It's all right," he tried to assure her. "It hurt like hell for a minute, but as long as I don't try to move it, it's okay."

There were thuds and bangs from the back of the pickup, and then Ramona rejoined them. "The door won't open. It's jammed shut. Roark, I'm sorry about this. I guess you were right. The truck should have stayed behind."

"Forget it. What's done is done. Ramona, you did set the brake before you left the truck, didn't you?"

"Absolutely. I can't imagine why it rolled like that."

Roark could. Either it had been an accident, the result of a steer slamming against the vehicle as he had earlier supposed, or else in all the commotion someone had—

He didn't have a chance to pursue his suspicion. Alex had returned, accompanied by Dick. The two men, together with the women, spent long minutes making every effort to either lift or rock the truck the necessary few inches Roark needed to drag his leg free. But no amount of straining budged the vehicle.

"She's wedged in here good," Dick complained.

"Maybe if we got Cappy," Alex suggested.

"Leave him with the herd," Roark said, knowing that

Cappy would make no difference. The vintage pickup had been made in the days when they used plenty of steel. Thick, *heavy* steel. "It's going to take machinery to raise her."

"There was a small ranch we passed a couple of miles back down the trail," Dick said. "And ranches have tractors."

"All right," Roark agreed, knowing there was no other choice.

And, meanwhile, he thought, turning his head to watch Dick bolt into the saddle and gallop off in the direction of the ranch, I'm stuck here and useless. He swore under his breath.

Samantha, who was crouched down again close by his side, heard his curses and misunderstood them. "Is your leg bothering you very much? Can you tell if there's bleeding?"

"The leg is going to be okay, once I manage to get it out. I can move it now under there from the knee down with barely an ache. Trouble is, I'm not going to be able to get it out until that tractor is here, and tractors move like snails." Frustrated, he was unable to prevent the bitterness in his voice. "And by that time, it's probably going to be too late to move the herd over the pass. It looks like the cattle drive ends here."

"Don't worry about that," Samantha said. "It's not important."

But he noticed her gaze drift in the direction of the pass that had to be crossed. There was both longing and regret in her expression. He knew she was wishing it didn't have to end here, that there was some way she could finish the drive. He knew he was failing her in his helplessness, and that made him angry.

"It *is* important to you," he growled. "It's always been the damn money, hasn't it? Sometimes I think that inheritance is more important than your own life."

She stared at him, stung by his accusation. His blazing

anger had been unreasonable, unfair. Roark was instantly contrite. "I'm sorry," he said. "You didn't deserve that."

"No, I didn't," she said, and he knew she was disappointed in him.

"Look," he said, trying to understand her own frustration, "I'm sorry it has to end like this, that you have to lose the inheritance."

"It isn't just that."

"It's proving yourself, huh? Hell, Samantha, you've already done that. You've managed to do it with every mile of this drive."

She nodded, but he could see she wasn't convinced. That his admiration for all the courage and resolve she'd demonstrated throughout each day of the difficult drive wasn't enough. But it was useless to argue with her about it. In any case, Cappy had appeared on his horse. An unhappy Cappy, who wasted no words of sympathy on Roark's plight.

"In case you've all forgotten," he reminded them around the wad of tobacco in his cheek, "there's a herd of longhorns on the other side of this here ridge, and they're growin' restless. *Real* restless. You don't want to lose them cows, then I need help to hold 'em."

Even with the ridge between him and the herd, Roark could hear the cattle bawling, expressing their discontent at being held so long in a tight place. He knew Cappy was right. And though he might be trapped under the Doorless Wonder, he was still the trail boss.

"Alex, there's nothing more you can do here. Go with him and take that fool heifer with you."

"I said *restless*," Cappy repeated with emphasis, gazing pointedly in Samantha's direction to indicate he needed more than one drover to effectively control the nervous cows.

"Uh-uh, no way. Samantha stays here." He glanced at Ramona, but she shook her head vigorously.

"Forget it, I don't ride, remember?"

"I'll go," Samantha said quietly, getting to her feet.

"Samantha, no."

"There's no reason for me not to help," she insisted. "It isn't as if I'll be in any danger, not with Alex and Cappy right there close by."

Damn it, why couldn't she understand that he didn't want to risk her in any situation, even with him helpless like this to adequately safeguard her? There was always the chance that Ernie Chacon might be out there somewhere. Ernie, who was their prime suspect and, for all he knew, was just waiting to strike at the first opportunity. Or, if not Ernie, who was still not a certainty, that one of the others could—

"Somebody needs to make up his mind here," Cappy said impatiently, "before we have us another stampede on our hands."

Roark made a fast decision. "All right," he reluctantly agreed, "but you go no farther than the top of the ridge where I can keep you in sight. You'll be able to stop any cow up there from straying back over the hill. Let Cappy and Alex handle them down below."

There was an advantage in having Samantha in that position. There would be no surprises, no enemy, either Ernie or anyone else, able to sneak up on her since the top of the ridge would permit her a view of the open country on all sides.

"You keep a sharp watch in every direction," he added.

She nodded, the meaning of his caution apparently clear to her. Roark, intending for her to take his pistol, started to reach for the weapon in his holster. She stopped him. "No gun. I wouldn't know how to use it."

He'd feel better if she had the gun with her, but he could see she wanted no part of it. There was something else he saw as she stood there looking down at him, torn at the last moment by whether to leave him or to remain at his side. All of her anger with him since he'd told her about Hank Barrie had been set aside in this crisis. But not forgotten, he knew. The issues between them were still there and would have to wait to be sorted out. If ever, he thought dismally.

Ramona, understanding Samantha's hesitation, offered her a hasty comfort. "Don't worry. I'll stick right here by him."

Alex had fetched her horse and Irma from below. Seconds later, she was in the saddle and following Cappy, Alex and the heifer up the slope. Sensing how anxious he was about Samantha, Ramona squatted down at Roark's side and tried to distract him.

"Dick won't give up until he finds a tractor. We'll soon have you out." She paused. "Roark?"

"Yeah?"

"I know the cook truck shouldn't have come with us on this last part of the drive. But I wasn't just being obstinate. I had a reason. I was planning to fix us a special dinner when we got to Alamo Junction, a surprise to celebrate the end of the drive, and I needed the truck for that. But now, of course..."

Roark scarcely listened to her. His attention was focused on the crest of the ridge where Samantha was stationed on Dolly, her back to him as she kept watch over the cattle.

"It's Ernie, isn't it?" Ramona said solemnly. "That's what you're so worried about. That Ernie will come back and try something. But he won't. He's far away by now."

"How do you know that?"

"Because he told me when he left he was going back to Texas. He was scared he'd end up being blamed for Shep."

"And you believed him?"

"He isn't bad, Roark. Not the kind of bad everyone thinks. He's just confused and unhappy."

"Ramona, your son has an explosive temper. Look at the way he was always turning on Alex."

"But he secretly admires Alex. No, it's true. Oh, I know the two of them were always scrapping, but Ernie confided to me he wished he could be more like Alex, because Alex wasn't defeated by his failure. He put it behind him, came home to Purgatory, and helped to run the family ranch. And never once was he bitter about being dropped from the program at the university."

What was she talking about? Roark wondered, only half-listening to her while keeping his eye on the figure of Samantha several hundred yards above him. If he hadn't felt sorry for Ramona, recognized her need to talk about her son, he wouldn't have paid any attention at all to her argument on his behalf.

"Not that Alex ever talked about it to anyone in Purgatory," Ramona explained. "Ernie only heard about it because of the two of them living up in Austin at the same time. Anyway, Ernie envies Alex for making the best of it when what he really wanted was to get his doctor's degree and be a successful— I don't know what you call it— that thing with animal bones."

His curiosity stirring for the first time, Roark turned his gaze on Ramona. "You mean husbandry?" That would make sense, considering Alex's background in ranching.

"Not that. Extinct animals. You know, dinosaurs. Oh, what do they call it?"

"Paleontology." She had his full attention now. "Ramona, are you sure of this? That Alex is a disappointed paleontologist?"

"That's what Ernie said. Why? Does it matter?"

Roark was suddenly afraid that it could matter a great deal. A slow flame of suspicion had begun to curl deep inside him as his PI instincts kicked in. A searing possibility that, if he was right, had all the potential of a blazing revelation. But *was* it possible? Was this the explanation for everything, including the mystery of the ravine back at the Walking W Ranch?

"Ramona, listen to me. This could be important. Where's my horse?"

"Down there, tied to a sapling where Alex put him when he went to get Samantha's horse and the heifer."

"I want you to go down there and bring something back to me. You'll find it in my saddlebag. A thick brown envelope with photographs inside. Hurry."

He could see Ramona was mystified by his urgent request, but thankfully she didn't question him. Getting to her feet, she trotted off down the hill.

Samantha, he thought when she was gone. He had to get Samantha back here at his side. There was perhaps no solid reason for the anxiety gnawing at him. It was, after all, only a suspicion, not a certainty. Maybe even an improbable one. But if the threat was real, the danger to her this close…

She was still up there alone on the narrow spine of the ridge. Lifting his head from the ground, Roark called to her.

She didn't hear him, didn't turn in the saddle to look his way. Either she was too far away, or, more likely, the bellowing of the cattle drowned out his shouts. He couldn't go to her. He was pinned here under the truck. Seething now with frustration.

Ramona. What was keeping Ramona?

THE LONGHORNS WERE still noisy but less restless now that Alex and Cappy had circled the herd from opposite directions, making efforts to settle them down.

They don't like being bunched up like this, Samantha thought. Not after the open trail.

She had headed off one straggler, turning the cow back down into the hollow, but otherwise she had been idle. Nothing to do but sit up here in the saddle, one hand resting lightly on the pommel while she worried about Roark. And tried, without success, to keep her gaze from wandering again and again to that fold between the mountains.

"Alamo Junction, huh?"

The voice was understanding, sympathetic. Alex's

voice. Samantha lowered her gaze to find him just below her on the flank of the ridge. Cappy was with him, both men astride their horses. She realized there must have been a yearning expression on her face, easy to read, as she looked off toward the pass.

"Poor Sam," Alex said. "It's got to be tough on you, having to give up like this when everything you've worked so hard for is just over there on the other side."

"I call it a damn shame," Cappy concurred in his gravelly voice. "Here we come all this way and get this close, then end up just throwing it away."

Samantha shook her head. "It can't be helped."

"Well," Alex said slowly, "maybe it can."

She looked down on him sharply. "What are you saying?"

He shrugged. "Only that we could still do it. There's enough time if we left right now."

"You mean just the three of us driving the whole herd? Alex, that's impossible."

"Maybe out in open country, yeah. But not over a mountain pass with a trail too narrow for the herd to bulge. See, we don't need anyone riding flank, and with, say, Cappy riding point, and you and me riding drag…sure, the three of us could manage it."

"Boy's right," Cappy spoke up. "Hell, it's only a few miles."

"I can't," Samantha said.

Alex nodded. "Because of Roark, you mean. No, I guess you couldn't leave him."

"Don't know why not," Cappy barked. "He's gonna be all right, ain't he? Nothing you can do for him anyway until Dick gets back with that tractor. Huh, by then we'll probably have delivered the cows. Maybe be back here before we're even missed."

It was a temptation. Alex and Cappy couldn't know just how much of a temptation. The chance to prove herself, to defeat those last, lingering fears of everything connected to her grandfather's world. The uncertainties about herself that had troubled her all her life. Oh, yes, she knew what Roark had tried to tell her. That she had already demonstrated her worth on the trail, overcome all the obstacles. But she hadn't. She needed to complete the drive, to achieve this last victory. And, yes, she also needed that inheritance.

Danger. Roark was worried about the danger. But Alex and Cappy would be with her. She trusted Alex. Alex wouldn't let anything happen to her.

No, she couldn't do it. Desert Roark when he was trapped down there? What was she thinking?

Twisting around in the saddle, she looked below her at the fallen truck. Ramona was there with Roark, watching over him, caring for him. A movement caught her attention. She lifted her gaze and saw in the distance the figure of Dick approaching on horseback. A tractor crawled just behind him. Help was on its way.

"So," Cappy called up to her from his side of the ridge, "are we doing this or aren't we?"

Alex glanced from Samantha to Cappy, looking indecisive now. "Maybe we shouldn't, Cappy. If Roark knew—"

"Well, he don't know, does he?"

"But he'd forbid it."

Alex couldn't know it, but he had just issued a challenge Samantha couldn't resist. From the day she had left her grandfather and his ranch, she had refused to let any man control her. Even one as stalwart as Roark Hawke.

"We're wasting time," she said, making up her mind. "Let's go."

Heels in Dolly's flanks, she and the horse surged forward, cantering down the hill to the waiting herd. Determined now but unable to silence her pangs of guilt.

Forgive me, Roark, but I have to do this. It's the only way.

Chapter Thirteen

Roark was on fire with impatience by the time Ramona arrived back at his side.

"Sorry," she apologized. "It took me a few minutes to find it. You have an awful lot stuffed in that bag."

Murmuring his thanks as he snatched the envelope from her hand, he checked again on Samantha. She was still up there alone on the top of the ridge, back to him. Maybe he was wrong about his suspicion. Maybe he was overreacting, and the photographs would tell him nothing.

Tearing into the envelope as a puzzled Ramona hovered over him, he removed the packet of the latest photos Wendell had shot of the ravine's walls. He went through them rapidly, dismissing most of them as being of little interest to anyone but a geologist. Nothing. He could find nothing. Unless…

He went through them again, selecting two photographs that Wendell had labeled as the face of the wall about fifteen feet above the floor of the ravine. Separately, they meant nothing, but when he lined them up, placing one close above the other—

This was it! The images that had nagged at him when he had examined them earlier, but which had escaped his understanding until the two halves were put together to form a whole! He had the full picture now!

To a casual observer in the ravine, it would mean nothing. But to someone professional, it would be a startling find. Even Roark's untrained eye, now that he knew what to look for, could make it out—ridges of rock suggesting rib bones, the shape of a large head with an eye socket. Faint, but there. A Tyrannosaurus rex? Looked like it.

This was the secret of the ravine. Not ancient artifacts in caves but something far older than that embedded high in the walls of the ravine and overlooked by all but one man. Dinosaur fossils, possibly even a rare complete skeleton among them. Fossils that somehow had been discovered in that remote ravine by a failed paleontologist who had recognized their immense worth and been willing to go to any lengths to safeguard his trove.

All the while the explanation had been right here, but until Ramona had triggered Roark's attention in this direction—

He stopped, staggered by the realization that Samantha was vulnerable. Alex McKenzie, who must have managed to release that brake when no one was looking, hoping the truck would strike Samantha down. She was up there with the little bastard close by, not knowing, trusting him. Because Alex was a friend who'd once had a crush on her.

Thrusting the photographs to one side, Roark elevated himself on his elbows, his gaze shifting frantically to the top of the ridge. His heart dropped like a stone. Samantha was nowhere in sight. It couldn't have taken him more than two minutes to make sense of those photos, but in that brief time she had disappeared.

"Samantha," he rasped. "Where did she go?"

But Ramona had been watching him, not the ridge. "I don't know. Probably down to the herd. Roark, what is it? What's wrong?"

There was no time to explain. He had to get Samantha away from McKenzie. "Go up there, Ramona. Find her. Tell her I need her back here. *Now.*"

Sensing his new urgency without understanding it, Ramona headed for the crest of the ridge. When she was gone, Roark cursed his helplessness again and made another effort to free himself. But all his tugging and straining earned him nothing but a fresh spasm of pain in his trapped leg. He lay back, his fists pounding the ground with the anger of his defeat.

If he lost Samantha…

The anguish of that possibility was more than he could bear.

What was taking Ramona so long? He tried not to panic, tried to realize it was a hard climb on foot to the head of the ridge. But it seemed to take forever before she scrambled back down the hill and came to him out of wind. One look at her face told him the worst.

"Gone," she reported when she could breathe again. "All three of them are gone, and the herd with them. They left only the remuda behind."

The pass, Roark realized. They had to be on their way to the pass and Alamo Junction beyond. Samantha was out there with Alex McKenzie. A desperate McKenzie who would do anything to keep her from qualifying for that inheritance. Even though there were still missing pieces to this puzzle, he just *knew* that much had to be true. And unless he could get to her in time—

"Dick is on his way," Ramona added, offering that hope. "I could see him coming from up there. And he has a tractor with him."

Tractors were slow. Agonizingly slow. This one was an eternity in reaching him. Then there was a maddening delay while Dick and the lanky young rancher who owned the machine decided on the best method for freeing him.

That established, the powerful tractor moved into place. It was equipped with a front-end loader, and when its nose had finally been positioned facing the underside of the fallen truck, Roark could hear the two men attaching chains from the loader to the stout frame of the pickup.

Dick came around to the downed side of the vehicle where Roark lay. "All right, he's ready to raise her."

Roark, too, was ready. All he needed were a few inches of clearance to withdraw his leg. Dick went back to conduct the operation while Ramona stood by to offer assistance if Roark should need it.

The tractor went to work at Dick's signal. Over its roar, Roark could hear the rattle of the chains pulling taut as the front-end loader heaved upward. Bracing himself, he listened to the grinding of metal straining at its seams and a sudden banging that sounded like the jammed camper door popping open under the pressure.

Slowly, slowly, with Dick calling out directions to the tractor's driver and Ramona admonishing all of them to be careful, the Doorless Wonder rose from the bed of rock where it had been wedged. Roark waited tensely, and when the load was finally hanging a foot or so in the air above him, he went into action, scooting himself backward on the ground until he was clear of the truck.

"He's out!" Ramona shouted.

Dick relayed the message to the driver, and the tractor roared again, lowering the load. When the pickup had been eased back to the ground, the young rancher cut the engine and joined Dick and Ramona, who were crouched beside Roark.

"It's all right," he assured them, waving them off as he lifted himself into a sitting position. "The leg is going to be fine."

He didn't know that. There was a tear in his jeans which disclosed a gash in his flesh above the knee. The blood had already caked and dried around the wound. But, injury or not, he had no intention of letting that stop him. He was going after Samantha.

"Man, you need a doctor," Dick said.

"What I need is my horse. No questions. Get him for me, will you, Dick?"

The horse wrangler and Ramona exchanged glances. "The cattle are gone," she said quietly. "Alex and Cappy and Samantha have taken them over the pass."

"Dick, I'll explain everything later. Just get my horse."
The horse wrangler offered no further resistance. He rose
and went off down the hill to fetch the roan from the sapling. The puzzled rancher offered his support, helping
Roark to his feet.

"Should you be doing this?"

"I have to," Roark said grimly. The leg hurt when he
tested it, putting weight on it. But then he wouldn't need
to put his weight on it. Not once he was in the saddle.

Come on, Dick, where are you?

While Roark hobbled around a few steps, waiting impatiently for Dick, he learned that the lanky rancher's
name was Buzz Scultz and that he would accept Roark's
thanks, but he would not accept any payment for his rescue.

Alex McKenzie, Roark kept thinking. He had to get Samantha away from him. And if that bastard touched her...

Dick finally reappeared with the roan. "I'm coming with
you," he said, mounting his own horse after seeing Roark
settled in the saddle.

Roark nodded and leaned down, handing Ramona his
cell phone. "Try to contact the nearest sheriff's office.
Buzz can probably help you with that. Tell them what's
happening and where we've gone." Gathering up the reins,
he turned to Dick with steel in his voice. "Let's ride."

THE FIRST FLAKES that drifted down from the overcast sky
were entirely unexpected. But then Samantha decided there
was no reason why she should be surprised. After all, this
was Colorado, where early snowfalls weren't unusual, especially at the higher elevations like this.

The stuff was thickening now, a heavy, wet snow that
began to cling to the ranks of the conifers that lined both
sides of the trail. Despite the warmth of her leather jacket
with its sheepskin collar and her Stetson, which shed trick-
les of melting snow, Samantha shivered in the cold air.

Alex, riding close beside her at the rear of the plodding

herd, offered his encouragement. "Don't worry. We should reach the summit of the pass in a few minutes. It's bound to improve when we descend on the other side."

Samantha wasn't worried. Poor weather or not, they were making excellent time. Nor did she question the unfamiliar quality of Alex's voice, low and soothing. She was much too busy with the thoughts that attacked her mind, whirling at her from every direction like the snow.

It was nearly here. The end of the cattle drive. She had begun the long haul with timidity and self-doubt, but she was no longer that woman. The trials of the drive had strengthened her, taught her new skills and a confidence in herself. Roark had been right about that.

The snow was coming faster now, collecting on the backs of the lumbering cattle pushing steadily forward in front of her. The boughs of the pines, laden with it, began to droop. Samantha paid it little attention. Scarcely listened to Alex at her side.

"I knew if you got this close, Sam, you wouldn't be able to give up. That even without Roark, you'd find some way to complete the drive. So in the end I made use of your need."

Roark, she thought. He had believed in her. Had helped her to believe in herself. Even to finally respect the ranching she had always feared and loathed. Why hadn't she appreciated that about him?

"Cappy just hated throwing in the towel, so I figured he would back me. All I had to do was plant the idea, and the old man would be hot for it. Which he was."

What was Alex going on about now? She wished he would just be quiet and let her sort out her confusion. The end of the drive. He was talking about the end of the drive. Why wasn't she happy about that? Happy about the new Samantha Howard? Why was she so miserable?

Because the end of the drive will mean the end of Roark and you. You'll part and go your separate ways.

Isn't that what she wanted? To be free of the temptation

of a man who valued everything she had resisted all her life? Everything that had made her unhappy.

But she wouldn't be happy without Roark. How could she be when he was everything she needed? When she couldn't bear the prospect of a future without his love?

Oh, why hadn't she understood this back at the canyon when he had told her the truth about Hank Barrie, and she had pushed him away in anger and kept him there? Never seeing that Hank was just a bittersweet memory without substance. That Roark Hawke was the only reality.

It was this reality, and the full acknowledgment of her love for him, that shook Samantha out of her reverie. She looked around with a sudden awareness of what was happening. The snow was coming faster now, a swirling curtain of white. Just off to her left, emerging from the haze, was a precipice. Where had that come from?

And what did it matter? Only one thing mattered now. Roark. She neither wanted nor needed anything else. Not the inheritance, not to prove herself by pushing relentlessly on like this to Alamo Junction. They weren't important.

"I'm going back," she announced to Alex. How could she have left Roark like that under the truck, ridden away to satisfy what essentially had been a selfish motive? She was going back to him, and she'd spend the rest of her life making it up to him for her terrible error. If he let her.

"No, Sam, I can't let you do that. Not after all the trouble I went to to cut you out of the herd." Alex grinned at her, enjoying his metaphor. "See, I couldn't take the chance of Roark getting free in time to take you on to those stock cars. I needed for us to be alone."

What was he trying to tell her? Whatever it was, she realized for the first time that it wasn't innocent, that she ought to have been listening to him more carefully. Sensing that something was very wrong, she experienced both alarm and anger.

"Get out of my way!" she ordered him, intending to

turn her horse. But as she started to swing Dolly around, Alex caught the animal by its bridle, preventing her retreat.

"I hate to do this, Sam," he apologized. "You know how much I always cared for you. No, it's true. I never meant for you to be anything more than scared off, or maybe just injured enough to put you out of the running. But whatever I did, you just wouldn't give up, would you? Now I don't have any choice about it."

Samantha stared at him in shock and horror. He was a stranger suddenly. An Alex she didn't know, with a twisted mouth and a vicious gleam in a pair of eyes that had never looked at her before with anything but gentleness.

"Of course," he said, "that business with the truck was meant to hurt you, not trap Roark. But if it hadn't worked out the way it did, Roark ending up under the truck and you wanting to complete the drive, I would have just figured out some other way to stop you. I know, it's confusing, isn't it? I wish there was time to explain everything, but there isn't."

His bigger, stronger horse was crowding Dolly now, squeezing her toward the long drop at the sharp edge of the narrow trail.

"No one will ever be able to prove it was anything but an accident, Sam. Just like Shep's sad accident."

Dolly, as frightened as Samantha, tried to back away, but the larger horse blocked her escape, kept pressing them toward the precipice.

"Cappy!" Samantha screamed.

"No good, Sam. He's at the front of the herd, remember? Too far away. He wouldn't hear you, anyway. Haven't you noticed the old man's hearing is no longer what it should be?"

The snow continued to fall, making the trail slippery. As treacherous as the man who was determined to kill her. Who must have been responsible for everything—her grandfather's fall in the ravine, the rattlesnake planted in the mansion back in San Antonio, the shadow in the night

at the Morning Star Ranch, the stampede, the figure who
had shot at them in the narrow gorge, the stalker in the
fog. All of it Alex McKenzie.

An Alex who would destroy her if she didn't act. But
when she attempted evasive tactics, trying to fall back or
move ahead, he anticipated her, cutting her off. And all
the while working her toward the edge.

In desperation, she dug her heels sharply into Dolly's
side, this time surging forward, managing to break free.
But only for a moment. The herd was directly in front of
her, stopping her flight. And Alex was right behind her.

Samantha would never know if the heifer's action was
merely a result of panic or an animal obeying a primal
instinct to rescue the woman who had so often rescued
her. Whatever the explanation, Irma, who as usual was at
the tail end of the herd, twisted around and charged into
Alex's horse. Butting his mount so forcefully that it reared
back in fear, unseating its rider.

Samantha seized the opportunity to pivot Dolly and
started to race back down the trail. Too late. Springing to
his feet, Alex caught her by the leg as she passed, dragging
her from her horse.

THE SNOW IN THE PASS was blinding at times, hindering
their progress. But Roark kept telling himself that the cattle, who never moved with speed, anyway, would also be
slowed by the snowfall. He and Dick would overtake the
herd. They *had* to overtake the herd. He wouldn't let himself believe otherwise.

They were riding as hard as the slushy trail permitted,
but it wasn't fast enough for Roark. He kept urging his
horse to quicken its pace, heedless of the dangerous conditions. Heedless, too, of his injured leg, which was throbbing now. He ignored the pain. Nothing mattered but
reaching Samantha.

God, don't let him touch her. Let her stay safe until I

*can get to her. Where are you, sweetheart? Where
are you?*

They had reached the summit of the pass, and there was
still no sign of them. Straining forward in the saddle, he
peered through the snow, cursing its veil. Where were
they? He kept searching, searching for—

There!

Heart slamming against his ribs, he saw them. Samantha
and Alex were struggling on the brink of the precipice.
Obeying Roark's ferocious command, the roan leaped forward with a last burst of speed.

Roark didn't wait for Dick. Didn't wait to rein in his
horse and dismount. Reaching the scene, he launched himself from the saddle while the horse was moving. A startled
Alex, releasing Samantha, whirled around at the instant
Roark smashed into him.

The two men went down on the ground, locked in combat. But Alex was no match for Roark. Not in Roark's
fierce state of rage. The younger man landed two ineffective blows, then collapsed like a deflated balloon when
Roark delivered a furious, decisive punch to his jaw.

And then Dick was there, lariat in hand as he crouched
beside the stunned Alex. "Looks like I've got an ornery
steer here that needs lassoing," he said, busying himself
knotting the rope around Alex.

Roark got to his knees, looking around wildly for Samantha. She was there. She was all right. She came to him,
dropping to her own knees, and he reached for her, folding
her in his arms.

"Your leg," she said.

"Never felt better," he lied, because it didn't matter.
Nothing mattered but the woman in his arms. He covered
her face with feverish kisses, his nerve endings on fire with
each one of those kisses.

"I was turning around and coming back to you," she
said between their kisses.

"Were you?"

"I was. I realized that nothing would be worth anything without you. And, Roark?"

"What?" His mouth caressed her cheek, wet from the snow.

"I could manage just fine on a ranch. Don't you think? I mean, I'm pretty good now on a horse."

"And you're not bad at herding cattle, either." The tip of his tongue teased a particularly inviting area in the hollow of her throat.

"Maybe I could even learn to rope a steer."

"Why not, when we have the rest of our lives for me to teach you?"

He might have been tempted to teach her other things in that moment, even with the snow collecting around them, even with a grinning Dick looking on. If, that is, a thundering Cappy, who had ridden back along the line of stalled cattle, hadn't interrupted them.

"What in cowpat's name," the old man demanded, staring in disbelief at the couple on the ground clinging to each other, "is going on here?"

"A cattle drive, Cappy," Roark assured him, lifting both himself and Samantha to their feet. He found he could manage the leg when he was standing, at least as far as his horse. "And I think if we get moving, we can still make those stock cars."

Samantha looked at him, eyes wide. He nodded back with certainty, his heart swelling with his love for her. But that love would have to wait to be expressed.

"We don't have any time to waste," he said, "because once we've delivered these cows, we have a wedding to talk about."

He prayed Samantha would have no objection to that. And she didn't.

Chapter Fourteen

The savory aroma of barbecuing beef came from the pits out back, mingling with the fragrance of flowers on the warm Texas air. The blossoms were everywhere, entwined in the latticework of the arbor where the ceremony was to take place, decorating the porch of the ranch house and heaped lavishly in baskets on the picnic tables under the live oaks where the fixings for the banquet were already being spread.

For all Roark knew, even Irma might be wearing a garland around her neck. Not that Samantha's beloved heifer was present, but everyone else was.

The yard was filled with people consisting of guests from San Antonio, a sizable share of Purgatory's population, neighboring ranchers and the entire Hawke clan, who had flown in for the occasion. The crowd included a pair of fiddlers and a caller for the square dances to follow the banquet. This was to be an old-fashioned Western wedding in every respect.

It was all here and waiting. Everything, that is, but the bride. Where is she? Roark wondered, beginning to worry in earnest.

To his enormous frustration, no one in the yard seemed to be concerned that she was missing. "Gave me a little wave and took off in her car," Dick informed him when Roark asked him if he'd seen Samantha. "Yeah, she was alone. I don't know, about fifteen minutes ago maybe. Hey, man, you'd better have a beer with Cappy and me. You're looking like a nervous bridegroom.''

He had similar responses from all of them. None of them could explain her mysterious absence, and none of them doubted she was anything but safe and would turn up in plenty of time for the ceremony.

Roark was out of his mind with worry and ready to go after her, wherever that was, when his mother and father appeared on either side of him, linking their arms with his.

"Come up on the porch and sit with us," Moura Hawke urged.

He knew what was his mother was after. She wanted him to rest his leg. The leg didn't need resting. It had healed nicely, without complications. "Ma, I don't have time to relax. I've got to find out what's happened to Samantha."

Casey Hawke chuckled. "Now, son, you don't think your bride's run out on you, do you?"

Roark was beginning to wonder if he *was* being jilted at the altar. Samantha had told him she was happy with his decision to concentrate on ranching, even though her faith in him had restored his belief in himself as a PI. Told him she was prepared to live here on their spread and, like him, commute to San Antonio a couple of days each week to supervise their real estate and private investigation operations. But what if she had reconsidered? What if she had decided that she couldn't endure an existence as a rancher's wife? The possibility scared the hell out of him.

It continued to gnaw at him as his insistent mother and father dragged him off to the porch where they settled side by side on the wide seat of the old swing while he perched unwillingly on the porch railing facing them.

"It was all about money and glory," Casey said. "But then it usually is. At least the money, anyway."

"What are you talking about, Pop?"

"Alex McKenzie."

"That sheriff of yours is such a nice man," Moura said, indicating the rotund figure of Tom Poltry on the far side of the yard. "He told us that much, which I understand he got from the Colorado sheriff, who finally got it out of McKenzie, but he left the rest for you to tell us."

"Ma, this isn't the best time for me to—"

"You have to, dear. We're just dying to know the details."

Roark wasn't deceived by her eagerness. His mother and father were obviously trying to keep him distracted. He was in no mood to accommodate them, but he did his best to fill them in on the whole story, though his explanation didn't lessen his concern about Samantha.

"Alex McKenzie's father has been charged with collusion," Roark said, "and that's why our local sheriff is involved in the case, though, of course, Alex will stand trial in Colorado where he's being held."

Casey nodded. "Yes, Sheriff Poltry did mention that. Something connected with the McKenzies having serious money problems, I think he said."

"Right, which is why the dinosaur fossils were so important to them. They knew Joe Walker would never part with a single acre, but if he was eliminated and his ranch went to the Western Museum, as he'd always said it would—"

"But the ranch was to go to Samantha, wasn't it, dear?" Moura interrupted him.

"Not at first. That only happened after Joe survived the attack on him and changed his will in the hospital. That meant Samantha was eligible to inherit the estate, and even if she put the ranch on the market, the McKenzies wouldn't have been able to afford to make an offer on it. But if Samantha failed to qualify, the Walking W would go to the Western Museum, and since the senior McKenzie had friends on its governing board—"

"Ah, I'm beginning to see the cunning at work here," Casey said. "Your hand bothering you, son?"

Roark looked down at his hand, realizing that he had been exercising its fingers again. Nerves, he thought. "No. And the McKenzies were cunning about it. They realized that if Samantha was out of the way, they could make use of their original plan."

"And what was that, dear?" Moura asked him.

"Since the monastery would get all of Joe Walker's other assets," Roark explained, "it would leave the museum needing operating funds for the Walking W. Alex's father would have had no trouble convincing the board for a nominal sum to sell him a corner of the ranch to add to his own spread. A corner that happened to include a ravine rich with dinosaur fossils worth a fortune on any market, illegal or otherwise. And when enough time had passed to make it look like nothing more than a lucky find, Alex would have pretended to discover those fossils."

"But until then his discovery had to be protected," Casey realized.

"Exactly. Alex was desperate about anyone getting anywhere near his secret. Like Shep Thomas. My interest about ancient artifacts, and the possibility of them existing in the caves in the ravine, got the trail boss thinking. He remembered how weeks ago, when he was on his rounds, he found Alex in the ravine. Alex told him he was looking for one of his father's missing beeves, and at the time Shep accepted that. But what if it was something else Alex wanted in that ravine?"

"Like dinosaur fossils," Moura said.

"No, Ma, Shep wouldn't have guessed that. He would have thought it was valuable artifacts. He made the mistake of going to Alex the night he died, wanting a cut of whatever Alex might have found."

"So Alex pushed him into that canyon," Moura said, understanding what must have happened.

"And threw the books he'd taken from my bag after him so it would look like Shep was trying to destroy those books in a drunken rage and fell to his death in the fog."

The envelope containing the earlier photographs Wendell had taken of the ravine had also been in his saddlebag, Roark remembered. They had been right there with the books, and if Alex had known of their existence... But he hadn't, of course.

"That makes it murder, all right," Casey said. "Not that I hope McKenzie's full confession will do him much good when he stands trial."

"What about Ernie Chacon?" Moura asked, leaning forward in the swing she shared with her husband. "Where did he come into it?"

"Ernie was dangerous to Alex," Roark said. "He knew all about Alex's paleontology studies, and that threatened his secret. That's why the sly bastard wanted him gone from the cattle drive. Which he achieved by making sure we all knew of Ernie's bad-boy reputation and that he was probably responsible for the troubles on the drive."

"Ruthless young man, wasn't he?" Roark's mother could switch topics in midstream faster than anyone he knew, and she did so now. "I never noticed it before this."

"What, Ma?" he asked, stirring restlessly on his perch, impatient to be out in the crowd again seeking an explanation for Samantha's vanishing act.

"Madeline," she said, gazing into the yard where Roark's sister-in-law stood chatting with the other members of the family while her husband, Mitch, hovered nearby, keeping a solicitous eye on his hugely pregnant wife. "I think she's bigger with that baby than our Christy was with hers at this stage."

"Big babies run in the family," Casey reminded her, proud of the height of his three sons and eldest daughter, Eden, even though he, himself, was of a short stature.

Roark twisted around on the railing to view his brothers and sisters and their children. Devlin and his wife, Karen, had three youngsters chasing happily around the yard while Christy's husband, Dallas, held their infant son in his arms. Looking at them, Roark thought sourly that maybe he would never have a brood of his own. Not if the woman he wanted to be the mother of his children had skipped out on him.

"Anyway," Moura said, "where were we? Oh, yes, you were telling us what we didn't learn from your local sheriff."

"Which Roark has already done," Casey said. "So it's all settled now. Except for the Walking W. What happens to that?"

"Samantha is keeping it in the family as her grandfather wanted," Roark told them. "It'll be operated under the direction of the Western Museum, which will keep it open to educate the public on ranching in Texas. Place should be of real interest now that the longhorns are in place. As for the fossils in the ravine, they'll be responsibly excavated by professionals. The profits from them will benefit everyone, including the St. James Monastery. It's all Samantha's idea."

"Speaking of which," Casey said matter-of-factly, nodding in the direction of the driveway, "here's your bride now. Safe and sound, just like we all told you she would be."

Roark was off the porch as if shot from a cannon and racing toward the driveway where Samantha had just emerged from her car. She looked radiant in a silky full-skirted creamy affair, with flowers woven through her lustrous chestnut hair. And he was furious with her. Which it was difficult to be since the smile she directed at him was doing exciting things to his heart, never mind several other areas of his body.

"Where the devil have you been?" he thundered when he reached her, taking her hands in both of his just to be sure she was really here and still belonged to him.

"Why, just down the road, of course," she said mildly.

"I've been sick with worry."

"I'm sorry, darling. You were so busy thanking Wendell for his legwork and for taking all those photographs that I didn't want to interrupt. But I told Ramona where I was going and why. Didn't she give you my message?''

"Ramona," he informed her in exasperation, "is in no state to remember anything. Ernie arrived just after you disappeared, and he wasn't alone. The director of the Western Museum was with him.''

"His father?" Samantha said, her eyes glowing with pleasure. "You mean he's finally recognized his son?''

"Looks like it. Anyway, the three of them are over on the other side of the yard engaged in a family reunion. Down the road? Where down the road?''

"The cemetery. It was all the flowers here. I looked around and decided that it couldn't wait, that I had to take some and lay them on his grave.''

"Your grandfather," Roark said, beginning to understand her errand.

"It was time to make peace with him, lay all the ghosts to rest. I knew suddenly that I had to do that before we were married, a clean start, and it was something I had to do alone. Did I do the right thing?''

"Yes, you did the right thing." Roark drew her toward him, releasing her hands in order to gather her into his arms. "You are one hell of a woman, Samantha Howard, and I am the luckiest guy in Texas.''

He kissed her long and deeply, demonstrating his love for her with every nuance of his body molded to hers. There was no telling how much more he would have eagerly expressed, and in what manner, if they hadn't been interrupted by the husky voice of his eldest brother, Devlin.

"I think as best man it's my duty to point out to you that all this is supposed to wait until after you've exchanged the 'I do's.'''

Roark reluctantly ended the kiss and swung around to face his grinning brother. "Bad timing, Dev. Okay, lead the way then so we can take care of that little formality.''

He was suddenly impatient to have the ceremony and

banquet ended and all of them gone so he could carry his wife into their bedroom, where he hoped to get a start on that brood of their own.

Meanwhile, he thought, catching up Samantha's willing hand in his own and hurrying her in the direction of the arbor, he would have to be content with an exchange of their vows sealed by a kiss that he intended to be a promise of forever.

Come to think of it, that wasn't such a bad thing to settle for.

HARLEQUIN®
INTRIGUE®

Our unique brand of high-caliber romantic suspense just cannot be contained. And to meet our readers' demands, Harlequin Intrigue is expanding its publishing schedule to include **SIX** breathtaking titles every month!

Check out the new lineup in October!

MORE variety.
MORE pulse-pounding excitement.
MORE of your favorite authors and series.

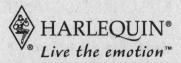

HARLEQUIN®
Live the emotion™

Visit us at www.tryIntrigue.com

HI4T06T

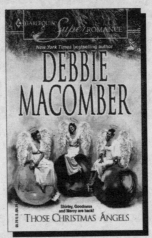

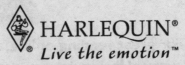

Your opinion is important to us! Please take a few moments to share your thoughts with us about your experiences with Harlequin and Silhouette books. Your comments will be very useful in ensuring that we deliver books you love to read. *Please take a few minutes to complete the questionnaire, then send it to us at the address below.*

Send your completed questionnaires to:
Harlequin/Silhouette Reader Survey, P.O. Box 9046, Buffalo, NY 14269-9046

---

1. As you may know, there are many different lines under the Harlequin and Silhouette brands. Each of the lines is listed below. Please check the box that most represents your reading habit for each line.

Line	Currently read this line	Do not read this line	Not sure if I read this line
Harlequin American Romance	❑	❑	❑
Harlequin Duets	❑	❑	❑
Harlequin Romance	❑	❑	❑
Harlequin Historicals	❑	❑	❑
Harlequin Superromance	❑	❑	❑
Harlequin Intrigue	❑	❑	❑
Harlequin Presents	❑	❑	❑
Harlequin Temptation	❑	❑	❑
Harlequin Blaze	❑	❑	❑
Silhouette Special Edition	❑	❑	❑
Silhouette Romance	❑	❑	❑
Silhouette Intimate Moments	❑	❑	❑
Silhouette Desire	❑	❑	❑

2. Which of the following best describes why you bought *this book?* One answer only, please.

the picture on the cover	❑	the title	❑
the author	❑	the line is one I read often	❑
part of a miniseries	❑	saw an ad in another book	❑
saw an ad in a magazine/newsletter	❑	a friend told me about it	❑
I borrowed/was given this book	❑	other: _____	❑

3. Where did you buy *this book?* One answer only, please.

at Barnes & Noble	❑	at a grocery store	❑
at Waldenbooks	❑	at a drugstore	❑
at Borders	❑	on eHarlequin.com Web site	❑
at another bookstore	❑	from another Web site	❑
at Wal-Mart	❑	Harlequin/Silhouette Reader	❑
at Target	❑	Service/through the mail	
at Kmart	❑	used books from anywhere	
at another department store or mass merchandiser	❑	I borrowed/was given this book	❑

4. On average, how many Harlequin and Silhouette books do you buy at one time?

I buy _____ books at one time	❑
I rarely buy a book	❑

MRQ403HI-1A

5. How many times per month do you shop for any *Harlequin and/or Silhouette* books?
   One answer only, please.

1 or more times a week	❑	a few times per year	❑
1 to 3 times per month	❑	less often than once a year	❑
1 to 2 times every 3 months	❑	never	❑

6. When you think of your ideal heroine, which *one* statement describes her the best?
   One answer only, please.

She's a woman who is strong-willed	❑	She's a desirable woman	❑
She's a woman who is needed by others	❑	She's a powerful woman	❑
She's a woman who is taken care of	❑	She's a passionate woman	❑
She's an adventurous woman	❑	She's a sensitive woman	❑

7. The following statements describe types or genres of books that you may be
   interested in reading. Pick *up to 2 types* of books that you are most interested in.

I like to read about truly romantic relationships	❑
I like to read stories that are sexy romances	❑
I like to read romantic comedies	❑
I like to read a romantic mystery/suspense	❑
I like to read about romantic adventures	❑
I like to read romance stories that involve family	❑
I like to read about a romance in times or places that I have never seen	❑
Other: _____	❑

*The following questions help us to group your answers with those readers who are
similar to you. Your answers will remain confidential.*

8. Please record your year of birth below.
   19 ____

9. What is your marital status?
   single ❑   married ❑   common-law ❑   widowed ❑
   divorced/separated ❑

10. Do you have children 18 years of age or younger currently living at home?
    yes ❑   no ❑

11. Which of the following best describes your employment status?
    employed full-time or part-time ❑   homemaker ❑   student ❑
    retired ❑   unemployed ❑

12. Do you have access to the Internet from either home or work?
    yes ❑   no ❑

13. Have you ever visited eHarlequin.com?
    yes ❑   no ❑

14. What state do you live in?
    _____

15. Are you a member of Harlequin/Silhouette Reader Service?
    yes ❑   Account # _____   no ❑   MRQ403HI-1B

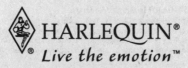

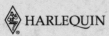

INTRIGUE®

COMING NEXT MONTH

#729 FAMILIAR DOUBLE by Caroline Burnes
Fear Familiar

When Familiar, the famous cat detective, signed on as a stunt double for a movie, he soon found himself up to his whiskers in another mystery! Nicole Paul had been framed and arrested for a theft she didn't commit. After her sexy boss, Jax McClure, bailed her out of jail, the two were swept into discovering who really stole the cursed diamond twenty years ago...*and* the secrets of their hearts.

#730 THE FIRSTBORN by Dani Sinclair
Heartskeep

When Hayley Thomas returned home to claim her inheritance, she found strange things happening around her—doors locked by themselves and objects disappeared before her eyes. The only thing she wasn't confused about was her powerful attraction to blacksmith Bram Myers...but did the brooding stranger have secrets of his own?

#731 RANDALL RENEGADE by Judy Christenberry
Brides for Brothers

Rancher Jim Randall never expected to hear from his college sweetheart again. So when Patience Anderson called him to help find her kidnapped nephew, Jim knew he had to help her...even if it meant facing the woman he'd never stopped loving. This Randall had been in danger before, but the battle at hand could cost him more than his renegade status.

#732 KEEPING BABY SAFE by Debra Webb
Colby Agency

After Colby Agency investigator Pierce Maxwell and P.I. Olivia Jackson were exposed to a deadly biological weapon that they were sure would kill them, they gave in to their growing passion. But when they miraculously lived, they were left with a mystery to solve...and a little surprise on the way!

#733 UNDER HIS PROTECTION by Amy J. Fetzer
Bachelors at Large

When a wealthy businessman was murdered, detective Nash Couviyon's main suspect was Lisa Winfield, the man's wife and the woman Nash had once loved. Would he be able to put aside past feelings—and growing new ones—to prove Lisa was being framed?

#734 DR. BODYGUARD by Jessica Andersen

Someone wanted Dr. Eugenie "Genius" Watson dead, so her adversary, the very sexy Dr. Nick Wellington, designated himself her protector. But when painful memories of the night she was attacked began to resurface, Genie discovered some shocking clues regarding the culprit...and an undeniable attraction to her very own bodyguard.